W9-DIZ-784

DEAD RINGER

A TRUTH SEEKERS NOVEL - BOOK ONE

SUSAN SLEEMAN

EDGE OF YOUR SEAT BOOKS, INC.

Published by Edge of Your Seat Books, Inc.

Contact the publisher at contact@edgeofyourseatbooks.com

Copyright © 2019 by Susan Sleeman

Cover design by Kelly A. Martin of KAM Design

This book is a work of fiction. Characters, names, places, and incidents in this novel are either products of the imagination or are used fictitiously. Any resemblance to real people, either living or dead, to events, businesses, or locales is entirely coincidental.

1

Blood-infused water circled the shower drain in Caitlyn Abbot's bathroom and disappeared. Like Caitlyn. Like her life. Like everything she touched.

"This is your last chance, Caitlyn." Her captor lurked in the shadows, his large nose seeming even bigger in an otherwise unremarkable face. "Tell me where she is, or I swear I'll kill you before the night's out."

"If I knew, don't you think I'd have told you by now?" She struggled against her restraints—twisting, turning her wrists as she sat tied to a chair in her bathroom shower. The heavy duct tape held firm—had held firm for five long hours of pain and mental battering by the man she'd come to think of as Igor.

He lumbered across the tiny bathroom. The white coveralls he wore whispered against his legs as his rubber boots thumped on the tile floor. He circled his calloused fingers around her neck. Rough, sandpapery fingers rested lightly against her skin, a grin overtaking his wide mouth.

She stared up at his face, zoning in on a chipped upper tooth as she'd done for hours to keep from recoiling in fear. He rubbed a hand over his blond hair, and it came to rest behind an ear that protruded like Dopey's ears, though this man was far from a dwarf. He was sturdy and tall.

His smile vanished, and he curled his fingers tight, his nails piercing her skin, adding to her already unbearable pain level.

"Stop lying to me." Spittle clung to the corners of his mouth.

Cait bit her lip to keep from crying out and giving him the satisfaction of knowing he was hurting her. "I'm not lying. Please. You have to believe me."

Anger and hatred emanated from narrowed eyes the color of the blackest of coal. This was personal to him. He wouldn't be able to restrain his anger for much longer. This could be it. The end for her. Her ability to hold back faded into a wisp of smoke.

"Help me," she screamed, her voice reverberating and bouncing off the tiled walls. "Someone, please help me."

His fingers tightened into a noose. Crushing, bruising, tearing her skin. Cutting off all oxygen. She bucked against the wrist and ankle restraints. The sticky tape cut against skin already raw from her struggles.

Memories ricocheted through her head, and she knew she had to keep her secret. Just had to. No matter what.

Please, please, please, don't let me crack. Not now. Not after I just found them.

"Tell me, Cait."

Her throat closed. Gurgled. She felt her body relax, saw herself floating up and out of the chair.

This is it. The end.

She'd never get to see them. Know them.

Suddenly he let go and stepped back. She dragged in air, filling her lungs, coughing and sputtering, her chest heaving with exertion, a hot burning mass of pain.

Thick lips that had spewed hatred and obscenities split

with a sneer. "If you don't want me to do that again, you need to keep quiet. No more attempted screams. Got it?"

"Yes," she croaked out the single word, but when he wasn't watching, she would cry out again and hope one of her neighbors heard. Not that they'd do anything. She'd only rented this townhouse for a week now and had only met one of them, an elderly lady who wouldn't be of much help.

Her captor shot back up and walked to the vanity. Lifting a bottle of water to his lips, he drank greedily.

Her parched mouth and throat longed for just one of the drops running down his chin, but she'd never beg for water. He went to a cooler he'd brought along with his other supplies and pulled out another bottle. He came close and rested the cold plastic against her cheek. She wanted to turn, to taste the cool damp condensation forming on the bottle, but she closed her eyes and willed the desire to the back of her mind.

"What's the matter, sweetheart?" He bent down, his mouth near her ear, his fetid breath curling toward her nose. "Don't you want a little sip?"

He sounded like the very devil, and she was beginning to think he might be, but she didn't move.

"Fine." He grabbed her hair and jerked her head back. He poured droplets of water into her open mouth.

Paradise. One taste felt like paradise.

"Want more?" he asked.

She nodded. He tipped the bottle. A rush of cold liquid filled her mouth, clogging her throat like the squeeze of his hands. She couldn't swallow fast enough. The icy water ran over her face and into her hair. She coughed. Gasped. Gagged.

She was drowning. Right here in her own shower.

Empty, he tossed the bottle across the room.

She fought for a breath again. Fought a sudden wave of nausea. Pulled in air and coughed out water. Tears filled her eyes as she struggled to breathe deeply.

He got in her face. "Now, I'll ask again. Where is it? What's her name, and where is she?"

"I don't know. Really, I don't. Please." She hated that she'd started to beg, but she couldn't survive much more. "I don't even know what you're talking about. I told you that. Why won't you believe me?"

"This is why." He lifted a manila folder from the counter and waved it in the air.

"Like I said—I'm searching for my birth parents. If they took something from your family, I don't know anything about it."

He slammed the folder onto the counter and dug out his phone.

"She won't talk, and it's getting too risky to stay here." He listened, his narrowed focus never leaving her face.

"You're sure?" He listened again. "Fine."

He ended his call and shoved his phone into his pocket, then retrieved the length of fabric he'd used as her gag.

"No please. I won't say anything. Won't cry out."

He twirled the cloth, stirring the air into a whispering breeze. She clamped down on her lips and clenched her teeth. He moved behind her and forced the material into her mouth, the smell of dirty gym socks emanating from the rag. Her chafed skin split, the pain adding to the hundreds of needles pricking at her body. She couldn't take it any longer. Tears slid down her cheeks. Seeped into the rag.

"No need to cry, my pet." After securing the gag, he stroked her hair. "We're going for a ride in the car, and that'll give you time to realize you need to cooperate."

He ripped the tape free from one of her arms. Skin and

hair peeled from her body, but she refused to moan or groan. He worked to loosen the other strips.

This was it. Her chance. What she'd been waiting for. Time to escape.

The last piece pulled free. She jumped to her feet. Barreled into him, knocking him back. She darted out of the stall and grabbed a jar from the vanity. Heart racing, she raised it overhead and crashed it into his skull.

Glass peppered the room. Cotton balls floated to the floor. He staggered back against the tile, hit his head, and slid down. A trail of blood followed.

She ran for the door. Clumsy. Slowed by stiff legs that had been restrained for hours. She heard him moving. His grunts. His struggle to get to his feet. His footfalls hitting the hallway. They pounded closer. He suddenly roared and lunged. Grabbed her by the hair. Spun her around and threw a solid punch to her face.

The force sent her to the floor, her head slamming against the wood. Pain sliced into her skull and stars danced like fireflies before her eyes. She blinked hard. Her lids refused to comply and remain open. The dark beckoned, cementing her eyelids closed.

"That's it, my pet," he said bending over to pick her up and hoist her over his shoulder. "Give in. Sleep. You'll think much clearer after a little sleep, and then I know you'll cooperate."

If she had any hope of escaping, she had to know where he was taking her. She pried her eyes open. Sliver by sliver they raised.

He took something from his pocket and blotted his head before tossing it into the bathroom and stepping through her master bedroom. The room was trashed by her earlier struggle to get free and into the family room. She grabbed at the wall, surprised to see blood on her hand leaving behind a long trail. Had she cut her hand on the jar or was it his blood?

She clutched the wall. Her slick fingers couldn't gain purchase. Her body was as floppy as a ragdoll, refusing to cooperate, laying limp against the iron bands of his arms. She struggled to move. Couldn't budge an inch.

He stepped outside, the cold October air doing nothing to help wake her. The sun had sunk below the horizon and the streetlight was burned out. No one would see them. The darkness called louder. Stronger. Demanded that she give in.

Her heavy eyelids carried the weight of the world. They closed in a final surrender to the dark and everything went black.

2

Sheriff Blake Jenkins wasn't responsible for finding Caitlyn Abbot in the past, but she'd become his responsibility today, and his duty weighed heavy on him. Heavier than normal—and that was saying a lot.

He ran his gloved finger over the front doorjamb that was perfectly intact, his gut tight. He'd recently closed a murder investigation and would rather be back on that case. The dead didn't depend on him. Didn't need him to save them.

But this woman? This victim, Caitlyn Abbot?

She needed him to bring her home before her life was ended. Exactly like his sister had once depended on him, and he'd failed big time. He had to do better here.

As soon as the call had come in, he'd set a perimeter and dispatched multiple units, but the abductor was long gone or switched vehicles and escaped capture. Blake would do his best to find Caitlyn, but he didn't want a terrified woman counting on him to save her life. He didn't want anyone counting on him ever again.

He couldn't fail another person. Just couldn't.

I wish you got that, God. I mean, I've told You more times than You could possibly want to hear. So why put me in this situation?

"This is a rough one," Detective Trent Winfield said as he approached, his expression intense.

Blake was always struck by the fact that Trent didn't look like a law enforcement officer. Sure, he had that confident swagger and posture that most LEO's possessed, but with his light complexion and nearly blond hair, he looked more laid-back. Add his abs of steel and rock-solid biceps that he worked many hours in the gym to maintain, and he looked more like an actor who played a cop. Blake razzed him about it all the time.

Gave him a leg up in the job, though. Where Blake intimidated people, they opened up to Trent. Blake tried to take clues from Trent but had yet to master the laid-back vibe.

"Witness is ready to give her statement." Trent paused by the door. "Thought you'd want in on it."

"Lead the way," Blake said and followed his detective across the perfectly manicured lawn to a townhouse two doors down.

Blake saw a plump woman probably in her late seventies standing under the light of the older building. She had curly gray hair and saggy jowls. Her lips were coated with bright pink lipstick even at the end of the day.

"Sheriff Jenkins." Blake offered his hand.

"Gladys Putman. I saw...this...it's just awful." She pulled her hand free to twist it with the other one, her gaze darting around as if she feared the abductor would come back and take her, too.

"Can you tell me what you saw?" Blake asked, trying not to sound demanding.

"A man. He was big. He had blond hair I think. And a

broad face. He...he...oh, it was horrible." Her gravelly voice broke.

Trent touched her arm. "I know this is difficult for you, but can you tell the sheriff what the man did?"

She grimaced. "He carried Cait like a sack of potatoes over his shoulder and dumped her in the trunk of his car. She lifted her head once, but then it fell. I think he drugged her, or she was weak."

"What kind of car?" Blake asked to quickly move her forward as she looked like she might break down.

"It was sort of gray. Or tan." She tapped her chin. "Or even silver. Midsized or full-sized. I'm sorry. So sorry. I'm not helping. It's just so...I...I just don't know."

Trent took out his notebook and pen. "Did you catch the plate number?"

She shook her head. "It didn't have a plate."

"And can you describe him other than he was blond?"

"I didn't see his face. Too dark. That darned streetlight's been out for a month now, and it gets dark so early this time of year." She sighed, a long hearty breath. "I told the city it was a problem, and now look—a man breaks in a few doors down and takes that sweet young woman."

"But you didn't see his face," Blake clarified as witnesses could sometimes be flighty, and Gladys seemed like such a witness.

"No. Not even after I screamed and he came back up the walkway. I bolted inside and locked the door. He took off and peeled down the road." She tugged her lavender quilted jacket closed. "That's when I called 911."

"Could you see what Ms. Abbot was wearing?"

"A bright yellow top. That I'm sure of. But I'm not positive about her pants. Jeans I think. I just..." She wrapped her arms around her body.

"What was the man wearing?" Trent asked.

9

"Well, I can tell you he wasn't wearing a jacket. Isn't that odd. I mean it's October and in the thirties right now."

"Yes, that is unusual," Blake said. "And his clothing?"

"He wore rubber boots. Like rain boots."

"And what else?" Blake felt like he was pulling teeth.

"You know those white suits the people in the house are wearing? Like on those CSI shows?"

"Yes," he said, knowing she was referring to the forensic techs dressed in protective Tyvek suits.

"That's what he was wearing."

"Way to bury the lead." Blake frowned.

"I beg your pardon?"

"Are you sure about that?" he quickly asked.

She nodded vigorously. "My grandson used to watch those Teletubbies, and I thought he looked like that."

"You mentioned that he was heading back toward the house," Trent said. "Any idea why?"

"I think he might have been coming after me." She shuddered, her large frame quaking. "What a day. I was in my kitchen thinking about what to make for dinner. I got distracted and looked out the window. That's when I saw the man. I didn't think and ran out to yell at him."

"Do you know Ms. Abbot?" Blake moved Gladys along before she worked herself up into even more of a frantic state.

"Cait? She only moved in a week ago. I brought her some of my famous chocolate chip cookies." She sniffed, her chin in the air. "It's a rental place. Lots of tenants coming and going over the years."

Blake could tell she obviously didn't like that. "See any friends come around? Maybe a boyfriend?"

"Two people helped her move. A man and a woman. They were all lovey-dovey, and Cait said they were a couple."

"You wouldn't happen to know their names, would you?" Trent asked.

"Sorry. I don't remember."

"Did you see any guys coming around for a visit after move-in day?" Blake asked to be sure she hadn't forgotten anyone.

She shook her head. "And no other friends stopping in either. I'm pretty observant, so I would have noticed."

"Except for when her abductor arrived," Blake pointed out.

"He must've gotten here while I was in bed sleeping because the car was out there when I got up and was parked there all day. I figured Cait had a visitor."

One who tortured her, Blake didn't say aloud as the poor woman would be distraught if she knew this man had been next door hurting Caitlyn all day long. "Thank you, ma'am. That's all my questions for now."

"I'm lead detective on this investigation." Trent handed her a business card. "Call me if you think of anything else."

Blake turned to head back to Caitlyn's place, and Trent walked alongside him.

"You think he was coming back for Gladys?" Trent asked.

"To abduct her, nah. But shut her up? Maybe." Blake stopped at the door to put on booties and stepped inside to continue their discussion as they were attracting the attention of neighbors. It wouldn't be long before cell phone cameras came out, and he didn't want his picture splashed across the Internet and local news shows.

He caught sight of the trashed living room and blood smeared on the wall and came to a stop. The flash of a camera went off on the far side of the room, reminding him they weren't alone. His two best forensic techs had arrived to process the place.

"You think this is Caitlyn's blood?" Trent asked.

Blake moved closer to the print. "It's high up. Backward. Like she tried to stop him from taking her from the house. Maybe the abductor was coming back to clean up the blood. I mean, otherwise why use the bathroom shower stall?"

"Makes sense, unless he thought with it being in the interior of the home it would be more soundproof."

Blake nodded his agreement. "If only Gladys was more specific. We can't issue an alert on the car or the abductor. And with this being a residential neighborhood only, there may not be any security cameras in the area. Makes finding Caitlyn exponentially harder."

Trent nodded. "Unfortunately, we don't have much to go on at this point."

Blake agreed but he didn't want to say so and risk impacting Trent's mood. "Still, we have a strong contingent of uniforms canvassing the neighborhood, and they could turn something up."

"We can hope."

"Time for a better look." Blake crossed through the living room holding stacks of unpacked moving boxes that had been dumped out, the sofa cushions pulled out and slashed, and other possessions strewn across the floor. He passed their photographer whose focus was set on something on the small desk in the corner and headed down the hallway to the bathroom. Behind him, Trent's bootie-covered shoes whispered over the wood floor that seemed original to the 1960's townhouse.

The bathroom looked recently remodeled and right inside the door was a four-by-six shower stall, three sides enclosed by glass. One of Caitlyn's dining chairs sat in the middle of the stall, strips of duct tape on the floor, and blood spatter covered the glass and white subway tiles.

Caitlyn had obviously been bound to the chair, and the

blood belonged to her. Anger rioted in Blake's gut. He curled his fingers into tight fists.

"How can any man do this to a woman?" Trent asked.

Blake couldn't fathom physical abuse of a woman. Never. No way. He didn't even want to think what this man did or the tool he used to produce the blood. "Not enough spatter for a life-threatening injury."

"Agreed," Trent said. "Most obvious explanation was that he was torturing her."

Blake's anger grew, and he wanted to punch a wall.

Focus on the facts. Each detail. That's what was important here. Otherwise the pressure of finding Caitlyn would be overwhelming.

He sucked in a deep breath, let it out, and took a hard look at the rest of the bathroom with a double vanity and big soaking tub. On the far side of the space, criminalist Helen Lindley swabbed blood on a window sill.

She was a tiny woman, not even five feet tall with a mousey-brown pixie haircut, reminding him of an elf drowning in her white Tyvek suit bunched up at the waist. She might be tiny, but she was mighty, an amazing criminalist, and he greatly respected her.

"You thinking that's blood from our victim or her abductor?" he asked her.

She looked up. "Honestly, I don't know, but because it's so far removed from the torture chamber, I think it's possible it belongs to the suspect."

"I hope you're right and we get a DNA match." Blake ran his gaze over the floor and spotted a thick rope. He squatted to give it a closer look, but refrained from touching it.

"I didn't see any blood on the rope," Helen said. "But then we might find traces of it when we run it in the lab."

"What's in the evidence bag?" Trent pointed at a large

plastic bag sitting on the floor with something white soaked in blood.

"A man's handkerchief."

Blake gaped at her. "Caitlyn's torturer was an old-fashion gentleman?"

"Odd, right?" Helen said.

"Very odd."

"If it does belong to him, we should be able to lift his DNA. And there's hope with the rope, too."

"Keep after the blood evidence. Let me know when you've finished with it." Blake headed back to the living area and faced Trent.

"Say you're right and the guy came back to clean up his blood so he didn't leave evidence behind," Blake said. "He could've used the handkerchief to clean up along the way, and it doesn't contain his blood. And I have to believe if he wore coveralls and rubber boots he also wore gloves so we won't likely recover his prints."

Trent stared at Blake with his eyebrows raised in perfect arches that Blake had learned was a common thinking expression for his detective. "You've been doing this job longer than me. What's your gut feel here?"

"My gut?" Blake took a look around the townhouse. "It says I wish this hadn't happened in my county."

"Me too, but you'll find her. You're the best, and I'm not just blowing smoke because you're my boss." Trent grinned.

Blake did his best not to frown. After all, he appreciated Trent's confidence, but Blake wasn't glad to hear someone else was depending on him to solve this mystery, too.

He nodded at the kitchen counter abutting the family room. "Go ahead and start with her purse."

Trent crossed the room and shoved a gloved hand in the large red leather bag that Blake would classify more as a tote bag than purse. He had no idea why women needed to carry so many things around with them, but he knew they often did.

He stepped past Trent to the back door, the last point of entry that had to be checked. He found the dead bolt secure, the nearby window intact. "No pry marks on this door either. So no sign of forced entry at all. She might've known her assailant and let him in."

Trent kept digging in the purse. "Could've been a delivery guy who barged his way in after she opened the door."

"Could be, but let's hope she *did* know him. It'll make it easier to find her instead of looking for some random guy." Blake moved toward the attached living area and noted there wasn't a pizza box or other delivery box sitting on the counter. Just a bright container with a bow on top. He opened it to find freshly baked cookies. Dirty cookie sheets sat in the sink. The cookies looked like a gift for someone. Maybe a "thank you" for the friends who helped her move.

Blake sat behind the small scarred desk facing out a window with closed blinds.

"Got a driver's license." Trent held it up and fanned the air. "Caitlyn Abbot, exactly like the neighbor said."

Blake nodded, but he didn't want to look at the picture yet. Made the missing woman far more real—real he didn't need or want. "How about a phone?"

Trent went back to the bag. If this wasn't such a horrific day, Blake might laugh at how out of place Trent's big hands looked pawing through a woman's purse. Blake turned back to the desk and started searching for family contact information. They'd have to notify and then question her loved ones in their time of distress. A low blow, but sadly, this task had become routine for him. Not easy. Not better. Just something he'd done many times in his years in law enforcement.

"No phone," Trent announced. "I'll go look for it and a larger picture of Caitlyn for our missing persons alert."

Many people kept addresses and pictures on their computers, not to mention email communications, but Blake wouldn't turn on her laptop or access it at all. Protocol in processing computers at a crime scene required a computer tech to take the machine into evidence and image the hard drive before anyone accessed the computer.

He turned his attention to the drawers. He found a work ID card for the University of Minnesota and various office supplies but no address book. He dropped her ID card into an evidence bag so he could follow up, though she had likely left that job if she was now living here in Cold Harbor.

He spotted a folder labeled Veritas Center.

Interesting.

Blake knew all about the state-of-the-art lab in Portland. Their DNA expert, Dr. Emory Steele, helped him with a murder investigation last year.

He opened the folder, flipped through, and found a DNA report for Caitlyn Abbot along with a report for another woman that the letter said wasn't a match as Caitlyn's mother. It also included a letter from Caitlyn to the center stating she'd only learned that she was adopted about a year ago when she was going through her deceased mother's belongings.

"No phone, but I got a better picture." Trent held out an eight-by-ten frame and handed it to Blake.

He could hardly refuse to look at the photo without some sort of explanation, so he took the frame. The woman stood with an older man in a snowy urban scene. She was striking with large brown eyes and a dazzling white smile. Glasses were perched on top of her head, holding back honey-red hair that was cut right above her shoulders.

He took the photo out and shoved it into his folder

without comment. What could he say? A beautiful woman was missing. Abducted. And they needed to find her. Fast.

Pressure weighed down on him—incredible pressure—and his stomach cramped.

Trent tilted his head and sniffed. "Am I smelling cookies?"

Blake nodded. The scent of warm cinnamon and brown sugar hung in the air, belying the tragedy that had befallen Caitlyn.

"There's a container of cookies in the kitchen with a bow on top and pans in the sink," Blake said. "Like Caitlyn planned to give them as a gift."

Trent shook his head. "It's things like that that get to me in this job, you know? A life interrupted."

Blake understood his detective's angst, but he couldn't dwell on it and not have his gut tied up in tighter knots. Better to focus on things he could do something about.

"What about the desk?" Trent asked. "You find anything there to tell us more about the victim?"

Blake handed over the Veritas file.

"Veritas, huh?" Trent cocked his head. "That private forensic lab in Portland, right?"

Blake nodded. "They got their start in connecting adopted and missing loved ones to their families. They still do that, but they've branched out to being a full-service lab for law enforcement, too."

Trent looked up. "Is that the place who did the DNA for the Hollis murder?"

Blake nodded his acknowledgement of the investigation that Dr. Steele participated in.

"This is surreal." Trent shook his head. "One day Caitlyn wakes up, and she's suddenly not who she thought she was for thirty years."

Blake nodded. "I can't even imagine what that would be

17

like. Parents have such an influence on their children. Good or bad. And, it's almost like the girl she was meant to be was missing that whole time. Had to have messed with her head and caused her to do some real soul-searching."

"Which is why she went to Veritas."

"And that's good news for us because we have her DNA profile, and it'll help us determine if the blood samples we collect today belong to her or our suspect."

Trent frowned. Maybe he was expecting a more definitive lead, but having the victim's DNA on file was a huge advantage to their investigation. Even if they didn't find a match for her in the FBI's DNA database, they might find a familial match, giving them an idea as to her true parentage and maybe a lead in the investigation, too.

Helen entered the room, evidence bags in hand. She lifted her free hand as if she wanted to run it through her hair, but then remembered she still wore latex gloves and dropped her arm. "You asked me to tell you when the blood samples are ready to go, and they are."

Blake never acted hastily, but the pressure was almost oppressive, and he made a spur-of-the-moment decision. He stood. "I'll be signing them out to deliver them to the Veritas Center for processing."

"Say what?" Trent gaped at Blake. "That place is pricey, and you're always harping on us to watch the budget."

He was right, but Blake didn't care. "Can't put a price on a woman's life."

"Oh, I get it," Trent said. "It'll take a minor miracle to get the DNA run done fast enough in any lab, even Veritas, to bring Caitlyn home alive."

"Let's not go there," Blake said, but he too thought the odds were good that she may not still be alive. "Give me the log to sign it out, Helen."

"Fine, but I'm taking additional samples for OSP, too.

Just in case." She frowned, narrowing an already-angular face. "And you need to know this wet evidence can't stay in the bag for more than two hours. You can't get to Portland that fast. So who will process it properly?"

"True...unless...I might have the solution we need." Blake grabbed his phone and tapped the icon for Samantha Willis at Blackwell Tactical located right here in Cold Harbor. The private company was made up of former military and law enforcement officers who'd been injured on the job and had to leave due to their injury. Blake's good friend Gage Blackwell founded and ran the business. They trained law enforcement and handled private protection and investigations, and Blake had worked with them many times in the past.

"Sam," he said the minute she answered. "Blake Jenkins. I need a favor."

"Ah, you need my help, huh? So the tables are turned for once." She chuckled.

He had no time to joke around. "Just hear me out. A woman's been abducted. I need to have DNA processed ASAP if we hope to bring her home alive. I was hoping you'd call your friend at Veritas to run the tests, and I can get Gage to let Coop or Riley fly me to Portland with the sample."

"Of course, I'll call Emory." Her tone had sobered. "And you're in luck. Hannah has a doctor's appointment in Portland first thing in the morning. Coop is flying her and Gage there to spend the night."

"When?"

"They're at the helipad now. How soon can you be here?"

He made a quick calculation on how long it would take to get to Blackwell Tactical's compound. Of course, he'd run with lights and sirens. "Ten minutes."

"Then hurry," she said, her tone agitated now. "And I'll run down there to stop them from leaving. I'll call Emory on the way. I know she'll do the DNA work."

"Thanks, Sam." Relief flowed through his words, and under any other circumstances he'd be embarrassed at showing such emotion in front of his team, but a woman needed him to find her, and he had no time to be worried about what others thought.

"No thanks needed." He heard a door slam in the background of the call. "You know I wouldn't refuse to help find a missing woman."

He disconnected and snapped off his latex gloves. "Give me the form, Helen. I've got a helicopter ride, and I'll be there in less than two hours. I'm sure their DNA expert knows how to handle wet evidence."

She held out the clipboard with her log and gave him a skeptical look.

He didn't care if she liked it or not. He would take this evidence to Dr. Steele in Portland. No question about it. It was the best chance of bringing Caitlyn home alive.

3

Emory Steele peered through the two-story glass blackened by nightfall. The dark, foreboding parking lot froze her feet on the Veritas Center staircase. Fear pressed against her shoulders, weighing her down and quickening her breath. After one hundred and eighty-three days of dreading sunset, the weight felt familiar. Like an old but very scratchy and constricting sweater.

Just like that day. That horrible life-changing day. And today for some reason she'd been unsettled more than usual, and she couldn't pin it down.

Another look outside and she shuddered, then turned to go back to the lab.

"Want me to walk you to your car, Ms. Steele?" Security guard Pete Vincent called up to her from the lobby.

She glanced down on his silvery-gray hair and friendly smile. He grinned back, his wizened eyes showing her he appreciated her formal attire for the upcoming ceremony.

His smile widened. "It'd be my pleasure to have such a fine-looking woman on my arm tonight."

She pulled in a breath and forced out a laugh. "You are such a flirt, Pete Vincent."

"And I'll never stop no matter how old I get." He suddenly frowned. "Though my wife says with all the harassment lawsuits these days, I should be careful...but it's not like you all take me seriously, right? I mean, you know I'm all bark and no bite. Have to be or my Valerie would use my sidearm to take me out." He chuckled, delight shaking his body.

Emory laughed, this time in earnest. She adored Pete. He was kind and compassionate, yet could be firm when needed. He had likely once been an excellent police officer before he retired to security work. He'd been employed at the lab for all five years it'd been in existence, and her partners in the business agreed with her assessment of his skills.

"With those spiky heels, you need me to come up and take your arm?" he asked, serious now.

"I can manage." She descended the open stairway toward the spacious lobby decorated in cool blue and gray tones. She might have told Pete she could handle the three-inch heels, but she wasn't used to them, especially not at the lab. So she tucked the files she needed for the event under one arm and held tight to the contemporary steel railing until both feet were solidly placed on the polished concrete floor.

"So tonight's the night for the big award." Pete stepped closer. "You all should be so proud of what you've accomplished."

"To tell the truth." She started across the lobby, staccato clicks sounding from her heels and echoing through the two-story space. "I feel like a fraud attending the ceremony. I wasn't even a partner here until nine months ago."

"So what?" He unlocked the door. "You deserve to relax for a night. No one else puts in the hours here that you do."

A fraud again. Sure, she worked hard, and she made a difference, but many of the hours spent in the lab were meant to keep herself busy. Hours when her mind still automatically went to that night six months ago and terror followed.

Pete gestured for her to step into the clear evening, but as usual, she paused—her feet not crossing the threshold until she thoroughly scanned the parking lot.

"C'mon, now, Ms. Steele. You don't want to be late." He held out his arm, as he typically did to get her to leave the building at night. He'd never asked why she couldn't breeze outside like the other staff, but he patiently helped her take the leap across the threshold.

She slipped her arm in his. They were both five-seven, but with heels on, she was taller. Still, he was stocky and solid and highly trained, so she clung to his arm and kept in step with him. Nearing seven o'clock, the parking lot held only Pete's beat-up van and her black VW Bug. She had her key fob in hand, and as they reached the car, she pressed the remote locks.

"I don't know why you drive such a little bit of thing when a bigger car would be safer." Pete opened the hatchback as he always did for her. "Gas mileage?"

"Something like that," she answered vaguely and settled everything except her tiny evening clutch in the back. She scanned every inch of the small space before closing the hatch.

Pete went to the driver's door and bowed at the waist as if she were royalty. "Your chariot awaits, Cinderella."

He was such a nice man, and she wanted to keep joking with him, she really did, but as she bent toward the seat, her heart started beating wildly. It took every ounce of nerve she possessed to check the back seat without hyperventilating.

She ran her gaze over the space, facing the real reason she chose a small car. No room for an attacker to hide in the back and spring out of the darkness at her.

Empty.

She blew out a breath and slid behind the wheel, her pulse now racing.

"See you later." Pete watched her carefully for a few minutes then slammed the door and stood back.

A quick press of the locks and the solid click eased her concerns a fraction. She fumbled with her keys, but finally inserted the right one into the ignition and started the engine. She plugged her phone into the car to receive any calls through her dash, and after fastening the seatbelt, she shifted into gear and lurched out of the lot.

Once on the highway heading toward downtown Portland, she relaxed and counted one more time she'd overcome her fear enough to get back into a car. She'd expected with time and choosing a smaller car that her terror would recede, but the opposite had happened. It was getting worse.

She checked every time she got in. Irrational fear was a bugger to live with, and she'd lived with it now for months. Obviously, her stellar plan of avoidance wasn't working, and she might have to see someone about the problem or soon she might not be able to leave her condo or the office at all.

Her phone rang, jolting her body as if an electric shock traveled through her. Seriously, she really had to fix this problem soon. She accepted the call from her best friend, Samantha Willis.

"Either you didn't get my voicemail or you're ignoring me." Sam's tone filled with accusation came through the dash speakers.

"Sorry. I'm stressed about attending the awards ceremony tonight, and I forgot to check my phone," Emory answered, forcing her tone to be light and carefree. "But now that you called, you can keep me company while I drive into Portland."

"You're alone?"

"Yes, why?"

"Um, it's dark out and—"

"Let's not go there, okay? So what does your message say?"

"I don't want you to miss your ceremony, but I have another favor. This time for Blake Jenkins."

"The sheriff?" Sam's friend Andy had been murdered in February, and Emory helped on the investigation, but she never met the sheriff in person.

"Yes. A woman has been abducted in Cold Harbor. Caitlyn Abbot. He's hoping you can run DNA on blood evidence as soon as he gets there. Coop is flying him in the helo and should arrive soon if you'll do the DNA."

"Of course I'll do it. And I can thank him in person for letting me help out on Andy's investigation." Emory whipped onto an exit to navigate her return trip.

"Thanks, Emory. You're a peach." A long sigh filtered through the phone. "As your friend, I feel like I need to warn you, though. He can be a bit intense."

"As are most people in law enforcement." Emory turned left to cross over the highway.

"Okay, fine, I was trying to be diplomatic." Sam laughed. "He's over-the-top intense. He won't share a thing about the investigation, and he'll probably insist on waiting while you run the test."

She didn't mind that at all. He was simply dedicated to his job. "More power to him if he wants to sit in the lobby for a day until the tests complete."

"No, sweetie. You misunderstand. He'll want to sit by your side while you work."

"No. Absolutely not. That I won't allow." She wished she wasn't driving so she could cross her arms for emphasis.

"Well, good luck in telling him that."

A hint of apprehension settled in, but Emory dismissed it. "I'll let our guard know to expect the sheriff."

"Thanks for agreeing to run the DNA," Sam said. "Let me know if you need anything."

Emory disconnected the call with a flick of a finger on the steering wheel control and got her car back on the highway heading toward home. The sheriff sounded like a force to be reckoned with. No worries. Emory had worked in the FBI lab in Quantico for five years and interacted with some of the most intimidating agents in that job. She handled them just fine and could handle Blake Jenkins. Of that, she was certain.

~

"She could die if you don't get this thing in the air," Blake said to Coop over his headset.

"Yeah, well," Coop replied his focus remaining on his controls. "We could die if I don't finish my preflight checklist."

Blake didn't like that they were spending much of the valuable time he needed for the investigation on the checklist. Still, Coop had a point, and Blake settled back in his seat, his knee bouncing as he waited for the helicopter to lift off.

On the other side of the passenger area, Hannah shifted in her seat next to her husband, Gage, and caught Blake's attention. Gage was a big guy with black hair, Hannah petite, her red hair wavy and full. Gage was a lifelong friend, and Blake couldn't be happier for them as they were expecting a child soon.

She smiled at Blake. "Why don't you tell us about the investigation."

"You don't want to hear about that, do you?"

"It'll take my mind off the appointment."

He didn't like Hannah's worried tone. She was usually so upbeat and bubbly, but she'd been contemplative since she climbed into the helicopter with Gage. "Everything okay with the baby?"

"We think so," Gage said, his voice breaking. "But we won't know until after the special ultrasound tomorrow."

"Hey, man." Blake's heart filled with their pain. "I'm sorry to horn in at a time like this."

"No." Hannah held up a hand. "We're glad to help in any way we can. Please tell us what's going on."

She really did seem to want to know, so Blake would share. "A woman named Caitlyn Abbot was tortured in her home and then abducted. The neighbor saw a man haul her off and dump her in the trunk of his car around dinnertime."

Hannah clasped a hand to her chest. "Oh, how awful."

"As of this moment, we have no idea why." Blake pointed at the floor where he'd dropped the duffle bag holding the evidence. "Sam's friend Dr. Steele at the Veritas Center has agreed to process the blood evidence for DNA so we don't have to wait on the state lab."

Hannah smiled. "Emory's a wonderful person, and I know she'll do a great job for you."

"And she's generous," Gage said. "She never charged us for the work she did on Andy's murder investigation."

"I didn't know that." Blake's impression of the woman rose several notches, and he already thought highly of her.

"We're good to go," Coop announced through the headsets.

"Thanks, Coop." Gage put his arm around Hannah to draw her close. "She doesn't like takeoffs and landings."

She clenched her hands in her lap. "*Doesn't like* is a mild way to describe it."

The chopper lifted off and whirled up into the air. Blake wasn't like Hannah at all. He loved the feeling of leaving his stomach behind and the sensation of weightlessness.

Gage turned his focus back to Blake. "So what else can we do to help you find Caitlyn?"

Blake gave it some thought. "Nothing at the moment. But you can be sure I'll call you if I can use your team's expertise."

Gage gave a firm nod. "Feel free to request the helo when needed."

"Hey, thanks, man. I know that's gonna leave you a man down, and then there's the cost of fuel."

Gage waved a hand. "No worries. Glad to help in any way we can."

Blake grabbed his duffle bag and set it on his lap. "I hope you don't mind me being rude for the rest of the flight and taking off my headset so I can concentrate. I've got some files I need to review."

"It's not rude," Hannah assured him. "We understand."

Blake was thankful for such good friends. Especially when he often gave Blackwell team members a hard time on their investigations because he wasn't able to release official information to them. There were many times he wished he was free from all the rules and laws dictating his investigative actions. The rules existed for a reason, and he understood the need to enforce them, but it would be so much easier to work in the private sector. Seemed like he was thinking that way more often of late.

He wanted to blow out his frustration in a long breath, but stopped to keep from drawing attention. He started to read the files he'd brought along from Caitlyn's desk. First up were her bank statements. He'd been glad to see that she got them in the mail or he would've needed a warrant to request them.

He reviewed them carefully, noticing that she was financially stable with a healthy savings and checking account balance. Could mean the abductor was after her money. Trent would have already put an alert on her accounts so if she accessed them, he would be notified. Blake ran down her monthly expenditures, which were mostly for Internet, utilities, rent, and a credit card. Nothing extravagant.

He grabbed his phone and started a text to Trent to ask him to request copies of the credit card statements, as those weren't included in the files. And he added another reminder to check out the prior address in Minnesota listed on the statements. He rested his phone on his knee and moved on to her unopened mail, minus junk mail, that he'd also tossed into his duffle. Next up was her billing statement for her phone. Trent had already requested full records and was having the phone pinged, but these records could give them a starting point until that came through.

Blake reviewed the calls, noting the repeated phone numbers. He made comments in the margins, snapped a picture of the log, and added it to the text so Trent could get IDs to go with the numbers. He couldn't send the message now as he had no service but would fire it off the minute they landed.

He reviewed the other mail, and finding nothing helpful, he put his headset back on and rested against the wall to close his eyes for a few minutes. Waiting for the samples to be processed and keeping in touch with Trent as he ran the investigation would make for a long night. Many sheriffs would take lead on such an important investigation, but Trent had more experience as a detective than Blake did, and Trent would do an excellent job.

"ETA three minutes," Coop announced.

Blake opened his eyes and saw Gage hold Hannah close again. A pang of jealousy hit Blake. He was happy Gage got married again after losing his first wife in a car accident. He was an amazing guy and friend, and he deserved all the happiness in the world. As did Hannah after her first husband was murdered. And they now had a wonderful blended family with a son and daughter from their prior marriages.

Blake wished he deserved to be happy, too, but after failing his sister, he couldn't allow another woman to depend on him, and he simply needed to be content with the job. Didn't mean he didn't want to get married—to have kids—but it wasn't in the cards for him.

He glanced out the window at the thick stand of trees below with a minuscule clearing. "What in the world? Coop, you're not planning on landing in that tiny spot are you?"

"Piece of cake." Coop laughed.

Blake shot Hannah a look. "No wonder you don't like the landings."

"My buddy Lee's place," Gage said. "He purposely leaves the space small so inexperienced pilots don't even try to land here. Says it keeps the traffic down."

"Makes sense I suppose."

Hannah shook her head. "Not to those of us who already don't like landing."

The helicopter slowed and lowered to the ground with only a slight bump, the trees cocooning them from the surrounding area.

"Nice landing, Coop," Gage said.

"Yeah, what he said." Hannah laughed.

"Thanks for putting us down safe." Blake grabbed his bag and hopped out. He turned to help Hannah, but Gage jumped out and lifted her down. Right. Blake should've known that would happen. His buddy was head over heels for his wife and very excited about the baby. No way he would risk her tumbling out of a helicopter.

The rotors above slowed and soon stopped. Coop opened his door. "I'll do my post flight check and then wait with Lee until I hear from you, Blake. I plan to head home tonight to Kiera and Grace. Let me know if you want to come along for the ride."

Blake nodded and liked the newer, less-tense man Coop had become since he'd married Kiera and they'd had a baby girl.

Blake's phone dinged, and he read the text from Sam. *Emory's glad to do the DNA. She's on her way back to the center. Security guard knows to expect you and will let you in.*

Blake thumbed in his thanks and sent his long text to Trent.

"This way," Gage said and led them to a battered old pickup. "You can take the truck. Hannah and I'll head across the road to borrow a car from Lee."

Blake eyed the dilapidated pickup. "You sure this thing will make it to town?"

Gage nodded. "Purrs like a kitten. Keys are under the front wheel well."

"Can I give you a ride to the road?" Blake asked.

Hannah shook her head. "It will do me good to stretch my legs."

Blake met her gaze. "I'm praying that everything turns out fine at the doctor."

She pressed her hands over her stomach. "Thank you. Say hi to Emory for me, and you should know—she's single."

Blake groaned. "What, you paired up everyone on the team, so now you're branching out?"

Hannah laughed, and he was glad he'd cheered her up. Her laughter trailed behind as she hooked her arm in Gage's and started down the road. Blake found the key, then got the truck going. It ran as smoothly as Gage had promised, and Blake made good time to the Veritas Center.

He grabbed his duffle and tucked the folder holding Caitlyn's picture and DNA results inside his jacket, then jogged through the spitting drizzle across the Veritas Center parking lot. He'd never been to the state-of-the-art facility, but he'd heard stories about the place and about the team of experts who owned the lab. Made him curious if the stories were true or exaggerated, and he'd always wanted to check the center out, but never had a reason to do so until today.

He scanned ahead, trying to get a preliminary glimpse through windows spanning both stories, but hazy fog obscured his view. From the nearly-empty parking lot, he couldn't tell if Dr. Steele was here. If not, thankfully, Blake wouldn't have to stand outside in the cold as the security guard would let him in.

At the front door, he peered through the glass at the lobby painted in a pale gray with blue accents. The space felt very spa-like and not at all clinical like the lab he was expecting. An odd choice of décor when experts worked behind closed doors to help locate killers, missing people, and lost relatives. At least odd to him. Maybe not for the six experts who owned the place. Maybe they wanted to put a pretty face on their work. Like lipstick maybe.

He spotted the security guard sitting behind a tall reception desk looking at the stairway. His head was covered in thick gray hair cut military short.

Blake tapped on the window. The guy pushed to his feet and lumbered around the end of the reception desk, tucking his white uniform shirt into black pants on his way. A sidearm rested in a holster on his belt, and an official badge hung around his neck. The cautious way he moved and his appraising stare had Blake pegging him as a former law enforcement officer.

Blake got a good look at his name tag, Pete Vincent, before he unlocked the door. Calming music drifted out, further emphasizing the contrasting nature of the place.

"You Sheriff Jenkins?" Vincent asked.

Blake nodded.

Vincent settled his hand on his sidearm. "I'd like to see some ID to verify that."

Blake didn't want to waste valuable time showing his ID, but it would take longer to argue, so he displayed his credentials.

Vincent gave them an intense study, then nodded and stepped back. "Let's get you signed in."

Blake entered the spacious lobby and trailed Vincent to the reception desk. His boots struck a steady beat, cutting the quiet with sharp retorts pinging off the two-story ceiling.

Vincent picked up an iPad, tapped the screen a few times, and set it on the upper counter in front of Blake. "Fill in the information and sign your name, and then we can get your visit with Dr. Steele moving in the right direction."

Blake grabbed the stylus. "Is she here?"

Vincent nodded.

"Is signing in really necessary? I have time-sensitive material here."

"If you don't want to talk to Dr. Steele, you can leave the evidence with me, and I'll get it right up to her."

Blake shook his head. "I need to see her. Chain of custody and all."

Vincent lifted his shoulders. "No need to worry about that. After twenty years on the force, I can handle signing a chain of custody log."

"I need to talk to Dr. Steele."

"Suit yourself." Vincent tapped the iPad. "Then fill out the form."

Blake wanted to groan. He rarely encountered anyone

more stubborn than a law enforcement officer except an ex-LEO. He set his duffle on the counter, recorded his information, and signed. He handed the device back to Vincent. "Go ahead and let Dr. Steele know I'm here."

Vincent took his time reviewing the electronic form before handing over a visitor's badge for Blake to clip to his shirt and then calling Emory. "Sheriff Jenkins has arrived."

Blake could hear a female voice respond but couldn't make out her words.

"Roger that," Vincent said and hung up the phone. "She's on her way down."

Vincent reached into a drawer. "You'll need a security pass if you're going up to the lab."

Blake picked up the duffle. "I'm not only going up there, I'm staying until the tests are complete."

Vincent's eyes lit with an inner glow of amusement. "Good luck with that."

Blake didn't need luck. He only needed powers of persuasion, something he had in droves since becoming a sheriff.

Vincent swiped the card in a reader and glanced at his computer screen. He handed the card with a shiny metal clip to Blake. "She sometimes gets caught up in her work so might as well have a seat while you wait."

"I'll stand." Blake clipped the badge on his jacket and pulled out the folder he'd protected from the rain.

"Suit yourself." Vincent took a seat, and his direct stare said he was trying to make a point.

Blake didn't know if Dr. Steele would come down the stairs or take the elevator, so he went to stand at the base of the open staircase seeming to float above a seating area. The center's logo—Connecting Loved Ones Around the World, in bold red letters circling a black globe—was painted on the wall above photos of happy smiling people. The pictures could be stock photos, he supposed, but he suspected they were of people the lab helped reunite.

Either way, private clients didn't likely know about the criminal work being done in this lab. They only wanted to find the truth about a family member, the reason for the center's name. Veritas meant "truth" in Latin, which Blake thought was fitting. They helped find truth by processing criminal forensics for law enforcement and for people wanting to find the truth about family members. Be it adoption, losing touch over the years, or paternity issues, the center used science to help bring families back together. A noble mission and he respected the owners.

The automated lock clicked on the second-floor landing. He looked up in time to see the door whoosh open. Expecting a frumpy woman with thick glasses and stained lab coat, he waited for Dr. Steele to step out. A woman, her back to him, clutched the door handle and finished a conversation with someone he couldn't see. Her red hair was pulled up in some kind of fancy hairstyle. She was wearing a white lab coat over a short skirt and had on three-inch red heels accenting long, shapely legs.

Nice. Not a frumpy lab rat at all. Or at the very least, the skirt and heels were the wrong choice for the woman he was expecting. Maybe she didn't fit the stereotype he'd already cast her in.

He waited for her to turn, but she continued talking. Losing patience, he started up the stairs. She suddenly spun as if she'd heard him. Their eyes connected. A flash of raw awareness traveled between them, the surprise totally unwelcome. He wanted to look away, but forced himself to take a long hard look at her.

No. No way. Impossible.

He was just too tired, too worn out, and was seeing things. He blinked a few times. Looked again.

No. Couldn't be.

He opened the folder and glanced at the picture of Caitlyn Abbot then rubbed his eyes and studied Dr. Steele again.

Was this some kind of a sick joke? If so, he didn't find it very funny.

Anger at being conned colored his vision red.

Caitlyn Abbot wasn't missing. She hadn't been abducted. She wasn't in danger.

She was very much alive and walking down the stairs to meet him.

4

Sheriff Jenkin's eyes turned as dark as his hair, as he ran his gaze down Emory's body, then back up to her face. She understood the look he was giving her. Happened all the time. She didn't match his perception of the person he was expecting. Most people expected scientists to be plain and carry a pocket protector. And to be older than her thirty years, especially when she'd always looked young for her age and earned her PhD in her twenties. She'd fought those stereotypes for years. Maybe if she'd changed out of her evening attire it would have helped, but she'd gotten caught up in her work as usual.

He locked his focus on her face, this time anger merged with his confusion and cut right through her. She instinctually took a step back. Sam was right. He was clearly a man you didn't mess with. Tall, six-three maybe, and wide-shouldered, he wore a heavy jacket, khaki uniform, and a casual style of boots favored in the often-rainy Pacific Northwest. A duffle bag dangled from one hand, a manila folder clutched in the other.

The rage radiating off his body was almost palpable.

What she'd done to earn his wrath, she had no idea, but it looked like she was about to find out.

She took the last few steps to stand before him, and his gaze locked with hers. His eyes the color of her rich morning coffee held firm. Her mouth went dry. Inexplicably. Just like that. Dry as the Sahara. He was good-looking, in a rugged, tough-as-nails kind of way, but she'd always preferred the scholarly type to this he-man physique.

Holding out her hand, she forced a smile and vowed not to be the first person to look away. "I'm Emory Steele. Glad to finally meet you."

He ignored her hand. "Trust me, Dr. Steele, if I'd known what you look like, I would've been over here even sooner."

Was he hitting on her? Not the first cop to do so, but seriously, she agreed to see him on short notice, and he hits on her? Unbelievable.

"Please call me Emory," she said trying to keep things professional and gestured at his bag. "I assume the evidence is in your bag."

He studied her like a blood sample under a microscope for several long beats then tipped his head at Pete. "We need to talk in private."

Letting him call the shots rubbed her the wrong way, but his sharp tone told her he didn't want Pete to hear what he had to say.

"This way." She spun on her heel to march up the steps. She felt his eyes on her back, and for some odd reason she was pleased. Pleased, for goodness' sake. A Neanderthal was staring at her, and she was happy.

She resisted shaking her head over her unwelcome reaction and pressed her finger on the print reader by the door. The lock popped open, the sound echoing through the lobby. She held the door for him until he grasped the metal with long fingers before she started down the hallway that ran the length of the building. She slowed and waited for the solid click of the door latch, then marched toward her lab that took up the entire back half of the second floor.

"On the right is our Toxicology and Controlled Substance Unit managed by Maya Glass," she said to cut the tension that was soupy thick.

She sensed him slowing to look into the windows at the large lab lit with defused lighting for the night. A quick press of her fingers on the print reader at the end of the hall gave them access to her lab, and she turned to face him. She usually felt comfortable, at home in this room where nothing could rile her, but his larger-than-life personality seemed to take up all the space.

"I can take those evidence bags now," she said to move them along and get him to leave.

"I'm not sure that'll be necessary." He widened his stance as if he planned to do battle.

Odd response. "I don't understand. Sam said you needed DNA tests run."

"I do...did, but now..." He paused and locked gazes. "I need to know why you would falsify your name and stage your abduction?"

"What?" She gaped at him. "What are you talking about?"

"You can cut the charade. I know you're Caitlyn Abbot."

"The missing woman? You think *I'm* the missing woman?" She gaped at him. "But why in the world would you think that?"

He set the duffle on a slate-topped worktable and pulled a photo from his folder. He made a big production of laying the picture on the counter before standing back, giving her a clear view of the woman.

It took only a second for her mouth to fall open. "Wow!

Oh, wow! She looks exactly like me." Emory looked up. "Is this Caitlyn Abbot?"

He nodded. "But she doesn't just look like you, she's a dead ringer. So what are you playing at here?"

"I'm not playing at anything."

"Then how do you explain the uncanny resemblance?"

"I...I can't, but that's not me in that picture."

"Do you have a sister?"

"Yes, but she looks nothing like me."

"What's your date of birth?"

"July 10, 19—wait!" Her mind spun, trying to figure out all of the implications.

He flipped through the folder, his jaw muscles working hard. He looked up, his gaze digging deep as if mining for the truth, and he held out the open folder.

She glanced at the page, a DNA report that declared Caitlyn's birthday matched Emory's. Matched. Exactly. They were born on the same day.

How could this be?

Emory's breath left her body, and she struggled to catch another one.

"Are you adopted?" he asked.

She held up her hand. "Wait. Now you think she's my adopted sister? I wasn't adopted."

He stared at her with that skeptical look she'd seen from officers before. "Perhaps your mother gave birth to twins, and she put one of you up for adoption."

"No! That's not possible. My mom had a hard time conceiving, and my younger sister was like a miracle baby. My parents wouldn't have given away a child." Shocked and unable to process this outrageous information, she continued to stare back at him.

Her stomach cramped and unease niggled at her mind, but she couldn't concentrate enough to figure out the

40

reason. She could call her mother to ask, but what if it was true? That wasn't a topic for a phone call. If only her father was alive she could question him, too, but cancer took him when she was in high school.

"We can figure this out real easily," he finally said. "You already have Caitlyn's DNA profile on file, and I know you'll have taken an elimination sample of your own DNA to prove you didn't contaminate samples here. You can compare the two."

"*If* we have Caitlyn Abbot's DNA on file."

"You have it." He pointed at their logo on the report in the folder. "She hired your company to find her biological parents last year."

"She's adopted," Emory whispered and that smidgen of unease grew into a brick of doubt.

"Yes, but she didn't know about it until after her mother died. About a year ago, Caitlyn located a woman she thought might be her birth mother and had your expert compare their DNA. Sounds like you don't remember doing the profile."

"I didn't work here then and don't have firsthand knowledge of the Abbot case."

His eyebrows rose in twin arches, and he tapped the report. "You can read, though, right?"

"I'd like to think they don't give out doctoral degrees if you're unable to read," she snapped and instantly regretted losing her professionalism.

She wished she could start this whole interaction over. She understood science perfectly—the empirical data, logical sequencing, and proven techniques. People—on the other hand—often baffled her. Especially law enforcement officers like this one. She couldn't tell if he was one of those officers who resorted to sarcasm when things didn't go their way, or if he was a jerk.

"I'm sorry." He curled his fingers into a tight fist. "That was uncalled for. I'm feeling the clock tick down on finding Caitlyn alive."

"I'm sorry, too. My sarcasm was unprofessional."

"Hey, I get it. I basically called you a liar and then claimed you have a sister you know nothing about. I'd probably have done and said far worse things." He smiled then, his whole face coming alive, and his eyes lightening to a warm chocolate.

She should look away. Of course she should, but was powerless to do so. A warm feeling settled over her. Like she knew him or at least shared something in common with him. *What* she didn't know, but he had this feeling of home for her. Odd. Very odd.

The blower for the heat kicked on, bringing her to her senses—him too, apparently, as he jerked his gaze away. "Caitlyn was abducted from her townhouse a few hours ago. We have no leads in the case or reasons for the abduction. A match to your DNA might give us something to go on."

Emory didn't want to compare her DNA with this woman. Not now, not ever, but Caitlyn's life was at stake. Maybe her sister's life...her sister? Might Caitlyn be her sister? Had her parents lied to her all these years? Did she have a sister...a twin?

It would explain all the odd feelings she got at random times and couldn't explain. Like today when she'd been out of sorts all day. Was Caitlyn calling out to her?

No, that was ridiculous. She didn't have a twin sister, and it was time to prove that.

She crossed the lab to the nearest computer. She pulled up Caitlyn's profile and her own profile then set the computer to compare the results. He came to stand behind her, and she felt the heat from his body, and her awareness of him nearly took over her thoughts again, but she willed herself to concentrate.

The computer hummed as it worked, and Emory looked away. She couldn't bear to see the results. Even if she'd believed the wrong thing her entire life and she had a twin sister, the poor woman had been abducted and might not even be alive anymore.

"So I've heard that DNA for twins is exactly the same," Blake said, startling her.

She would turn to face him, but he was only inches away, and she couldn't handle such a close up look into his eyes. "For the most part it is. At least that's what basic DNA testing shows, but newer technology allows us to find mutations that we weren't once able to locate. They can differentiate even between twin's DNA."

"And do you have access to this new technology?"

"Yes," she answered. "Our lab is one of the few across the country participating in an accreditation study for that very thing. In fact, we're receiving an award tonight regarding that." She took a long breath. "The reason for my attire in case you think I dress this way for work every day."

"And you aren't there because...?"

"Because I'm here."

"You have other staff who could've run the DNA, right?"

"I'm proud to say I supervise five amazing DNA analysts," she replied with enthusiasm as she respected each analyst she worked with. "But I'm the best, and you want the best when you're trying to locate a missing woman."

He leaned against the lab table, crossing his ankles like he owned the place. "In layman's terms, what exactly are you looking for in the comparison of your DNA to Caitlyn's?"

She looked up at him, briefly distracted by his eyes that held curiosity and an intense desire to know the answer. She respected officers who dug and questioned. They were usually the ones with strong closure rates.

But this guy? She reacted to him in a way that she couldn't explain, her heart fluttering just from his nearness. How could that be? First, she might have a twin sister who her parents hid from her for thirty years. Second, after the attack, she'd had zero interest in men. If you took her fear into account, it was less than zero. And third, she was a professional scientist here to do a job. To find a missing woman. No time for heart flutters or any other emotion he seemed to be raising.

She took a breath and focused on giving a complete yet understandable explanation. "What we're looking at here is basic DNA kinship testing. This process compares two people on a small set of autosomal genetic markers. These markers are randomly inherited from both parents. The values on these markers will indicate a high or low proba- bility of a close relationship."

"And this works in all cases?"

She nodded. "For identical twins, of course. The more markers tested for, the more likely the results will hold up in a court of law. I don't know how many markers we have on Caitlyn, but we're about to find out." She turned back to the computer and ignored the findings to set the analysis report to print.

"Time to learn if you have a twin." He stepped across the room and grabbed the page from the printer.

When he returned, she wanted to snatch the paper from his hands, but at the same time, she didn't want to see the results.

He silently scanned down the report. His head popped up, his expression blank. She felt like she might throw up but grabbed the report anyway, and her breath caught in her throat.

She took one look down the page and her entire body lost feeling. The paper slipped from her fingers and fluttered in the air. She watched it drift to the floor, barely able to comprehend the news.

A match. She was a positive match to Caitlyn in not only a few markers, but *all* of them.

There was no question. None. Emory had to face facts. Unbelievable, wild facts.

She had an identical sister. A twin sister. One who'd just been abducted.

5

"Hey, now." Blake took Emory's arm and helped her to a lab stool before she collapsed.

Her face had lost all color, leaving her large brown eyes seeming even bigger and also making her look like a young child who needed to be cared for. Surprisingly, he wanted to be the one to do the caring. He hadn't felt that way since his sister, Danielle, was mugged.

He shook his head to clear it. Emory wasn't a child. She was a doctor, a scientist, and was smart enough to be withholding information from him, and he couldn't be distracted. He had a job to do here.

He picked up the form and held it out to her again. "The DNA profiles are exactly the same."

She nodded woodenly. "Identical twins. The proof is irrefutable. Caitlyn Abbot is my twin sister."

"Now don't go all crazy on me, but how do I know you're not fabricating these results to cover up the fact that it really was you living under the name of Caitlyn Abbot and staging a crime scene?"

She gaped at him, her mouth wide open. Couple that with her reaction to the report, and his gut told him what he needed to find out. She didn't know anything about Caitlyn until just now. But as a sheriff, he couldn't go on feelings in an investigation. He had to deal in facts only. "You mentioned that there's a way to distinguish between twin's DNA."

She nodded, that same forced wooden bob of her head.

"And your lab can run that test?" he asked.

She nodded again. "We can do it."

"I still need to have the evidence processed to compare with Caitlyn's DNA on file." He tapped his duffle bag. "I recommend you call in one of your analysts to run the tests."

She crossed her arms as color started returning to her face. "Why on earth would I do that?"

"If we need to use the DNA in court, you don't want your conflict of interest to call the results into question. Second, you're in shock. You could mess up."

"I assure you, I wouldn't mess up, but you're right about the results." She got up and went to a desk in the corner where she quickly dropped into the chair and picked up the phone.

He didn't point out that since she didn't comment on compromising the results, she wasn't thinking clearly and could indeed mess up. Thankfully she was bringing in others to do the work.

"Lara, good. Glad I caught you. I need your help." She quickly and concisely explained that Caitlyn was missing, and Lara's help was needed to run MPS DNA, whatever that was. But Emory didn't mention her connection to Caitlyn.

Emory tilted her head and listened, her gaze intense. "Thanks. See you then."

She settled the handset in the cradle and came back to face him. "My best analyst, Lara Dixon will be here within thirty minutes. I'll have you do a cheek swab for my DNA and label it with 'Unknown Subject' to keep my identity from Lara."

Ah, so she *was* trying to hide something. "Why would you do that?"

"I don't want her to feel the pressure of running my DNA. Plus, I've been a partner in the center for less than a year, and I'm still getting settled in. The last thing I need is people around here gossiping. So I'd appreciate it if you didn't mention my connection to your investigation."

That would be good for the criminal proceedings too, as the analyst who would run the test couldn't be biased if she didn't know the swab contained Emory's DNA. "I won't say a word unless it's necessary to get the information I need."

"It won't be necessary." She grabbed a box of swabs that looked like large single-ended Q-tips and held it out. "Choose whichever one you want so you can't accuse me of giving you a specific one to taint the results."

He grabbed a random tube, and she opened her mouth. He ignored her smooth skin and full lips and ran the swab over the inside of her cheek. Satisfied he'd captured a large enough sample, he sealed the swab in the tube and labeled the container.

"Now the evidence." She gestured at the duffle.

He took out the bags and spread them out on the table.

She tapped the one holding the handkerchief. "How long has this been packaged?"

He lifted the bag and looked at the details Helen entered on the label then glanced at the wall clock. "We're nearing the two-hour mark."

Confidence replaced the unease in her expression. "We need to get it out of the bags before microorganisms grow and destroy or alter the evidence. We'll need paper to collect any trace evidence that falls from the clothing. Since I do have that conflict of interest you mentioned, you'll need

48

to remove the evidence, and we should document opening the bags with video. I'll grab the camera and paper."

He watched her go to the closet in the corner, her skirt swishing with each step. He found himself wondering what she normally wore to work, and if the fancy hairdo and beguiling red dress caused his attraction. Maybe with her hair down and lab coat over plain scrubs, she'd look...well... nerdy or something.

She came out with a roll of white paper and a camera on a tripod. Set unfolded the tripod legs and pointed the lens at him. She bent over the camera to focus, and the flirty little skirt of her dress skimmed her knees, catching his attention again.

Seriously? What was up with him tonight? He needed to concentrate on the task at hand, and he wished she would take the time to change clothes.

She got out an iPad and swiped to an evidence log. "Enter the case information from the bags on the log. I'm filming you so try not to look so grumpy."

"Grumpy?"

"Yeah. You've been that way since you saw me on the steps."

"I thought you were trying to pull a scam."

"And now? Do you still think that?"

"I don't want to, but..." He shrugged. "You know."

She jutted her chin out. "You're a law enforcement officer and LEOs have to remain skeptical until concrete evidence eliminates your every doubt. So you'll have to wait until the DNA results are done."

He watched her for a moment, assessing. "Sounds like you've worked with your share of law enforcement officers before."

She nodded. "I did five years at the FBI lab in Quantico before I came here. If you want to talk about grumpy and intense people, try not getting a sample processed as fast as an agent wants it. *Then* you'll see grumpy."

He had to laugh at her description, and she joined in, but it wasn't wholehearted.

"What brings you to Portland?" He made sure he sounded casually interested when he was questioning her for the investigation.

"Family. My sister specifically, but now I guess I have a second one, too." She took a long breath and slowly let it out. "I want to help you find her."

"I'm afraid beyond the DNA tests, there's really nothing you can do." He started listing the evidence items on the log.

"On the contrary. I've developed search strategies and techniques to mine Internet databases for matches and can compare Caitlyn's or my DNA profile to any profiles I find."

"I'm sure my tech people can do that."

"Um, no. These are proprietary searches that are well beyond your tech's capabilities."

"So our techs will search manually. How big of a job can it be?"

She scoffed. "I estimate there are ten thousand databases currently online. They contain between three to four hundred thousand profiles."

He looked up. "Seriously?"

"Seriously."

"Okay then, fine. Yeah. You have my permission to do that."

"I...ah...I don't actually need permission to search the web, but thanks. I want any data I locate to be taken seriously."

He appreciated her willingness to cooperate. "I'll have to sit with you when you create the search and then review the findings. That way I can prove you didn't alter any information."

"But why?" She tapped the container holding her cheek swab. "This will prove I didn't fake being Caitlyn or the crime scene at her house."

"But as of now, there isn't proof, right?"

She gave a reluctant nod.

He'd rather not have to keep doubting her, but that was just the way it was. For now. "How long will it take to run the twin comparison DNA?"

"Thirty-six hours or so."

"I can't wait that long to get going on this investigation." He tightened his fists. "I'll need the basic DNA run from the crime scene first."

"Then I'll need to call in another analyst."

"Go for it."

She went back to her desk and quickly made arrangements. He was starting to appreciate the way she ran her lab, and she had to be an okay boss if she was able to get additional staff to agree to come into work at a moment's notice.

"How long will the suspect's test take?" he asked after she ended her call.

"Since the DNA samples look pretty straightforward, I'd say around twenty-four hours."

"Seriously? I thought a big-time expert like you would be using the rapid DNA testing system I'm hearing so much about."

She rested a hand on a machine that was labeled RapidHIT. "We use this all the time, but crime scene samples aren't compliant with the FBI Director's Quality Assurance Standards, and they can't be uploaded to CODIS via this machine. Only buccal cheek swabs are allowed."

Blake was very familiar with the FBI's Combined DNA Index System and the swabs taken from the inside of people's cheeks, but not why crime scene samples weren't allowed in the rapid system. "Why the limit on samples it can run?"

"Buccal swabs always contain sufficient quantities of DNA, and they don't have potentially mixed DNA profiles that require a scientist to interpret. The blood samples you recovered could contain both the victim's and suspect's blood, so a human will need to look at and interpret the results."

He blew out a long breath. "So we wait, then."

She nodded and stood. "You know, I think the best way to handle this investigation is if you bring all of your evidence in-house for us to evaluate." She firmed her shoulders as if she expected him to argue. "We have experts in trace evidence, firearms, toxicology, and prints. We even have an anthropologist on staff. That should cover all of your crime scene needs."

Right. Like that would happen. "I can't possibly afford that."

"We'll process everything for no charge."

That was an unexpected offer. One he wasn't sure he wanted to entertain. "Why would you do that?"

"Because we're looking for my sister." Emory pushed back her lab coat and planted her hands on her waist. "And I also think it would be best to run the investigation out of our offices. That way when you do your daily updates, you'll have all of our experts available to weigh in and offer suggestions."

She had a good point, but with the way she kept distracting him, he didn't want to agree. Plus he needed to be in Cold Harbor working leads. "I can't do that."

"I have nothing against your local lab or the state lab for that matter, but we have far more experience and knowledge than any of the analysts in those labs. Means we can work faster and smarter. Find leads your people might miss." She locked gazes with him. "Don't you want Caitlyn found faster? Because I do, and I know if you partner with us, that will happen."

He couldn't argue with that. "Okay, fine. You can run the evidence faster here, so I'll agree to that, but I need to make a few phone calls for that to happen. The investigation will be run out of my office, though."

She opened her mouth to speak, but he was in no mood for an argument—especially one she had no hope of winning. He held up his hand. "That's not negotiable."

She crossed her arms. "Then I'm coming to Cold Harbor with you."

"No point in that." He widened his stance. "You and your team won't be involved beyond the lab work."

She stared at him for the longest time and suddenly pulled back her shoulders. "Then I'll be hiring Blackwell Tactical to run their own investigation for me."

He had to work hard to contain his sudden frustration with this very attractive woman. "Gage and I go back to our high school days. After I talk to him, I'm sure he won't agree to work this investigation for you."

"Refuse the request to find an abducted woman?" She snorted. "You may be friends with Gage, but I know he'd never say no to a woman in need. Never."

6

Emory's team was in place extracting and cleaning up DNA from the samples delivered by Sheriff Jenkins while he stood in the corner talking on the phone. She usually loved to watch her team work, but her heart was heavy tonight over Caitlyn. Not to mention her parents never telling her she was adopted. That cut clean through her and dread kept chipping away at her mood, leading her toward a panic attack. She couldn't very well freak out here. Keeping busy was what she needed. She had other DNA projects she could be working on, but not in her dress. A quick change of clothes was the answer.

She started to rise, but stopped when the sheriff stowed his phone and crossed the room toward her.

He planted those feet solidly on the tile just like when he'd taken a stand an hour ago. "We need to talk."

Would it kill him to be polite instead of ordering her around? "About?"

"Your connections to this investigation."

Lara glanced up. Questioning eyes a deep blue that matched her current hair coloring locked onto Emory.

"Not here," Emory whispered and came to her feet.

"Listen up, everyone. I'm going to go get changed, and the sheriff will take a break, too. We'll be back soon. Any questions or problems, call me."

Lara looked back and forth between them, but thankfully she returned her attention to her work without questions.

"Follow me," she said to the sheriff and took off across the room and out the door. She waited for it to close and latch. "I thought we discussed this, Sheriff. I won't have my team know Caitlyn's my sister."

"First, you should call me Blake," he said. "And I apologize if I raised concern with your staff."

Emory stopped in surprise at his apology. He seemed to be less controlling, but it could just be an aberration to the pushy behavior she'd witnessed so far and Sam warned her about.

"Is there somewhere we can talk privately?" he asked, sounding almost contrite.

"I need to change into work clothes. We can head over to my condo." She didn't wait for him to agree but took the hallway to the end and entered the elevator to push the up button.

Blake's eyes narrowed. "Shouldn't we be going down to leave?"

"Oh, right. You wouldn't know." The doors opened, and she pressed six for the skybridge. "All the owners live in condos in the other tower."

He shook his head and boarded the car. "A new definition to taking your work home with you."

"It's a great perk. I work long hours, and this allows me time to hang with my younger sister."

The doors slid closed, and she was totally aware of the man standing across the small space. She didn't like the tension so she rushed on with the first thing that came to mind. "My sister lost her husband and lives with me now. He was a marine. His chopper went down in a training exercise."

"I'm sorry for your loss," he said, his tone sincere. "I'm always thankful for military service and the sacrifices families make for our country."

"Thank you." She appreciated his sincerity. "We miss Will, but he died doing what he loved."

He cast her a skeptical look. "Sounds like you've got a healthy attitude about it. Not sure I could manage the same thing."

"Trust me, I didn't at first when I saw how hard the loss hit my sister. Took me some time before I wasn't mad at God for taking Will."

The elevator doors split open, and she led the way to the skybridge that connected the two towers. Stars sparkled in the night sky above the glass tunnel in a rare cloudless night.

Blake turned, taking in the bridge. "Must have cost a pretty penny to build this bridge and retrofit the building to include condos. Or did you have it custom built?"

"Actually, the building and condos were already here. This was supposed to be a mixed-use building. Retail on the ground floor. Offices in the east tower and condos in this tower. Maya inherited the building from her grandfather before it was leased, so they moved in and started the business five years ago."

"And you've been here for nine months," he clarified.

She nodded. "The founding DNA expert left to have a child and didn't come back. Maya contacted me and offered me a partnership. I grew up in Portland, so with my mom living here and my sister a widow, I thought it would be a good time to return."

And if she hadn't dated Robby after returning, it would

have been the best timing. Now? Now, she wasn't quite so sure. She stopped to unlock her condo door.

"I'll have to interview your mother first thing in the morning," Blake said.

Emory spun to face him and shook her head. "*I'll* be the first one to ask her about the adoption. If you don't agree, I'll go over there now and wake her up."

He planted his hands on a trim waist. "I can't have you talking to her without me. I need to see her reaction to the news to gauge her sincerity."

Emory couldn't believe his insensitivity. "You do realize this a highly personal thing, don't you? That I should be allowed to talk to her alone and ask her if I'm adopted?"

"I do." His hands fell to his sides. "And I'm sorry about the way things are going down. But I have to do everything within my power to find Caitlyn, and if that means making your life tough right now, that's what I need to do."

"Sam was so right," Emory muttered and pushed open her door.

"About?"

"How tough and focused you are. Like you don't feel a thing. It's all just a job to you. Procedures and by the book."

He gritted his teeth. "Don't doubt for one minute that all of this tears me up inside. But I can't let emotions get to me, because when I do, things go south. I won't let that happen here."

"Sounds like you're speaking from experience."

"Not going there." He tipped his head at the door. "Why don't we go in and talk about a game plan, so I can get back to work."

Glad to get out of her heels, she entered the space. Angela had left a small night-light on in Emory's large great room that connected to an open kitchen.

She pointed at the couch. "Go ahead and have a seat. I

want to check in with my sister and change clothes." *Maybe run away from you.*

"If you're planning to tell her about Caitlyn, please don't share any investigative details."

"I *am* going to tell her," Emory said and left it at that as she couldn't promise she wouldn't share anything about this situation.

She started down the hall and knocked on her sister's door before going in. Angela, who looked like their mother in her younger years with dark curly hair and a square face, looked up from a book she was reading in a comfy armchair.

"You're home." She smiled. "How was the awards dinner?"

"I didn't go." Emory sat on the end of the bed and had the urge to crawl under the covers and forget about everything, but Caitlyn needed her. Emory may have just learned about her twin, but she would work tirelessly to find her just as she would work to find Angela if she'd been abducted.

Angela met her gaze. "Fear keep you here?"

"No, I actually got on the road and then got a call from Sam Willis. The forensic expert for Blackwell Tactical."

"Of course. I remember Sam."

"She called to tell me a woman was abducted in Cold Harbor, and they needed me to process the DNA. So I came right back to meet with the sheriff."

"That poor woman." Angela closed the book, keeping her finger in the page. "I'm glad you can help, but I'm sorry you missed going out. You needed a night off."

"Actually, I'm glad I came back." Emory took a long breath and tried to form the words that would rock her sister's world, too. "I have something to tell you, and you're going to be shocked."

Angela's eyes narrowed, and she sat forward in the chair. "You're scaring me."

"I don't mean to, but as it turns out, the abducted woman —Caitlyn Abbot—is my twin."

"What?" Angela stared wide-eyed, her expression a mirror of the wild emotions swirling inside Emory.

She took a long breath. "Either Mom and Dad gave a baby away, or I'm adopted."

Angela set the book on the table and ran her hand over her face. "They would never have given a child away. They were desperate to have us."

"I know, so that must mean I'm adopted." Emory dropped to the floor and took her sister's hands. "Think about it. It makes sense. I don't look like you or Mom and Dad or even our grandparents. And you know I've always thought something was missing or odd at times."

Angela nodded. "But I can also tell you like a million reasons why I don't believe it."

"Believe it or not, the DNA doesn't lie. Nor does the picture." She'd taken a quick snapshot of Blake's photo, and she displayed it for Angela.

"Crazy! Just crazy!" Angela shook her head. "It's really true, isn't it?"

"See, that's another difference between us. You don't trust the science, but you trust the visual."

Angela continued to stare at the picture. "So what do you plan to do? Are you gonna talk to Mom tonight?"

Emory shook her head. "In the morning. With the sheriff. And speaking of him, he's waiting for me in the living room. I need to get changed and get back to work."

Angela pressed her hand over Emory's, the warm touch helping to thaw the ache in Emory's stomach. "You have to get some sleep."

"Not with Caitlyn missing."

Angela sat back and frowned.

Her look worried Emory. "What's wrong?"

"I'll have to share you. And with a blood sister. We're not...oh gosh...I don't like this."

Emory squeezed her sister's hands. "That doesn't matter. We've had twenty-eight years together and will have a ton more. Nothing can replace that, not even blood."

She nodded but didn't look fully convinced. She stood and hugged Emory. "I love you, sis. Please don't let this change anything between us. Please. And find Caitlyn. I can't wait to meet someone just like you."

Tears pricked Emory's eyes, and she swallowed hard to hold them at bay. She wanted to cry. Needed to cry, but crying wouldn't bring Caitlyn home. Working would. She'd get her clothes changed and then head back to the lab. She might not be able to run the DNA, but she could kick off her search program to mine DNA databases for comparisons to her own profile.

If she located a match to her DNA, it could very well give them a strong lead right off the bat and help find Caitlyn while she was still alive.

"You've put an alert on her bank and credit card accounts, right?" Blake asked Trent as he paced the living room while he waited for Emory to get changed.

A long sigh of air came through the phone. "Investigations 101, boss."

"I'm not doubting your skills. Just checking off all the boxes on my list."

"Then check it and the phone off. We never did find it, but I had her telecom ping her phone. No response. Must have been destroyed or the battery was removed."

"Just our luck," Blake grumbled.

"I should have call records soon, so we can see who she

talked to in the last few weeks. In the meantime, I'll get started on the bill you sent me."

"And email?"

"I'm waiting on computer imaging before I request it from her provider. I've also requested CCTV for the area, and Lorraine is reviewing Caitlyn's social media. You know how Lorraine loves these sites so I figured she'd be the best person for the job."

"Agreed." Blake's admin participated in most every social media platform and very few law enforcement officers went in for that stuff. That included Blake. They didn't have accounts and weren't as familiar with the ins and outs like Lorraine was.

"She started with Facebook," Trent continued. "But Caitlyn's security settings prohibit us from seeing her posts, so I've obtained a warrant for the information."

"They're not always quick with their responses."

"I'll start nagging them in an hour or so."

Blake appreciated Trent's quick work, but he wished they had more to go on. "Any theories on why she was abducted?"

"She has a large savings account, so money, maybe. Or maybe it has to do with the adoption, but I don't really have anything to base that on. If we had the evidence to prove the adoption is in play right now, we could get a judge to release the records. But we don't have anything other than a gut hunch to say it is."

Blake had the same thought, but likely because of meeting Emory. "Let's keep that in mind as we run down leads. Anything else I need to know?"

"Not at the moment."

"I'll be flying back with Gage Blackwell in the morning. I want a status report every hour tonight at a minimum, but check in with me anytime you learn anything. Should be back by eleven, and we can do an official status update then." Blake hung up and was about to go looking for Emory when she returned.

She'd changed into dark jeans, red Chuck Taylor's, and a purple knit top that clung to her curves. She let her hair down and had perched her glasses on her head, making her look even more like Caitlyn. He had to admit he'd found Emory attractive in her formal attire, but the casual clothes made her seem more approachable. More like the type of woman he was usually attracted to. One who might want to go camping or hiking with him. Or go to a football or baseball game.

"Sorry it took me so long," she said, but didn't explain any further.

He didn't want her to see his interest, so he quickly gestured at the sofa. "Have a seat so we can talk."

"That sounds ominous." A nervous laugh escaped as she chose a small leather chair and tucked her legs up under her.

Right. She didn't even want to sit next to him. Should dampen his interest, but he couldn't seem to focus on anything but the curve of her slender neck as she looked up at him. He swallowed and sat. "I want to make sure we're on the same page regarding this investigation."

She tilted her head. "If your page includes me visiting Caitlyn's house to look for additional evidence, then yes, we're on the same page."

He gritted his teeth at her tenacity. "You know I can't let you do that."

She raised her shoulders. "Why not?"

"So many reasons, but first, you're a civilian, and I can't let you compromise the integrity of the investigation. And just as important—maybe more so—you have a personal connection to the case and that would compromise things even more."

She lifted her chin. "I can be objective."

"I'm sorry, but you can't. No one could in your position." He held her gaze. "We could meet halfway, though."

"How?" Suspicion darkened her amazing brown eyes.

"I'll allow your trace evidence person to work the scene with one of my techs."

She frowned. "Sierra Byrd is our trace evidence expert, and she'll be as thorough as I would've been, but that's hardly meeting halfway."

He both hated and loved her persistence, but he wouldn't back down. "It's all I'm prepared to offer."

She tapped a finger on her knee. "When are you leaving?"

He almost blew out a breath of relief over her change of subject but something told him he hadn't heard the end of this. "Gage and Hannah are heading back right after their appointment in the morning. I'll go with them."

"Perfect. I'll contact Gage to see if we can catch a ride, too."

Did she mean him and her? "We?"

"Your decision doesn't change anything. I'm still coming to Cold Harbor to work this investigation. Either I do it by your side or on my own. That hasn't changed just because you're allowing Sierra to process Caitlyn's house."

Blake wasn't a sighing man, but this woman brought him close to becoming one. *Stubborn woman!* He crossed his arms instead. "What part about you being a civilian didn't you catch?"

"Not your average civilian. Veritas partners with law enforcement agencies all the time. The formal contract spells out chain of custody and procedure and will stand up in any court of law. So solving our dispute is simple. Just hire my company."

He frowned at her. "You know I can't afford to do that."

"Can you afford a dollar? Because that's my 'friends and family rate'—and Caitlyn's family." A mischievous smile claimed Emory's mouth, and she looked like a teenager pulling something over on her parents.

He wanted to argue on so many levels, but top of his list was that he was used to being in charge and running a team who knew that and acted accordingly. This woman, this feisty woman, was a loose cannon, and the minute he contracted with her lab, he knew he would have his work cut out for him.

But a woman's life was at stake, and he had to think of her first. Help from the Veritas staff gave him the best chance at finding Caitlyn alive. He would just have to be cognizant of and find a way to manage the conflict of interest.

He pulled out his wallet, slapped a dollar bill on the table and locked gazes with her. "I'll hire your team, but don't make me regret this decision, Emory, or I can't be held accountable for my reaction."

7

Blake admired Emory as she stood before her team, looking strong and in charge. She'd dressed that morning in black slacks, a lavender blouse with tiny leaf prints, and moderate heels. Her glasses rested on top of her head. He was starting to think she only wore them while working in the lab.

She smiled at her partners who she'd gathered at the break of dawn to inform them of her decision to commit their full resources for a single dollar bill. Blake still couldn't believe he'd agreed to the contract. Neither could Trent when Blake told him last night on one of the update calls.

"I'd like you all to meet Sheriff Blake Jenkins." Emory acknowledged him with a tip of her head. "Please, everyone, introduce yourselves. Why don't you start, Maya?"

The nearest woman, a blonde with shoulder-length hair and striking blue eyes nodded. "Maya Glass. Toxicology and controlled substances."

Blake believed a person's clothing said so much about personality, so he looked beyond her authoritative gaze to her navy blue knit shirt, a white lab coat over top. Said *all business* to him as did her assessing stare.

"Maya." He smiled politely when what he really wanted

to do was get moving so they could go interview Emory's mother and he could return to Cold Harbor.

"Nick Thorn, computer cybercrimes," the man seated next to her said. He had brown hair with a short beard, and great posture for a guy who must sit behind a computer on a regular basis. He was dressed in jeans and an orange shirt with what looked like tiny airplanes scattered over the fabric —kind of casual and unassuming.

Blake nodded a greeting.

The slender woman next to Nick sat forward and smiled. Her curly black hair was pulled up into a bun, and she dressed in a feminine frilly blouse with tiny hearts and ruffles, but her aqua-green eyes sized up every detail about him. "Kelsey Moore, forensic anthropologist."

"Nice to meet you." Blake quickly swung his gaze to the next guy seated across the table. Redheaded with a beard, he was ruggedly dressed in tactical pants and a plaid shirt.

"Grady Houston. You want to shoot someone or blow them up, I'm your guy." He chuckled, and his blue eyes crinkled.

Blake laughed. "Good to know."

"Sierra Byrd." The last owner, a woman dressed comfortably in jeans and knit top, tucked a strand of shoulder-length blond hair behind her ear. Her firm gaze held his. "Trace evidence and fingerprint analysis. I'll be joining you in Cold Harbor."

Blake smiled at her. "Thank you for agreeing to help so quickly."

"Let's cut to the chase," Maya said, her focus fixed on Emory. "What's this all about?"

Emory firmed her shoulders. "Last night Sheriff Jenkins asked me to run DNA for a crime scene where a woman was tortured and abducted. When he arrived, he thought I was trying to scam him."

"What? Why?" Maya glared at Blake.

"If you look at the TV." Emory paused and gestured at the large flat-screen television mounted on the wall, much like the TVs in Blake's situation room where they not only projected videos and reports, but kept abreast of local news reports. "This is the photo of the abducted woman."

She clicked a remote, and Caitlyn's face filled the screen. Gasps traveled around the table and mouths fell open.

"Whoa." Grady stared at the screen. "She's a dead ringer for you. Or *is* it you? I can't tell."

"Not me," Emory said. "But DNA confirms she's my twin."

Another round of gasps.

"You never said anything." Maya's accusatory tone cut like a knife.

"Because I didn't know until last night." Emory bit her lip and took a breath. "Either my mother gave up a baby, which I doubt would ever happen, or I'm adopted, and we were split up. I'll be talking to my mother as soon as this meeting's over."

"Man." Nick shook his head. "That's freaky."

"You must be in shock." Sierra got up and rested a hand on Emory's shoulder. "How are you doing with all of this, sweetie?"

Emory shook her head, her eyes glistening with tears, and Blake's heart constricted with her pain. He'd been so focused on finding Caitlyn and following proper protocol that he hadn't considered how this discovery might be affecting Emory. He needed to remedy that. She was a person first and foremost, not a robot running DNA samples for him.

"I'm doing okay, and we need to get to work." Emory turned her focus to the group, and Sierra took her seat. "I've offered our services in the investigation to find Caitlyn for a dollar. I hope under the circumstances that you all agree with my decision and can support it. If not, I'm glad to pay the bill."

"Of course we agree, don't we?" Maya looked around the group, and the others nodded.

"And I'm sure I don't have to add that finding Caitlyn takes top priority," Emory said. "We drop everything and work this case when needed. The sooner we find her, the more likely she'll still be..." Emory's voice broke off in a sob, and she lifted her face to the ceiling, exposing her slender neck as she swallowed hard.

She put her hand up stilling comments from others.

"I don't think the staff need to know about my connection to Caitlyn and want to keep it between us. I hope you can respect that." She stood taller and focused on her team as they nodded their agreement. "Sheriff Jenkins will provide details on the abduction and investigation. Then we'll take suggestions from each of you."

Blake nodded, and Emory took a seat. He was impressed with her ability to turn off her anguish and focus, but as she folded her hands together on the table, he saw them tremble. He wanted to forget about everything else and hold her hands until they stopped shaking, but he had a room full of experts staring at him.

"First, everyone please call me Blake." He smiled to try to relax everyone's concern for Emory. He ran through the facts on the crime scene, being cognizant of the fact that Emory was hearing the torture details for the first time.

"At this point, pretty much all we know is that Caitlyn learned she was adopted about a year ago, had her DNA run here to find her birth parents, and she has a male and female friend who helped her move. Other than that, we're just beginning to discover who she is." Blake paused to catch his breath. "The most obvious question I have no answer for or even a strong theory for is motive. Why torture this woman and then abduct her? What was our suspect wanting to know or gain from the torture?"

"Something she knows or has that this guy wants," Grady said looking disgusted. "Maybe both."

"I can do a deep dive on the Internet into her past," Nick offered. "Give you a complete picture of her life. But if you give me her photo I can do a search right now, and it might give you something to start with."

Blake grabbed Caitlyn's picture from his file and handed it to Nick.

He took it to a scanner on a table in the corner, and the machine whirred to life. "This will only take a sec."

Emory cleared her throat, grabbing everyone's attention again. "While Nick's doing that, let me update you on the DNA. There's some question that I might be posing as Caitlyn and faked my abduction."

"That's ludicrous." Kelsey firmed her shoulders and cast Blake an accusatory look.

He had no defense, so he said nothing, but all eyes were on him.

"I'm running MPS DNA in hopes of finding any distinguishing mutations to prove that I wasn't the woman at the crime scene," Emory continued. "We have other samples from the scene running, too. Hopefully one of the samples belongs to the suspect."

"Okay, check out the TV screen," Nick said without looking up. "You can see the search results as they populate."

Emory took a seat, and Blake turned to the wall-mounted television. A search page displayed on the screen. Nick clicked on the camera in the search bar and uploaded the photo. The icon churned and soon a list of links appeared.

"So these are the sites where a matching picture was posted." He ran his cursor arrow down the top items. "Facebook. Twitter. Instagram. Various ancestry websites. Since we already know she was searching for her birth parents that makes sense."

"What's that link just below your cursor?" Blake asked.

He clicked on it. "Now this is an interesting hobby."

Blake looked at story on photobombing as a hobby. "So basically she finds a TV news reporter doing a live feed, slips into the background, and makes sure she's captured on camera."

"It's odd, right?" Emory asked.

"Unusual for sure." Sierra batted long lashes. "Maybe this is the reason she was targeted."

Grady scratched his stubble-covered chin and looked at his partner. "What do you mean?"

"She could've seen or heard something she shouldn't have," Sierra said. "Or maybe a deranged person saw these stories, spotted her in the background, and took a sick liking to her."

Nick frowned. "It's awful to think an innocent woman was targeted just for appearing on camera, but we live in a sick world, and it's not farfetched."

Blake didn't want to respond, but he had to. "We have yet to determine she's innocent."

"Now wait a minute." Emory jumped to her feet and planted her hands on her hips. "Are you saying you think my sister is involved in something illegal or nefarious?"

Blake shook his head. "I'm just saying we don't know anything about her. I'm with Nick on this. No woman deserves to be targeted, innocent or not."

Breathing hard, Emory dropped back onto her chair.

Blake turned his focus to Sierra. "When you process the scene, can you look for anything related to photobombing?

Since we didn't know about this hobby on the initial search, we could've overlooked a lead."

"Sure thing." She jotted a note on a legal pad, her pink polished nails flashing in the light.

"I think this is a good lead," Blake said to the group. "An unhealthy infatuation is a strong motive for an abduction."

Grady sat forward, his blue eyes sharpened. "Were any weapons recovered?"

Blake shook his head. "And we don't know the extent of her injuries other than the blood found isn't indicative of life-threatening injuries."

Grady nodded. "I may specialize in weapons, but I have a basic forensic degree, so let me know if I can help in any other area."

"Same goes for me," Kelsey said. "I'm glad to pitch in wherever you need."

Blake smiled his thanks for the offer, but he couldn't even begin to think they'd find a body that required her anthropology skills. If they did, it meant the investigation had taken a seriously odd and deadly twist.

Emory's partners departed, strolling slowly out of the room, giving her sympathetic and questioning looks at the same time. She couldn't handle talking to them without crying so she faced Blake. *Great.* She was so upset that she'd rather talk to Blake than the people who had supported her for months. But she couldn't start crying or she might never stop.

"I'll be back in an hour tops," she told him, trying one more time to go see her mother without him. "Plenty of time to catch the helicopter back to Cold Harbor."

Blake's jaw jutted out. "I'm coming with you."

She shook her head hard. "We've been through this, Blake. This is personal. I can't have you there when I confront my mother."

"I'm sorry, but I'm coming along." His gaze sharpened even more. "I'll be sensitive to the situation. I promise. But I have to interview your mother. She could hold the key to finding Caitlyn."

Emory looked him directly in the eye. "Give me a list of questions, and I can ask them for you."

"You know that's not how interviewing works. I need to see how your mother reacts. Read her body language. And form additional questions based on her answers."

Emory *did* know that, but had hoped to win this argument. She wasn't one to give in so easily, but she really didn't have any other reason with which she could convince him. "Fine, but I'll be watching you. From what Sam said, you're not good at doing sensitive, so I'll call you on the carpet if you fail."

"Duly noted."

"Then let's get going."

She grabbed her backpack and marched to the lobby. It was only when she caught sight of Pete sitting at the reception desk that she remembered the sun hadn't come up, and her feet refused to move. She swallowed down her anxiety and faced Blake. "I'm assuming you want to drive."

He nodded.

She forced a blank expression to her face that she'd learned to employ when giving a client DNA results they didn't want to hear. "Would you mind bringing your car up to the door while I talk to Pete a minute?"

"Glad to." He struck out as if he was eager to be on the go and gave Pete a firm nod on the way past.

She joined the smiling security guard. "Sheriff Jenkins

will be working with us on an abduction investigation, so you may see a lot of him."

Pete frowned. "Please tell me it's not a child."

"No. A woman my age." She wasn't ready to share with him about her sister either, so she looked away before he asked additional questions. She saw the headlights on an old pickup approaching the door.

"Interesting ride for a sheriff, huh?" Pete asked.

Emory nodded, but relief swept through her. An attacker couldn't hide in the cab with them. "I'm going to Cold Harbor to work this investigation and may not see you for a few days."

"I'll pray this young woman is found safe and sound."

She squeezed Pete's arm, and he opened the door for her. By the time she stepped into the drizzling rain, Blake stood holding the passenger door open.

He frowned. "I should've warned you about my borrowed truck. It runs great, but it's pretty beat up. If you'd rather take your car—"

"No, this is fine." She glanced in the bed to be sure it was empty and climbed into the old vehicle. Nostalgia for her grandfather came rushing back. "My grandpa had a truck like this."

Her grandpa Steele. Not really her grandpa now, was he? At least not biologically. She might have another, maybe two more grandfathers out there now. The thought nearly made her head spin.

Head down against the rain, Blake hurried around front and got behind the wheel. "So where are we headed?"

She gave him the initial directions out of the lot, and he pointed the truck toward the exit. She focused on the wipers scraping across the window to keep from thinking about the darkness surrounding them.

He glanced at her. "So tell me about your mother."

Emory didn't know what to say. Did she even know her mother anymore? No matter the reason she hadn't told Emory about Caitlyn, her mother deceived Emory for her entire life. Tears pricked at the back of her eyes.

Father, please. This is so big. Huge. Help me to deal with this. To be open-minded and really listen to my mom.

"Emory?" Blake asked. "You okay?"

"Sorry. I'm still trying to process the news, and I was offering a quick prayer."

"If it helps, I said a few for you *and* Caitlyn on the way to the truck." He met her gaze for a moment. "I'm sorry that I haven't given much thought to what you're going through."

She shot him a surprised look. "So you're a man of faith?"

"Ouch." He mimicked a stab wound to the chest. "If it's such a surprise to you, I must not be a very good witness."

"No. No." She waved a hand. "Sorry. You're just so...um... well...decisive. Maybe rigid. I just didn't...not really sensitive to other people's feelings." She clasped her hands together and grimaced. "I'm making it worse, aren't I?"

"Pretty much." He grinned at her, his smile lighting up his face and leaving her gaping at his handsome face.

Her heart flip-flopped.

"Oh," the word slipped out as she tried to come to grips with her reaction.

"Oh, what?"

"Nothing...nothing," she rushed on and was sure she was blushing. "You need to turn right at the next stoplight."

His smile disappeared, and he took a long look at her before focusing back on the road.

She concentrated on taking shallow breaths to keep him from noticing her sudden discomfort. What was up with her? She was still terrified of men from the attack and hadn't even had a fraction of interest in a guy since then.

Boom—just like that, this man swoops in, and she's smitten.

Craziness. Crazy, crazy, crazy.

"I do understand how hard this must be for you," he continued. "You're probably wondering why it happened and you might even be mad at God. I get that. Trust me. I totally get it."

She both liked and disliked the idea that he was a man of faith. As a Christian, she would, of course, want him to know God, but as a woman who was captivated by him, if he wasn't, it would have been a great obstacle to keep her interest at bay.

Listen to her. Thinking like she needed an extra obstacle. After the attack she didn't need a reason not to get involved with men. She couldn't trust them. Or more precisely, she couldn't trust her judgement. She'd dated Robby for two months before realizing they weren't right for each other. He had other ideas and had become obsessed with her. He hid in the back of her car and attacked her. She'd barely escaped with her life.

So, no. She didn't need a reason not to follow her attraction to the good sheriff. She didn't trust men. Any man. And even if she stopped to consider Blake's profession and believed he was a good guy, after seeing Angela suffer such loss, Emory would never date a man with a dangerous job.

"I can understand it might be hard to talk about your mother," Blake said, oblivious to her true inner turmoil at the moment. "I just thought it would be helpful to know a little about her before we meet."

"She was a dancer," Emory said the first thing that came to mind to keep the focus off her. "She's still so graceful and slender. And she still dances. Not ballet, but other forms. My sister Angela is just like her. She was into dance for many years as a kid. Me, not so much. Bugs, creepy-crawlies, and how things worked was what I loved. And books. I usually had my face buried in one. I still read a lot. I was more like my..." *Father*, she was about to say, but didn't really know if that was true or not.

He cast a quizzical gaze her way, but she held her tongue. She wasn't about to discuss her inner turmoil with him.

"What do you like to read?" he asked.

"I thought this was about my mother?"

"It is, but I'm just curious."

"You're going to laugh, but right now I'm into fiction. Gets my mind off things. And my current favorites are sweeping historicals from a time gone by." She sighed as she thought of gentlemanly manners back in the day. Sure, men attacked women then, too, but it seemed like a safer time to her.

She waited for him to gape at her or laugh, but he simply nodded. "What do you like about that genre?"

"The manners. Order to society. A simpler time, I guess." She smiled, thinking of some of her favorite stories.

"If you lived in those bygone days, you surely wouldn't have been allowed to work in the science field, and you'd be out of a job."

"True," she said, wondering if she would trade what she loved to do for a feeling of safety. She had to admit at this time in her life, she would. But only for personal security. She loved her work. Her partners. Her lab. Loved it all and wouldn't give it up for any other reason.

He turned the corner, heading into the neighborhood where she'd grown up. For many years when she'd worked with the FBI in D.C., she'd left behind this quaint city neighborhood where neighbors sat on porches and stoops to talk.

The sun was rising over the homes on the familiar street in glorious red and orange striations with a hint of purple blended in, and she was surprised to discover it no longer felt like home. Finding out she was adopted had likely taken that from her, too.

She pointed at the craftsman home with stone pillars and big porch. "It's the big green house on the left."

Just looking at the place, the light flowing from inside and spilling onto the porch, sent her breakfast churning in her stomach. What was she going to say to her mother?

Please. Please help me to do this the right way.

Blake parked at the curb and faced her as he took out the keys. "How do you think your mother will react to this news?"

Emory opened her door, but kept her gaze on his. "There's only one way to find out."

8

An elegant woman with black hair in shoulder-length curly waves opened the door. She wore pressed jeans with sharp creases and a white button-down blouse, her posture perfect. She was a few inches taller than Emory and looked nothing like her daughter. Either Emory looked like her dad, or they would indeed learn that Emory was adopted.

"Hi, sweetheart." She reached out to hug Emory.

Emory frowned and stepped back out of reach. She'd put her glasses in her backpack, and her eyes were dark and wide as she watched her mother.

Hurt and confusion flashed in her mother's eyes for a beat before she recovered to smile at Blake. "And who is your guest?"

Blake held out his hand. "Sheriff Blake Jenkins, ma'am."

"Karen Steele." She shook hands but cast her gaze back to Emory. "Has something bad happened, Emory?"

"Why don't we go inside and sit down?" Blake suggested.

"Emory?" she asked.

"We can talk inside." Emory's voice came out in the barest whisper but held a hard edge.

"Sure. Let me take your coats." Karen held out her hands.

Emory and Blake shed their jackets, and Karen hung them on a hall tree, the air saturated with tension and unspoken questions. Without a word, Karen spun gracefully and crossed the foyer to a hallway.

Blake stood back to let Emory enter before him and closed the door. She jumped, telling him she was more nervous than he first thought. It stood to reason that she would be, and her posture and responses suggested she was very angry at her mother. Another logical reaction.

He followed her down the hallway. He'd never been in a situation remotely like this with his mother. Not even when he'd let an argument with his sister, Danielle get heated, stopped to let her get out of the car, and then she'd been attacked as she walked home. When his mother heard, she'd responded with tremendous grace and compassion for him. His guilt wouldn't let him receive it, and he felt even guiltier for not being there for his sister.

He shook his head to erase the memory for now. He knew it would be back, as it returned at the oddest times, but right now he had an interview to conduct.

He trailed the women down a hallway that opened into a large kitchen with a monstrous island topped with white marble. Four wrought iron stools sat on one side of the rich wood cabinets. Emory pulled out a stool, and he slipped onto the one next to her.

Karen gestured at the coffee pot. "Could I get either of you a cup?"

Having been up most the night keeping updated with Trent, Blake was dragging, and the coffee—a hazelnut variety if the rich scent lingering in the air told him anything—sounded good. "That would be nice. Black, please."

"Nothing for me," Emory said as she stared at her hands on the counter.

"You want me to do this?" he whispered.

She shook her head hard, her hair swishing in rhythm, but her face didn't hold half the confidence of her response.

Karen placed a large stoneware mug in front of Blake and went to sit at a stool on the side of the island nearest Emory. "Now suppose one of you tells me what this is about."

Blake got out his notepad and pen.

Emory took a long breath. "Sheriff Jenkins brought evidence from an abducted woman's home in last night to have me run DNA. Imagine my surprise when he shared her picture, and she looked like this." Emory reached into her backpack and slapped Caitlyn's photo in front of her mother.

Karen pulled it closer, and her head shot up. "But I don't understand. This is you."

"More precisely." Emory took a long breath. "My identical twin."

Karen's lips covered in the palest of pink lipstick turned down. "What kind of a joke is this, Emory, because it's not funny."

"Am I adopted?" Emory asked, her tone sharp.

"What?" Karen clutched her chest.

"Am. I. Adopted?"

Karen glanced at Blake as if looking for help.

"Don't look at him," Emory snapped. "Just answer. If you can't say it aloud, then nod your head."

Looking stricken, Karen nodded.

"It's true, then. Really true." Emory stood and planted her hands on the countertop, her breath coming in shallow bursts. "I'm adopted, and I have a twin sister."

"I don't know anything about a twin." Karen reached out to place a hand on Emory's.

She jerked her hand back. "Why didn't you ever tell me?"

"I...we...we wanted to. But when you were younger, the time never seemed right. And then it got to a point when you were too old, and we couldn't do it." She clutched her hands together. "I know we should have, but sweetheart, please try to understand."

Emory raised her eyes to the ceiling then back to her mother. "If Caitlyn hadn't been abducted, I'd be walking out that door. But because I want to find my twin, I need you to tell us everything you know about the adoption and answer any of Blake's questions. A life is at stake here. Can you be truthful about that at least?"

"Sweetheart, please." Karen stood and took a step.

Emory moved to Blake's other side and sat. He didn't mind being her buffer, but it was distressing seeing pain consume both of these women when there was nothing he could do to help. All he could do was try to find answers so he could locate Caitlyn.

He gentled his voice and turned to Karen. "Was this a private adoption?"

She nodded and dropped onto the stool. "A closed adoption through Draywall Adoption Agency in Tigard. I haven't had contact with them since the adoption was finalized. I don't even know if they're still open."

"I'll need to see the paperwork."

Karen gave a firm nod. "It's in our safe deposit box at the bank."

"Then I'll need you to get it for me as soon as possible."

"I can do it right away."

"Perfect." He smiled, hoping to ease some of her turmoil. He wanted to assure her that Emory would get over her anger, but he couldn't possibly do that. "You said you know nothing about Caitlyn."

"Nothing." Karen's eyes glistened with tears. "If we'd known Emory had a twin sister, we would have adopted both babies."

Emory sucked in a quick breath, and he glanced at her to be sure she was okay before continuing. "Tell me what you know about their birth parents."

Karen clutched her hands together. "Nothing, really. We never met them. The agency told us they were married, but couldn't afford to raise a child. They wanted Emory to have a better life."

"Did my *real* parents name me or did you?" Emory asked, her tone sharp and biting.

Karen cringed. "They did. You were only nine days old when you came to us, but I loved the name, and you seemed like an Emory so we kept it."

Emory gave a single nod.

"Were the parents from Portland?" Blake asked.

"I don't know."

"What *do* you know?" Emory asked.

"That your dad and I have loved you since we first saw you. That I'm sorry for not telling you. That it was wrong. Please forgive me—us." Her pleading gaze hurt Blake's heart, and he had no reference in his own life to know what Emory might be feeling.

"I mean about the adoption," Emory replied, emotionless now.

Her mother took a long breath. "We had an attorney but he passed away, and his office closed more than twenty years ago, so he can't help. I don't know, maybe you could find someone who has his old records, but I don't think he knew anything more than we did. Other than that, Emory came to us dressed in a cute but inexpensive onesie, and she had a yellow-and-mint-green-striped blanket that was hand-knit. Also a small bracelet, an engraved silver frame with her baby picture from the hospital, an engraved silver comb-and-brush set, and a small ruby ring. Her birth stone. We were asked to give them to her when we told her she was adopted. Obviously, we never did, so we kept them with her adoption papers."

"Do you have the blanket?" Emory asked almost breathlessly.

"Yes. I'll go get it." Karen bolted from the room.

Blake turned to Emory. "She's really hurting."

"*She's* hurting?" Emory gaped at him. "What about me?"

"Of course. That's to be expected, and I'm not taking her side, but from looking around this house and spending time with you, I can see you had a good life and turned out to be an exceptional person. Karen and your dad took excellent care of you, and I have to believe your mother really loves you."

Emory tilted her head and was quiet for so long that Blake thought he'd really offended her.

"Yeah. You're right they did," she finally said. "They loved—she loves—me without reservation, and they gave me an incredible life." Emory took a long, anguished breath and let it out. "I hope once I process this shocking news that I'll see that again, because I don't want to hurt Mom the way she hurt me. The pain is just too deep to ever be the same again."

In the living room, Emory fingered the soft blanket lying in her lap, tears brimming over and dropping onto the yarn. Her mother had gone to the bank, and Blake arranged for Gage to wait for an extra hour. Emory had called Sierra to go straight to the heliport. That way Emory and Blake could leave the minute her mother returned with the paperwork.

Emory's adoption paperwork.

Seriously, she was thirty years old, and she just learned her birth parents weren't her biological parents. That she had other family members. Surely this was about to change her life in ways she couldn't even imagine. Her head spun with all kinds of scenarios, and the same emotions she'd seen while matching up families by DNA in her job shredded her heart.

"Anything I can do to help?" Blake asked from the sofa Emory had played on as a kid.

Emory shook her head.

"I know this must be a huge shock."

"Shock. Yeah." She stared at the sofa's floral pattern as she couldn't look at him or she might throw herself into his arms for comfort. "My mother had this sofa recovered several times, but it still holds so many family memories. She always curled her legs under her and sat in the corner reading. I did the same thing. Tucked my legs up."

"I noticed that last night."

Surprised he'd paid her so much attention, she looked up at him.

"Noticing all the little things is a side effect of being a law enforcement officer." He smiled.

"Right." She looked at the sofa again. "I loved that sitting like that came naturally to me because it was one of the few things that I did like her. All these years, I thought I'd inherited it, but now I know it was learned behavior."

"Doesn't make you any less her daughter, though, does it?"

Emory eyed him. "Why are you taking her side?"

"I'm not taking anyone's side. Simply trying to point out things that might make it easier for you. Good things."

"How about thinking about your own life? Putting yourself in my place? What if you found out today that your parents aren't your parents?"

He didn't respond right away, but something she'd said had hit him hard, and he was suffering.

At his anguish, she wished she could take it back. "Did I say something wrong?"

He shook his head and got up to go look out the window. "You've probably seen others discover the same thing, right? I mean in your work."

"Yes," she said.

And from that at least, she knew the way she was feeling was normal. She'd had to break this news to many adults. And she'd talked with parents who'd kept the adoption a secret, too. She'd been able to empathize with them as their intentions were all good. But not now. Now that the ball was in her own court, she couldn't empathize with her mother.

Emory's phone chimed. "It's a text from Nick. Draywall Adoption agency closed in the early nineties. He's trying to locate their old records along with the attorney's files."

"He works fast."

"That he does." She sent Nick a thank you text and stowed her phone.

"Karen's back," he announced and let the curtains fall.

Emory's gut tightened, and she clutched the blanket, wondering about the man and woman who'd given it to her. What did they do with Caitlyn? Did she get a blanket, too? Why didn't they want their babies?

But wondering about them wouldn't help her right now, nor would it help bring Caitlyn home. Emory got up and tucked the blanket back into the storage bag. "The blanket and booties are hand-crocheted, but it's possible my team can trace the onesie back to the retailers who sold it. That could help."

Blake turned. "We won't have time to drop it off and still get to the chopper on time. Could they trace it from pictures?"

"Maybe." Emory took a few snapshots and texted the photos to Nick who quickly agreed to do an Internet search on the onesie.

The door opened, and Emory forgot how to breathe, so she focused on tucking the onesie and booties into the bag with the blanket. Her mother came into the room, her eyes red and blotchy from crying. Sadness crept into Emory's heart, and she felt bad for being the one to cause this unhappiness, but she could still hardly look at her mother. Partly from anger, the other part from guilt. She'd been so rude to her when she didn't have to be. She'd even prayed not to be, but the moment she'd laid eyes on her mother, Emory's emotions took charge. Correction—Emory *allowed* her emotions to take charge. Maybe she could do better now.

"Here's the paperwork." Her mother held out a thick envelope and small box. "I made a copy for my records."

"Thank you." Emory took them and picked up the blanket. "They're holding the helicopter for us, and we need to go."

"When will I see you again?" Her mom's tone was so tentative it hurt Emory's heart even more, and she wished she could assure her mother that they would be fine, but she didn't know that yet.

"Not likely until after Caitlyn's found." She took a long breath. "I'm sorry I was so harsh, but it's..." Tears clogged her throat, and she had to stop to breathe. "I'll think about things. Let you know."

Her mother lifted her hands like she wanted to hug Emory, but let them fall to her side, her gaze dejected and rejected. "Does Angela know about this?"

"I haven't talked to her since you told me I'm adopted, but she knows about Caitlyn and that the DNA proves she's my twin."

"And is she mad at me, too?"

"You'll have to ask her. Now I really have to go." Emory clutched the items to her chest like a shield and slipped past her mother, honestly wondering if she would ever come back to this house again. She didn't care that she was adopted. That she was fine with, as she believed adoption was a wonderful gift people could give to children. But she did care about being deceived every day of her life—correction, every day minus the eight days she'd spent with her birth parents.

She rushed away from the house like running from a bullet and climbed into the truck, for once not caring if anyone was lying in wait for her. She jerked the door closed and waited for the familiar fear to come. To suffocate her. But it didn't make an appearance at all. Sure, it was light out now, but she felt uneasy every time she got into a vehicle.

Had learning that she'd been adopted eliminated her fears for good or only for this moment? Wouldn't that be something if this latest shock erased the earlier one?

Blake slid behind the wheel and glanced at his watch. "We better hope we don't hit much traffic or we'll be late."

"Will Gage wait for us?"

"I know he would want to, but they need the helicopter for a training today, and he has to get back." He shifted into gear and got them going.

"Blackwell Tactical is something else, isn't it?" she asked, hoping to direct the conversation anywhere but on her.

Blake got the truck on the road and merged into morning traffic. "Gage is quite a guy."

"How long have you known him?"

"We went to school together. Played football on the same

team. I was the captain, he was the quarterback." A fond smile crossed his face. "We lost touch when he was a SEAL but reconnected when he came back to Cold Harbor."

"And did you stay in Cold Harbor when he was off being a SEAL?" she asked, now genuinely interested in learning about him instead of just avoiding her past.

"I went to college, then came back and went straight into law enforcement. Been sheriff for seven years now."

"Is that an elected position?"

He nodded and cringed. "I don't much like the politics."

"And the job?"

He didn't say anything, keeping his focus on the road. He was speeding through traffic, and she was glad he was focusing on that, but she also wanted him to answer her question.

"I'm making a difference," he finally said. "And I know I run a fine department."

"But do you like it?"

He didn't answer right away. "Honestly, not as much as I used to. We've had an uptick in drugs and the crime it brings in the last few years. It's disheartening to see a county I love go through that."

"You really care."

He nodded. "You sound surprised."

"I don't know...maybe a little, but not because of you per se." She searched for the words to explain herself. "I work with all kinds of law enforcement officers. Those who care. Those who once cared but are too jaded to care anymore, and those who never did care."

"It's hard not to get cynical," he said, sounding a little disillusioned himself.

"I can't even imagine. I mean, I do the DNA work for a lot of crimes, but I rarely know about the victims. It's more of a clinical thing for me."

"Until now."

"Yeah, until now." She didn't want him to linger on the topic and searched for something else they had in common. "So you said Hannah had a doctor's appointment. Is everything okay with her?"

"Not sure. She didn't want to talk about it. She's pregnant."

"When's she due?"

"Due?" He shook his head. "I don't know. She looks pretty big, so soon I think."

"I hope you didn't tell her that."

"No. Of course not." He looked at Emory and held her gaze for a long moment. "You really seem to have a bad impression of me."

"Sorry, but as direct as you seem to be, I just thought..." She shrugged.

"And here I thought I handled myself pretty well with your mother."

"Yeah," she said, thinking about it. "Yeah, I was too wrapped up in my own stuff to notice. But you did handle it well. You were compassionate and kind. Thank you."

"You're welcome." He smiled, and she locked on his gaze, finding it hard to look away.

He turned back to his driving. "You haven't talked about your dad."

"He died from lung cancer when I was in high school." She shook her head. "He never smoked a day in his life. His dad died from it, too. I was worried it might be a hereditary thing. I told my mom that. She could've told me about the adoption then."

"Was that right after your dad died?"

"Yeah."

"So she was probably grieving."

"No matter what you say, you really do seem to want to

take her side." She felt her anger rising. "Is there something in your past with your family that makes you want to do that?"

He tightened his fingers on the wheel. "That's a long story."

"We have time."

He pointed ahead. "Sorry. We're here."

"You're not sorry at all, are you?"

"Not really."

"Well, mister," she said, "You may need to know all about me to find Caitlyn, but trust me, I love puzzles, and I'm far more curious than you think. And I'm equally skilled at getting to the bottom of things, so I'm not giving up on asking about your life."

9

Feeling sorry for herself, Emory approached the helicopter, but when Hannah covered her pregnant belly with her hands as if protecting the precious life inside, Emory was ashamed for her selfish thoughts. There were far more important things to focus on. Not only Hannah and Gage's child, but Emory's missing sister, too.

Committed to do better, Emory stepped closer to the helicopter with blades spinning in a *whomp, whomp, whomp* above and prayed Hannah and Gage hadn't received bad news during the doctor's appointment.

As Blake loaded their bags in the cargo area, she glanced at Riley Glen in the pilot seat. She nodded a greeting at the Blackwell team member who she'd once spent a long afternoon with at the morgue before he'd flown her home from Cold Harbor.

"Riley," Blake greeted and climbed inside.

He turned to offer his hand, and Emory took hold, the touch shooting right to her heart. She closed her eyes for a moment to erase her wayward and unwelcome response, then focused on Gage and Hannah. Gage sat with a protective arm around his wife, but he was smiling. Sierra was seated on the other side of the helicopter, smiling at the couple.

"Good to see you again, Emory," Gage said loudly to be heard over the helicopter rotors. "This is my wife, Hannah."

"Congratulations on the baby." Emory held her hand out to Hannah who was carefully watching her.

"Thank you." Hannah smiled joyously. "We just had an ultrasound and our little peanut is as healthy as can be."

Gage let out a relieved breath.

"Good to hear, man." Blake clapped Gage on the back.

Emory sat next to Sierra, and Blake took a seat next to Gage. Maybe that meant Blake would chat with Gage and wouldn't try to talk to her in flight.

"How'd it go with your mom?" Sierra kept her tone low, meant only for Emory's ears.

Emory really didn't want to talk about it, but Sierra was such a kindhearted and compassionate person, always looking out for her partners, so Emory wouldn't refuse. "She admitted I was adopted."

"Oh, gosh! Like wow." Sierra was usually serene and optimistic with everyone. Her shocked surprise made things worse for Emory, and she didn't know what to say or do.

"Sorry. I shouldn't have said that." Sierra wrapped an arm around Emory's shoulders and gave a quick squeeze. Those incessant tears that had been threatening since she'd learned of Caitlyn pricked at her eyes again. She closed them tight until she could gain control.

Sierra met Emory's gaze. "Are you totally shattered?"

"Pretty much." Emory found compassion in Sierra's gaze, but Emory would break down if she said anything else, and she didn't want to do that in front of Blake or the others. "If you don't mind, I don't want to talk about it."

"I totally understand." She gave a final squeeze and removed her arm.

"All systems are a go," Riley announced.

Gage pointed at the wall behind Emory. "Headsets are hanging beside you. Put one on if you want to communicate during the trip."

Emory reached back for her headset and settled it in place as did everyone else. Not that she really wanted to talk to anyone, but after Will's death in a chopper crash, she was a bit leery of flying.

The helicopter rose into the sky and whirred away from the ground like a bird in flight eager to migrate to a warmer climate. She took a moment to enjoy the feeling of weightlessness, to let go of her concerns, and look out the window.

"Any news on Caitlyn?" Gage's voice came over her headset.

Emory figured he was talking to Blake and didn't answer, but when she looked at Blake, he'd fixed a questioning look on her. Was he asking if it was okay to mention Caitlyn was her twin? If so, she appreciated his consideration.

"Blake showed me Caitlyn's picture," Emory said, willing her voice not to break. "We look exactly alike, and DNA proves she's my twin sister. I didn't know I had a twin until yesterday or that I was adopted until today."

"Oh, my...oh, goodness." Hannah reached her hand out as if wanting to comfort Emory, but was too pregnant to bend far enough forward to touch. "I'm so sorry your sister is missing."

"Thank you, though honestly, I'm still processing the whole twin sister thing."

"I can imagine." Hannah's compassionate gaze said she really understood. "I'll pray for you both, but tell me how else I can help you."

"Prayers are the best thing right now." Emory gave her a shaky smile. "And prayers for my mom, too. I hate to admit it, but I let my anger get the best of me. I know I hurt her. I tried, but I couldn't control it."

Sierra shook her head. "Don't be so hard on yourself."

"Agreed." Blake met her gaze. "You'll work through this and so will she."

"How can you be so sure?" Emory asked.

"I've only known you for a day, but I can tell you're a person who not only will get through this, but come out stronger." He smiled, and she felt the warmth clear to her heart.

Hannah looked between them, her gaze like a ping-pong ball, and her expression perked up. "Oh, so it's like that."

"What?" Emory asked, confused.

"Oh, nothing." She sounded like a teenager with a secret. "So where are you and Sierra planning to stay while in Cold Harbor?"

"With Sam."

"Oh, oh, good. Perfect." Hannah swiveled to look at Blake. "Sierra said she and Emory are here to help you with the investigation."

He nodded.

"Wouldn't it be a good idea if you stayed at one of our cabins until Cait is found? That way you can use our meeting facilities, be close by if you need to fly back to Portland, and it's closer to your office, too."

He narrowed his gaze. "I'll only go home to change and shower, so I don't think that's necessary."

"But you'll waste time, and time is precious, right?"

He took his time answering. "Yes. Time is precious."

"Then it's settled. You'll stay with us." A cat-that-ate-the-canary grin spread across Hannah's face.

Gage looked at her and shook his head.

Emory didn't know what she was missing here, but Hannah had some sort of agenda.

Gage shifted to look at Blake. "Have you thought of anything we can do to help?"

"I've already called Sam and asked her to accompany Sierra to Caitlyn's house. The more eyes we have on potential evidence the better. I hope that's okay."

"Of course. Anything else you need?"

Blake lifted his eyes to the ceiling for a moment, and then shifted his focus back to Gage. "This is a big ask, but having the chopper and a pilot on standby to rush evidence back to the Veritas Center would be amazing."

Gage faced the front. "You good with that, Riley?"

"Absolutely."

"Then you got it," Gage told Blake.

"Hey, thanks, man." Blake held out his hand to Gage for a fist bump.

"I'm looking forward to seeing your compound," Sierra joined in. "I've heard a lot of good things about your team."

"Ditto about Veritas," Gage said. "Sam gushes about you all."

"Well, then." Emory clapped her hands. "Together we should be able to bring Caitlyn safely home."

The others nodded, but the helicopter filled with a somber tone. She'd sounded so confident a moment ago, but would they really be able to figure this out in time? Would Emory really get to meet Caitlyn? A sense of urgency to find her twin sped up Emory's heart, and she felt a panic attack coming on. She had to occupy her mind before she lost control.

She put on her glasses and dug in her backpack for the envelope her mother had given to her. Something jingled inside. She first pulled out an engraved silver frame with her baby picture from the hospital and ran her fingers over it to study her face. She'd hoped to find details that would tell them where she was born, but the photo was a cropped close-up with little in the background. She looked at the engraved silver comb-and-brush set, ring, and bracelet that looked like a set. Except for the sterling silver links, the bracelet had three white beads with the numbers forty-five, twenty-eight, and twenty-two in the middle section.

Odd. She would think the bracelet should hold her birthdate.

"What's that?" Sierra asked.

"A bracelet my birth parents gave to my adoptive parents and asked them to give it to me."

Sierra touched the round beads. "It's beautiful, but what do the numbers mean?"

"I have no idea."

Sierra continued to stare at it. "Maybe it's the combination for a safe."

Emory gave her idea some thought. "But why would they give me that when I don't even know where they are or where their safe might be?"

Sierra shook her head. "It's a mystery all right."

"I wonder if Caitlyn got one, too," Emory mused aloud. "Maybe that's what her abductor wants from her."

"Her adoptive father would know, right?" Sierra asked. "I'm sure we'll find him soon, and we can ask."

Emory nodded and looked up to see Blake watching her. She held out the bracelet to him as he had to have been listening to the conversation on the headsets. He studied it from all angles and shook his head. "Safe combination sounds like a good choice. Or a locker combination. Or for a padlock used to lock up almost anything."

Emory took the bracelet back and slid it back in the envelope. She drew out the papers and read through the adoption attorney's paperwork, and then looked at her birth certificate. She'd seen it before, of course, but now it held new meaning for her. Now it was the second such certificate issued since she'd been born.

She rubbed her fingers over the lettering and thought about her morning. She'd started the day as one person and would end the day as another one. At least that was how she felt. How did she get over her parents' duplicity? Put it behind her and figure out whatever she could about her biological parents—if anything?

She bit her lip and tried to still her racing mind. She took even breaths and blew them out to relax. She'd slept very little last night, so she settled her glasses on top of her head, closed her eyes, and leaned back. The rhythmic hum of the engine put her to sleep, and she dreamed of Caitlyn. Of meeting this woman who was a mirror image of her. The joy in finding each other.

"Three minutes to touchdown," Riley announced, his voice startling her.

She jerked awake to find Blake, Hannah, and Gage all watching her.

She smiled to ease their concern. "I must've fallen asleep."

Riley set the helicopter down, and Emory spotted Sam leaning against her Jeep at the trail leading to the cabins and training center. Sam was three inches taller than Emory, and she was thinner with long blond hair pulled up into her usual work ponytail. She wore black tactical pants and a gray knit shirt with the Blackwell Tactical logo embroidered on the chest.

Just the sight of a close friend who would offer moral support brought tears to Emory's eyes, and she blinked hard to stop them. Not usually prone to crying, she'd become a tear-producing machine in less than a day.

The rotors started to wind down, and Blake scooted past her to open the door and help her down. His concerned look lingered on her face, but before she could react, Sam stepped up to them drawing Emory into a tight hug.

"I'm so sorry, sweetie," Sam said, her hug fierce and protective. "You know I'll do everything I can to help find Caitlyn."

"Thank you." Emory pushed free and drew Sam off to the side while Blake and Gage hauled the bags to the utility vehicle parked by Blake's county SUV. Hannah, her arm linked with Sierra's, was making a beeline for them, and Hannah looked like a woman on a mission.

Emory had to hurry to get her request out before Sam's attention was divided. "I was hoping you'd take pictures at Caitlyn's house for me."

Sam cocked her head to the side. "Aren't you coming with us?"

Emory shook her head. "Blake says the conflict of interest is too great. Plus he's concerned seeing the scene will bother me."

Sam shifted to look at Blake. "I totally get the conflict of interest, but he usually doesn't concern himself with anyone's emotions."

"Maybe it's an added excuse to keep me away." Emory faced him, wanting to see what Sam was seeing.

His gaze locked onto Emory, transmitting his concern. She had to look away from the warm tenderness in his eyes before she did or said something she'd regret.

"Oh...oh," Sam said, but she was still staring at Blake. "He means it all right. He's looking at you like you're the only woman on the planet."

Emory glanced back at him and found the interest Sam mentioned sparking in his eyes. Emory was shocked that he was feeling the same attraction she'd been feeling. Shocked and pleased. Seriously, how could she be pleased about something that she wouldn't do a thing about?

Sam clapped her hands and grinned. "Blake's got a thing for you. How fun!"

Hannah stepped up to them. "I saw it on the helo, too. And if I'm right, *you*, my dearest Emory, are equally interested."

"You?" Sam's voice rose. "Does that mean you're over... well...you know?"

Sierra smiled. "That would be so wonderful if it does mean that."

"You're mistaken." Emory took a long breath and decided to shift the attention back to the business at hand. "So about those pictures, Sam."

A knowing expression crossed Sam's face, but she moved on. "Glad to help, but why stop at stills. Gage just bought a 3-D laser scanner, and I can give you a virtual look at the place."

"Perfect." Emory squeezed Sam's hand and hoped she was up to seeing the 3-D image of the location where her sister had suffered under the hands of a crazed madman.

10

Blake marched toward Emory, his steps purposeful. She held her breath. She had no idea what he might say. She only hoped it didn't encourage the others to think something personal was happening between them.

He took the firm stance she was coming to associate with him. "We should get moving."

"Will you be going to Caitlyn's place with us?" Sam asked.

Blake shook his head. "I'm headed into the office to catch up with my detective on the investigation."

"Sierra and I can take my Jeep," Sam said. "But someone will have to let us into the townhouse."

"I've arranged for our most experienced tech to meet you there. Her name's Helen Lindley. She'll log any evidence you find, and then we'll meet after you finish to decide the best and fastest way to process it."

Sam nodded and looked at Sierra. "I assume you brought equipment. I can help you load it into my Jeep."

"I did," Sierra said.

"I'll drop the other baggage off at your place, Sam," Gage said.

"Thanks." Sam faced Emory. "I guess we'll see you when we see you."

Emory didn't plan to sit here at the compound twiddling her thumbs. "I'm going with Blake to his office. We can connect there when you finish."

"Now wait a minute." Blake crossed his arms, that stubborn lawman back in place.

She met and held his gaze. "You hired me, remember?"

"He *what*?" Sam's shocked surprise returned.

"For a dollar," Emory added.

"Still..." She locked gazes with Blake. "Who are you and what have you done with the Blake Jenkins we all know?"

Blake rolled his eyes. "No need to be so dramatic. A woman is missing, and we need all hands on deck to bring her home alive."

"Then let's get going," Emory said to move them along. "Thanks for the ride, Gage. Tell Riley thanks too, and I'm so thrilled you all got good news at the doctor."

Gage nodded, and Emory headed for Blake's vehicle. He unlocked and opened the passenger door for her then charged around front proving he was as eager to act as she was. She took a moment to look around his vehicle that was clean and tidy and held a computer mounted between the front seats. A police radio filled the console area, and she caught sight of rifles or shotguns mounted on the sidewalls in the back.

Guns. She'd once detested them. She'd never fired one before the attack. Then she bought a cute purple Ruger handgun, also known as the Lady Lilac, and took lessons at a local range. She went every Friday after work to practice. And yet, she was still afraid.

She faced Blake. "So your long guns in the back. Rifle or shotgun?"

Hand on the ignition, he flashed her a surprised look. "I didn't take you for a gun enthusiast."

Of course he'd ask about it. Dumb topic unless she wanted to tell him about the attack, and she sure wouldn't do that. "An interest I acquired recently."

"I actually carry three long guns. A shotgun for close support. The shock-and-awe aspect is just a bonus." A little-boy grin lit his face. "A rifle for that long-range ability. And by that, I mean anything beyond twenty-five yards and reasonably within about two hundred yards. And an automatic rifle for the ability to respond with heavier firepower, and/or at least approach if not match what the bad guys are carrying."

She didn't like the thought of him needing to carry all of those guns, and it underscored how she couldn't get involved with a man who constantly put his life on the line. "That's a lot of firepower."

He nodded, serious now. "An officer involved in a gunfight has to end the encounter as quickly as possible. Especially a situation like a mass shooting. Unless you get lucky with a handgun and hit a major organ or major blood-carrying artery or vessel, you won't cause massive bleeding and circulatory collapse. Means the assailant will likely continue shooting."

"But a rifle will cause that collapse?"

"You have a much greater likelihood."

She shivered. "I don't like to think about you in a gunfight, but I'm thankful that you and other officers are willing to protect us from such shooters."

"So you own a gun, then?"

She nodded.

He shifted into gear and got the vehicle going. "Have a concealed carry permit and are carrying now?"

"I do and I am." She watched him ease the vehicle down

the road that was more like a wide driveway leading past a mock town. On their flight back to Portland last year, Riley, a former sniper, had told her all about the storefronts used for urban training classes.

He glanced at her. "And you know how to use it?"

"I took lessons and go to the range every Friday to practice. I've gotten pretty good."

"You'll have to demonstrate for me."

"Sounds like you don't believe me."

"I do, but I still don't see you carrying and shooting." He shook his head. "Mind if I ask why you decided to start?"

"Personal safety," she replied, purposely remaining vague. She faced out the window to look at the compound and to end the topic. "This is some place, isn't it?"

Blake didn't speak for the longest time, so she looked back to find his suspicious gaze on her.

"Have you ever taken any of their law enforcement classes?" she asked to keep them on the same subject.

He nodded. "And I schedule my deputies, too."

The SUV approached two rows of cabins. Basic log cabins for their trainees sat on the left, and the team members' cabins were located further down the road.

She took in their very unique designs. "I forgot to ask the time I passed through here which cabin is Sam's. Do you know?"

"First one on the right." He pointed out the window at the one painted a calming green. Simple, clean, and modern, the small building sat atop steel piers and had tall glass doors that led to a large deck.

"She said the team members designed and built their own cabins with help from each other. And tradespeople for electrical, plumbing, etcetera."

"I pitched in a few times, too. I swing a mighty hammer."

He laughed and drove past Gage and Hannah's house to the exit protected with a high-tech security gate.

He opened his window and punched a code into the lock.

"Wow, Gage must really trust you if you have security clearance for this place."

"Like I said. We go way back. Hannah, the kids, and Gage are like family. And since he's gotten more involved in criminal investigations, we cross paths a lot."

"That's great that you all support each other. It's just... well..." He raised an eyebrow and turned onto the road. "What?"

"*You*. I keep expecting the guy Sam warned me about. Sure I've seen him, but there's more to you than that."

She didn't know if he looked hurt by her comment or just pensive, but his expression tightened. "I'm not one to defend myself, but Sam has a limited viewpoint. I've only interacted with her when she wanted information that I couldn't share or when she wanted to process crime scenes that I couldn't let her touch due to personal involvement that would jeopardize evidence integrity. I've had similar interactions with other team members, too, so they typically only see that side of me. I work a lot, but I'm not sheriff twenty-four seven. Then I'm just a regular Joe who I think is pretty easy to get along with."

Emory gave that some thought and could honestly see what he was saying. "And what about actual family?"

"I have a sister and parents who live in Cold Harbor. Never been married so no kids." He glanced at her, his eyes narrowed. "This is starting to feel like one of my interrogations."

"As far as I know, you haven't broken any laws." She chuckled. "But what about hearts? Are you single because you're a heartbreaker?"

He frowned, his fingers tightening around the wheel. "Nothing like that."

She didn't miss the fact that he didn't explain anything, and she would respect his decision not to talk about it. She actually hoped he was keeping some big terrible secret that, when revealed, would erase her attraction to him. It was hard enough to live with her own fear. Another thing altogether to bring someone else into the situation.

Her phone chimed, and she looked down to see a text from Angela. *Mom told me about your talk this morning. She's devastated.*

She's devastated? Emory shook her head and typed, *So am I.*

I can't even imagine. Can I do anything to help?

Check in on Mom. I know I was awful to her, but am still processing. Will call her when I figure things out.

Actually, I'm going to stay with her for a few days. Any word on Caitlyn?

We're working on it, but she's still missing.

Let me know if you need anything.

Will do, Emory answered, but honestly, what she needed more than anything was time to think this through. She sighed.

"Everything okay?" Blake flipped the blinkers on.

"My sister Angela told me how upset our mother is. Angela's going to stay with her."

He turned onto a county road. "That's good, right?"

"Yeah, but I wish I was big enough to get over this so I didn't keep hurting my mom."

"It's mind-blowing news." He sped up. "It'll take time. Your mother should understand that."

"She probably does." Emory sighed again. "Why does life have to be so messy and complicated? Why can't it be more straightforward like science with proven rules and precepts?"

"Because we have free will, and we can really make a mess of things at times."

"God probably rolls His eyes at all the crazy things we manage to do." She actually felt a bit better after this conversation. Blake was easy to talk to and seemed to understand her. She could relax around him, even forget her fears for a moment.

She rested her head against the seat, stealing glances at him, until they entered Cold Harbor. It was a typical beach tourist town with seafood restaurants, quaint souvenir shops, a candy store, and bakery all on the main road. He turned off, wound toward the beach, and then the road climbed up a hill where a large building that looked like it was constructed in the 1800s sat with a sheriff sign out front.

She took in the old clapboard siding, brightly colored awnings over windows, and a solid wood door painted vivid blue. "What a charming building."

"Great." He rolled his eyes. "Charming. *That's* the image I want to project as sheriff."

She swatted a hand at him. "How old is this place?"

"It was built in 1852 as a rooming house for miners who extracted gold from hundreds of placer mines. We've remodeled it just a bit." He laughed.

"Still, it fits in with the town atmosphere and tourists don't see a stark police station."

"It does and was what the county administrator was going for when he bought it. That, and it overlooks the water. We have a marine patrol as part of my department, and it's good to be able to see the water from my office."

"You really have a wide-ranging county, don't you?"

He nodded. "Beach, foothills, and lowlands, mostly

rural. And then we have the Rogue River, too. Makes patrolling interesting to be sure."

He pulled to a stop at a security gate behind the building and punched a code into the lock. The lot held several patrol cars and a large speedboat on a trailer with the county emblem painted on the bow.

"Do you take the boat on the river and ocean?"

He nodded. "Here's an interesting fact for you. We have a mailboat that still delivers mail upstream and has been running that service since 1895. It's one of only two rural mailboat routes remaining in the U.S."

"That *is* interesting."

He parked in a spot reserved for him by the door, and they got out. He went to the back of his vehicle and removed his long guns.

At the door, he paused and faced her. "You should know. I had to tell my department that Caitlyn's your sister. I couldn't afford for one of them to see you and think you were Caitlyn. They might have let down their guard in finding her."

"That's fine," she said.

"But the only people who know you just found out about Caitlyn and that you're adopted are my admin and the detective taking lead on this investigation. I figure no one else really needs to know."

She was unreasonably happy at his consideration, and that he didn't air her dirty laundry for everyone. She smiled at him. "You really are a softie, Blake Jenkins."

"Shh. Don't let that get out or I'm done for as sheriff." He flashed her a mischievous grin.

Her heart cartwheeled in her chest, and she couldn't breathe under the intensity of his charm. Emory had to wonder, really wonder, why a man this attractive and seemingly kind was still single. He had to have some fatal flaw that she would intently watch for to keep from falling for his charms.

He jerked his gaze free and opened the door to step inside. She followed him. She felt flushed and overheated and knew her face was beaming red.

They entered through the back of the station. Right inside the door sat a neatly organized desk. A woman Emory thought to be in her early sixties sat behind it. She had short blond hair that looked like her natural color in soft waves framing her face. She was slim and wore a powder-blue button-down shirt rolled up at the sleeves. She looked up and smiled, her lips covered in a rosy lipstick.

"Emory," Blake said. "Meet my admin, Lorraine Burkas."

Lorraine stood, and Emory saw that Lorraine was indeed trim in her khaki slacks. She held out her hand, and her smile widened. "Nice to meet you, Emory. I watch all those CSI shows and am completely fascinated with people who work with forensics and DNA."

Blake groaned. "Whatever you do, Emory, do not repeat that my right-hand person watches shows that are so far from fact that it's laughable."

Lorraine rolled her eyes, her lids covered in a power-blue shadow. "Don't be surprised if I try to pick your brain while you're here."

Emory nodded. "You'll have to come visit our lab sometime."

Lorraine charged around the desk. "Really, you mean it?"

"Of course."

She clasped Emory's hands tightly, and Emory tried not to wince but didn't manage it.

"Oh, sorry." She released Emory's hand. "I get a little excited."

"A little?" Blake shook his head, but he smiled fondly at his assistant.

Lorraine's expression turned serious. "Trent has the situation room all set up, and he's been keeping up with all the leads as I know he's told you. He's really been proving his abilities on this investigation, but I know he'll be glad to share the workload."

Blake's eyes narrowed and gone was the fun-loving boss —the man Sam warned her about was front and center. "Would you mind taking care of Emory for a few minutes while I change into a fresh uniform?"

"Glad to." She circled an arm around Emory's shoulder. "Let's go to the breakroom and grab something to drink."

She didn't give Emory a choice but escorted her down the hall and into a small room that smelled like popcorn and coffee. "What can I get you?"

"Black coffee is good."

She went to the pot and grabbed a mug that said *Police Officers Can't Fix Stupid But We Can Arrest It.* Emory wanted to laugh at the quote, but Lorraine was looking extremely serious, so Emory resisted.

"I'm very sorry to hear about your sister," she said. "But if it's any consolation, Blake is the best sheriff I've worked with. If anyone can find her, he will." She handed the mug to Emory. "Now if you tell him I said that, I'll deny it." She smiled, her eyes crinkling.

Emory blew on the mug. "How long have you worked here?"

"Six sheriffs or twenty-four years. Take your pick." She filled another mug.

Emory took a sip of the surprisingly good coffee. "You must be good at what you do if they all kept you on."

She waved a hand. "I made sure I was indispensable. But Blake really is a cut above the others. The deputies respect him because he's tough but fair, and he never asks them to do anything he wouldn't do. And he has a heart of gold. Always takes a personal interest in their families."

"But he's never married and had children of his own." Emory felt bad about making this personal, but she really wanted to know why he was still single.

Lorraine frowned. "He has his reasons, and I'll not share out of turn, but I suspect he just hasn't found the right woman to make him want to change his opinion."

Emory was about to ask "opinion on what," when he stepped into the room looking fresh and so appealing that she couldn't take her eyes from him. His khaki shirt and forest green pants were pressed and crisp and fit his muscular frame oh-so-well.

"Time to meet Trent and get started." He pivoted with precision and exited. She trailed him down the hallway and into the room Lorraine had called the situation room.

Whiteboards covered several of the walls. A large flat-screen television was mounted on another wall and above it three smaller televisions were tuned to news programs. Computer stations ringed the walls below, and a long table filled the middle of the room. The final wall was covered by a map of the county.

One of the whiteboards held pictures of Caitlyn and her apartment. Emory started toward it, and Blake stepped in her path. Frustrated by his need to protect her, at least that was what she thought he was doing, she looked away.

Her gaze caught on a large digital clock, counting down with seven hours and fourteen minutes. "What's the clock for?"

Blake looked at her, his face rigid. "The first twelve to twenty-four hours are the most critical in a missing persons investigation. When this clock hits zero, Caitlyn will have been missing for twenty-four hours."

11

Blake hated telling Emory about the clock, but with her work, she had to know the statistics on bringing a missing person home alive. Twelve to twenty-four hours for an adult was tough to work under, but it was only three hours for a child. Blake hated the facts, but most abducted children were killed within that timeframe.

And the other stats weren't any better. On any given day, ninety thousand people were missing in the United States, forty thousand of them under the age of eighteen. Blake had never been able to get his head around that staggering figure. But right now he didn't need to get his head around ninety thousand. He needed to focus on one.

He introduced Trent to Emory. They shook hands, but she seemed to shrink a bit and looked uncomfortable. Blake had no idea why. He'd like to know, but had no time to investigate the reason.

He motioned for Emory to sit before taking a seat next to her and facing Trent. "Bring us up to speed."

"You want new information only or a recap for Emory?" Trent sat on the other side of the table.

"Go ahead and do the recap. She might pick up on something we've missed."

Trent concisely recounted arriving at the townhouse, a description of the scene, and Gladys's statement. "She was traumatized, so she could very well be mistaken, but I do believe her when she said the man was wearing a Tyvek suit. I doubt she could make that up or be confused on it."

Emory frowned. "He knew enough to not leave forensic evidence."

"On the bright side, it could mean he committed past crimes and the odds of his DNA being in CODIS is higher." Blake used the Combined DNA Index System that was managed by the FBI plenty of times, and Emory would in her work, too, so he didn't need to explain.

Emory nodded. "My analyst updated me this morning, and we'll have the DNA profiles before the day is out."

"Any way to rush it?" Trent asked.

She shook her head. "It's running on the Genetic Analyzer, and that takes at least twelve hours to finish."

"Let's move on, then," Blake said to Trent. "Were you able to locate next of kin or Caitlyn's current place of employment?"

"I just now found her employer, and I haven't interviewed anyone there yet. I'm closing in on the family and hope to have that information soon." He slid a piece of paper across the table toward Blake.

Emory snatched it up. "She works at Cold Harbor Marina. We're free to interview her boss, right?"

Blake met her gaze. "*I* am yes, but you're—"

"Don't say not official law enforcement," she interrupted. "You contracted our agency's services for this very reason."

He sighed. "I wouldn't say for this reason exactly."

"Still, it means I can come along on the interviews." She continued to hold the page, but kept her focus on him.

He was powerless to say no to that earnest face.

"I can go on my own if you prefer," she added before he could respond.

"We'll go together." He shifted his gaze to Trent. "Tell me about her job."

"She's the marina manager, which seems odd as she has a PhD in Aquaculture and Aquatic Sciences."

Blake shook his head. "Pretty fancy degree to manage a marina."

Trent nodded. "She was a researcher at the University of Minnesota until she moved here. I'll call them to see if she left under difficult circumstances that would have prevented her from finding a job more commensurate with her degree."

"Let me know what you learn." Blake moved on. "What about phone data?"

Trent tapped a stack of papers on his desktop. "Just got the call logs and will get started on them right away. The computer image giving us access to her email should be done any time now."

"We should send a copy of that image to our computer expert," Emory suggested. "Nick can locate deleted files that your techs could miss."

Trent frowned and opened his mouth to speak, but Blake held up a hand. "No point in trying to defend our guys. They're good, but the experts at Veritas can probably run circles around them and do it faster. So for the most part we'll have them process the forensics for this case."

Trent nodded, but he didn't look happy about it.

Nothing Blake said would ease his mind, so he shifted his attention to Emory. "Give Trent Nick's contact information."

She grabbed a notepad and pen lying on the table and

jotted down Nick's email and phone number then slid the pad across the table.

"Thanks," Trent said, his tone reserved.

Blake understood Trent's hesitancy, but Blake couldn't let it interfere. "Make sure you deliver that file to Nick the minute you get it."

Trent nodded, and Blake knew even if his detective wasn't happy with Veritas stepping into their territory, he would comply. "Any hits on her bank account?"

Trent shook his head. "So it's not looking like the abduction is money motivated."

"Not yet anyway." Blake got to his feet. "We'll head out to the marina and come back to see what you've learned on those phone records."

Emory stood, and Blake motioned for her to precede him. She stepped into the hallway.

"Hey, boss," Trent called out and joined him by the door. He glanced at Emory and lowered his voice. "You should know. I'm also running a background check on Emory. Figured her connection might give us a lead."

Blake wasn't shocked at Trent's actions, but hiding it from Emory? That was a surprise. "Your point in keeping this from her?"

"There could be more to this sisterly bond than Emory's letting on. She may actually know more of their history and isn't being forthcoming with us." He eyed Blake. "Honestly, boss, I didn't think you'd question this. If you were lead on the investigation, you'd be doing the same thing. I hope you'll respect my decision."

Blake didn't want to keep the background check a secret. He wanted to be up-front with Emory and the very thought surprised him. He knew it was in the best interest of the investigation to respect Trent's decisions.

Emory turned back. "You coming?"

He nodded and looked at Trent. "Fine. For now. Let me know what you find."

Emory smiled at him before continuing down the hall.

Blake was doing his job, so why did he feel like he was betraying Emory's trust when she was just getting over the very thing from her mother and keeping this quiet would come back to bite him?

~

Emory tried to memorize everything about the scene unfolding in front of her as Blake wound his SUV down the hill toward the marina where Caitlyn worked. Her twin worked here. Her twin! Would she ever tire of thinking that? She couldn't see how. Because as shocked as she was over her mother never mentioning the adoption, the upside of all of this was that Emory had a twin sister. If they could find her. Hopefully they'd learn something at the marina.

Emory looked ahead at the tall trees lining the winding driveway that opened into a large parking lot abutting a sparkling lake. A truck and trailer were parked near the boat ramp, and the driver was unloading a large speedboat. Several SUVs with empty trailers sat in the lot. At the water's edge, a building with a crisp white coat of paint floated on the water and a long dock led to additional docks with numerous slips holding a variety of boats.

"I don't get it," Emory said as Blake parked. "How can someone with a PhD choose to manage a marina?"

Blake shifted into park. "I'm the wrong person to ask. Just a bachelor's degree. You would be better able to answer that."

"But see, I can't. I worked hard to get my degree, and I wouldn't want to do anything else."

"Hopefully we'll understand once we gain additional

background information on Caitlyn." He turned off the ignition and pulled out the keys. "Interesting though that you both have PhDs in the sciences."

"Yeah. I was thinking the same thing." For the first time, she felt a nearly overwhelming desire to be able to get to know this woman and find out what else they had in common.

Please, God!

Blake got out, and she joined him in the cool breeze coming across the lake and whipping the white sails on a navy blue boat heading for the dock. If Emory's sister wasn't missing, she would take time to enjoy the view, but she had no time for sightseeing.

She hurried down steps leading to a floating building and marched inside, Blake right behind her. A skinny, stooped man with thinning gray hair looked up from behind a long counter holding colorful fishing lures. Emory pegged him at his late seventies or early eighties.

"Cait," he cried out. "Thank goodness you're here. We were so worried when you didn't come to work this morning and didn't answer your phone."

Shocked, Emory came to a sudden stop, and Blake bumped into her. He grabbed hold of her waist to steady her, but she barely noticed. This elderly man thought she was Caitlyn, and for some reason that suddenly made everything more real. Sure, Blake had confused her for Caitlyn but that was from a photograph. This man actually knew Caitlyn—"Cait" as he called her—and he was confused.

"Cait?" he asked. "What's wrong?"

She couldn't form the words.

Blake released her and stepped around to display his ID for the man. "Sheriff Blake Jenkins and this is Emory Steele, Caitlyn's twin."

"Oh, oh. Sorry." He waved a hand. "Cait never mentioned she had a twin sister."

"I see." The only words Emory could form slipped out on their own accord.

The man's gaze suddenly shot back to Blake. "If you're here, does that mean something bad has happened to Cait?"

"We believe she was abducted."

"Oh, no." The man's face paled, and he dropped onto a stool. "Poor thing. Who would want to do that?"

"That's what we were hoping you might help us with. Mr.—"

"Emerson. Walter Emerson." He stood gaping at Blake much the way Emory suspected she was gaping at him. "I've only known Cait for a month or so—if you count email and phone communications as knowing someone—and she's shared very little about her personal life."

"So she's worked here for a month?" Blake asked.

Emory was thankful for his questions when she was too rattled to think, much less speak.

"Two weeks," Walter said. "Moved here from Minnesota."

"Where she was a researcher at the University of Minnesota, right?" Blake asked.

Walter nodded.

Blake took a step closer. "And she was hired to do what here?"

"Manage the marina. I'll turn eighty this year, and I can't handle things like I used to. So I looked for someone who wanted to manage the place with an option to buy. Which is why she left her fancy job at the university. She said she had family in the area and wanted to be closer to them while putting down solid roots. Plus she loves the outdoors and couldn't imagine being cooped up inside all of the time."

Blake swung his gaze to Emory who saw his surprise. "Did she say what kind of family? Parents? Siblings?"

Walter tipped his head to the side and tugged on his ear. "She didn't say, but I know for sure she didn't mention a twin. Sorry."

"No need to be sorry." Emory smiled.

"Wow, the resemblance is just uncanny. Cait even has a similar haircut."

Emory nodded as there was nothing she could think of to say in response.

"A couple helped Cait move into her townhouse," Blake said. "Do you know who that might be?"

Walter shook his head. "She's made friends with other young people who work around here, but I don't know who or where."

"Can you think of anyone who might want to abduct her?" Blake asked, and Walter blanched at the question. "Perhaps someone she upset when she took the job?"

Walter gripped the counter so tightly his fingers turned white. "She did have to fire one of my newer dock workers. He quickly developed a thing for her. Made sexual advances and innuendos all the time. I don't abide that kind of behavior so I offered to fire him." He shook his head in disgust. "I should have known when he couldn't keep a job that he'd be trouble, but I was desperate for help."

"So Caitlyn fired him or you did?" Blake asked.

"She insisted on doing it. Said it was her job and she wouldn't shy away from it." He chuckled. "She added that she just might enjoy it, and who was I to stand in the way of that?"

Blake glanced at Emory. "Sounds like something you might do."

Emory smiled as she loved to hear that Caitlyn had such spunk. "What's this guy's name, and can you describe him?"

"Floyd Otter. Tall, maybe six-two. Blond hair. Kind of a square face. Muscular."

Emory met Blake's gaze, and he gave an almost imperceptible nod acknowledging that Otter fit the description provided by Gladys.

Blake shifted his stance. "Does Otter live in Cold Harbor?"

Walter nodded. "I can get his contact information for you if you'd like."

"That would be great," Blake said. "It would also be nice if we could have a copy of Caitlyn's job application."

"Sure. Sure. Be right back with them both." Walter vaulted from his stool with the energy of a child and raced out of the room.

Emory looked at Blake. "Can't you just look Otter up in the DMV?"

He nodded. "But Walter mentioned the guy couldn't keep a job and that could mean Otter's more likely to move around. He'd also be more likely to keep his work address updated than his DMV address."

"Oh, right. That makes sense."

His gaze suddenly warmed. "Are you okay? Something obviously threw you for a loop."

She appreciated his concern more than he could know. "Being mistaken for Caitlyn made the abduction seem more real somehow."

"I can see that." He lifted his hand as if he wanted to touch her, but Walter came bustling into the room, and Blake's hand dropped to his side.

Walter held the forms out to Blake. "His application has his current address and most recent jobs. Maybe they can tell you more about him."

"Thanks, Mr. Emerson." Blake gave the older man a

genuine smile. "Is there anything else you can think of that I should know about Caitlyn?"

Walter planted his hands on the glass-topped counter. "I...well...she didn't like to talk about her past. Or family. Which is why I don't know much about them. Me, I'm an open book and thought I could get to know the person who was buying my business. You know, so I could keep in touch after the sale went through, but..." He shrugged.

Blake fished a business card from his shirt pocket and handed it to Walter. "Call me if you think of anything."

"Will do." Walter frowned. "And you'll let me know what you find out?"

"I'll do my best."

"I'm sorry about your sister, Emory." Walter cast her a sympathetic smile. "I'll be praying for you both."

"Thank you." Emory squeezed his wrinkled hand. She liked Walter and could understand why Caitlyn would want to do business with him.

Blake started for the SUV but Emory stopped to look over the choppy lake and take a long breath of the fishy-smelling air. She'd never been much of an outdoors person, so she might have the PhD in common with Caitlyn, but then they differed wildly.

Blake returned to her side. "You're awfully pensive."

"I'm thinking about Cait," Emory said, surprised at how natural it sounded to shorten her name. "Sounds like Cait is what she goes by."

He nodded. "It's going to be interesting for you to learn all these little nuances about her."

"That's actually what I've been thinking about. Like the fact that she has a PhD, but a lot of her work must be done outdoors while I prefer to sit in a lab. Makes me wonder if her adoptive family loves the outdoors while mine prefers indoor activities like concerts, ballets, and plays."

"There's bound to be a lot of differences due to upbringing."

"I wonder if we'll get along." Emory sighed then realized she was just wasting time and firmed her shoulders. "Doesn't matter if we don't find her, now, does it? Let's get going."

She hurried up the hill to the parking lot. Blake pushed past her and unlocked the passenger door. She smiled her thanks. He gave a crisp nod and climbed behind the wheel.

"I want to check Otter's DL picture." He started typing on his computer and after frowning at it, he swiveled the computer to face her.

Otter had stringy blond hair to his shoulders with a reddish mustache and goatee and scowled at the camera. Not telling in itself when a lot of the time the DMV managed to capture the worst pictures.

She looked up at Blake. "Gladys didn't mention facial hair, but it could've been too dark to see it."

"Agreed, and Walter didn't mention it either, so maybe he's clean-shaven now." Blake swiveled his computer back in his direction. "He's registered at the same address that Walter gave us. It's only a few miles down the road."

"Let's head over there now, then," she suggested.

Blake didn't say anything for a few moments, but then faced her, his expression tight. "He has a record. Could be dangerous and I can't put you in a potentially volatile situation."

She crossed her arms and raised her chin. "It's not a good idea to dawdle in finding Cait either. If I don't go with you, you'll have to take me back to the station and then come back out here."

"You have a point there." He tapped the wheel with his thumb. "Tell you what. I'll have Trent meet us there. We'll assess the situation, and if I decide it's not problematic, you can approach with us. If not, you wait in the vehicle."

"Okay," she said, but had no idea what she might do when they arrived at this guy's apartment. He could be holding Cait captive. If that was true, Emory wouldn't sit back. Not even for a moment.

12

Trent was already waiting outside the apartment in a run-down neighborhood when Blake parked at the curb. Emory looked at the fourplex buildings with peeling white paint on clapboard siding sitting on patchy grass dotted in clumps of sandy soil. They were tired looking and greatly in need of a face-lift.

"Wait here." Blake got out and hitched up his duty belt then rested his hand on his sidearm as he talked to Trent.

He stood tall with the confidence she was coming to associate with him, but she now knew there was a vulnerability to him as well. He didn't want others to see it, but she did, and she wanted to ask what put it there. But that was too personal for this point in their relationship.

Relationship, hah! What was she thinking? Their only relationship was investigator and DNA expert. Period. That was it.

He signaled for her to remain in the vehicle, and he and Trent set off down the walkway to the first building. She waited until they disappeared around a corner, and then climbed out to follow. She would hang back, but not miss out entirely.

Blake pounded a fist on the door and stood back. She saw him flick off the strap on his holster and keep his hand firmly planted on his weapon. She didn't like the thought that he faced danger. Didn't like it at all.

The door opened and a man matching the driver's license picture came to the door.

"Floyd Otter?" Blake asked.

"Who wants to know?"

Blake showed his ID while introducing himself and Trent. "We have a few questions for you."

"'Bout what?"

"About the disappearance of Caitlyn Abbot."

"Cait's missing?" he sounded genuinely surprised.

"Mind if we come in to discuss it?"

He stepped back, and Emory rushed forward. She didn't want them to disappear inside, making her miss this conversation.

Otter caught sight of her. "Hey, what are you trying to pull here?"

Blake turned and locked gazes with Emory. She'd have to be blind to miss his disappointment in her.

"I'm Cait's twin. Emory," she said. Up close, she saw he wore a stained white T-shirt over torn and baggy jeans. He was muscular with a square face that only boasted a five o'clock shadow. He had an evil air about him, and she wouldn't want to run into him in the dark. It was all she could do not to shudder now.

He cocked an eyebrow, the same reddish blond as his hair. "She never said she had a twin."

"Were you close to her?" Emory asked to keep from having to explain.

"Yeah, we had a thing."

"What kind of thing?" Emory asked.

"If you must know, she had the hots for me, and we were

going to start dating. Then old man Emerson canned me, and I had a hard time getting hold of her 'cause I didn't have her phone number."

"If she had the hots for you, wouldn't she have given you that?" Blake asked, his tone sarcastic.

He fired a biting look at Blake. "We just never got around to it. Emerson was watching me all the time and all."

Blake gave Emory a pointed look—which she took to mean she was to stay outside—before shifting to look at Otter. "Let's go inside and finish this discussion."

"Only if the chick comes with us." He gave her a lascivious grin.

With the way he ran his gaze over her, she felt unclean but nodded to be able to find out what he knew about Cait. She stepped past him and into the apartment. The smell of dirty socks times a thousand hit her the minute she entered, and she gagged. Blake gave her another pointed look, and she wanted to respond, but didn't want to put Otter off.

The only options for sitting were an old torn leather sofa, a grease-stained brown recliner, and a wooden bar stool. She suspected the stool held fewer germs and perched on it. Otter plopped down on the recliner. Blake and Trent remained standing, and the screen door snapped closed behind them. Emory had never seen apartments with screen doors, but maybe the owners hoped the places would air out with the fresh ocean breeze.

"Mind if I use your bathroom?" Trent asked.

"Course I mind." Otter glared at him. "You're just looking for things to haul me in for, but go ahead. You won't find anything. Down the hall. First door on the right."

Trent gave Blake a quick questioning look. Blake nodded, and Trent took off down the hall. Otter grabbed a cigarette and lighter.

"Mind holding off on that?" Blake took out a small notepad and pen. "Bothers Emory."

He couldn't have any idea about that, but it seemed like he was using Otter's attraction to her to work him.

She would do the same thing. She smiled at Otter. "When's the last time you saw Cait?"

A dopey grin on his face suddenly morphed into a scowl. "Not since I got canned a few days ago."

Emory was taken aback by his mean look, but she wouldn't let him see that. "You didn't try to contact her since then?"

He frowned.

"What?" Emory leaned forward and gave him a soft smile of encouragement. "You can tell me."

"Okay, fine. I went by the marina a few times. You know, to get a look at her and hope she'd be alone to talk, but she never was." He leaned toward her.

She had to fight her instincts to jerk back.

"So you followed her home," Blake stated, thankfully taking Otter's attention.

"No."

Blake widened his stance. "What would you say if I told you CCTV caught your car in her neighborhood?"

"That I know someone else who lives there." He smirked.

"Name and address of that someone?" Blake held pen over notepad and eyed Otter.

Emory would melt under his intense look if she was Otter, but the man crossed his arms and jutted out his chin. "I don't need to give you anything."

Blake widened his stance and rested his hand on his sidearm. "You do unless you want me to haul you in for questioning."

"No biggie. I'll be free in a few hours."

Blake's forehead narrowed. "I can hold you far longer than a few hours."

Otter glared at Blake, and Emory could see malicious intent in the man's eyes. She hated the thought that he'd been anywhere near Cait, but she would use his feelings for her to get him to answer.

"Forget about the sheriff." She waved a dismissive hand in Blake's direction. "I'm so worried about my sister. I have to find her. Help me, please. I don't care if you went by her house. I understand. Just say so."

"Fine." He blew out a long breath. "I did follow her one night. Must've been Saturday. She went inside, and I stayed until she pulled her curtains shut and then I left."

Memories of Emory's attack came rushing back. Her former boyfriend closing his fingers around her neck. His unwashed smell as he'd taken a dive into despair and stopped caring about anything except revenge for breaking up with him. Choking her. She could easily imagine this guy in the back seat of her car waiting to attack—far too easily— and she had to work hard not to let her revulsion show.

Blake moved closer and bent to grab Otter's attention. "Can anyone confirm that you left and Cait was still fine?"

"Yeah, the nosy lady a few doors down. She came out and told me to move on before she called the cops. I gave her a piece of my mind." He smiled, revealing yellow and uneven teeth. "She'll remember."

Gladys hadn't mentioned anything about seeing Otter, but then she'd been distraught. They would need to talk to her again.

"Do you have any idea of who might want to abduct Cait?" Emory asked.

Otter shook his head, and his stringy hair slapped against his face.

Trent came back into the room and gave an almost

imperceptible nod in Blake's direction. He'd obviously checked the rest of the apartment out and didn't find Cait.

"You coulda at least flushed to make it seem real," Otter muttered.

A snide smile slid across Trent's mouth.

"Where were you yesterday?" Blake asked.

"What time?"

"All day."

"I was at the unemployment office from nine to noon, then hung with my buddies at a bar until nine. Stopped for some Mickey D's then crashed here. Alone."

"I'll need the name and phone number of people who can vouch for you." Blake handed his notepad and pen to Otter.

Otter started writing, his tongue peeking out the side of his mouth as he concentrated. A perfect opportunity for Emory to watch him when he didn't know she was looking. She scanned his hands and arms for any injury that could account for the blood found at Cait's house. She saw nothing, but couldn't see his entire hand. She would have to shake hands with him to get a better look.

"Don't know the unemployment office number," he mumbled. "But I'll give you my all-star worker's name. She had me searching for openings all morning long."

"And your buddies, too," Blake said. "Especially them."

Otter grumbled but got out his phone and started scribbling on the pad.

"You'll want to add your cell number on the page as well," Blake added.

Otter continued writing then shoved the pad back at Blake who glared at Otter. "Anything else you want to tell me about Cait before I leave? If I learn something you haven't told me and I have to come back here, you won't like that one bit."

"Nah, man. That's it."

Blake motioned for Emory to exit. She stood and held out her hand to Otter. "Nice to meet you, Mr. Otter."

He got up, rubbed his hand down his pant leg, and then offered it. She shifted back so he couldn't connect with her.

"Odd," she said and tried to sound surprised. "Are both your palms like that?"

"Like what?" He turned them over to look at them.

She noted they were injury free and made up a story to pacify him. "The lines. I'm a DNA expert, and I'm always fascinated by how genetics creates such individual characteristics like your palms."

He stood staring at them. She hurried out the door, wondering how long he would stand there trying to figure out what she was talking about.

Outside she drank in the fresh air and finally released that shudder she'd been holding.

Blake grimaced. "That's why I wanted you to wait in the vehicle."

"I'm sorry." She honestly felt bad for not listening to him, but Cait came before following his rules. "You have to admit he talked more freely because I was there."

"Yes, but you can never un-see those disgusting looks he kept giving you." Blake's lip curled.

"I can handle a few wayward looks if it helps find Cait." She fixed a confident stare on him. "And I was able to determine he didn't have any injuries that could have produced the suspect handprints on the walls at Cait's place. So if the DNA says it was the abductor's blood and not Cait's, then we know that Otter isn't our guy."

"Good work," he said, but it was with a begrudging tone. "But I need to know that in the future you'll listen to me. I won't allow you to do anything that risks your safety."

She opened her mouth to tell him that she was capable

of evaluating the danger any situation presented, but Trent joined them.

He held out a small evidence envelope. "This should move the investigation along."

She found several strands of blond hair inside.

"He's not real neat," Trent said. "His brush made me want to barf, but if Sierra or Sam find any blond hairs at Cait's place, you can compare them, right?"

"You know we can." She smiled at Trent and stopped short of hugging him for his fast thinking.

"Good work, Trent," Blake said, but he didn't look happy about it.

Emory had no idea why, but she wouldn't ask.

"Let's regroup at the station," Blake said. "Go ahead and call Otter's buddies, and then be sure to request security footage for McDonald's from last night."

Trent nodded and hustled off.

Emory watched him go. "He seems very competent."

"He is. He'll make an excellent sheriff when I retire."

"You're pretty far from retirement age."

He didn't speak, and his face clouded over as he started across the parking lot.

She caught up to him. "Are you still mad that I didn't stay in the car?"

"Mad? No." He met her gaze. "But I am concerned that going forward you won't do the same thing again."

"I'll do my best to listen to you, Blake," she said sincerely. "But I like to think for myself, and I've got to follow my hunches."

He intently studied her. "Even if your hunches get you killed?"

"The only harm Otter inflicted on me was his suggestive looks."

"But he could have hurt you." He sounded frustrated

with her. "You had to see that, right? See that he could have been dangerous."

"Yes," she admitted reluctantly.

He took a long breath and slowly let it out. "As I said, I can't let anything happen to you. I could never forgive myself if it did. So if you won't listen to me for your own safety, listen for my mental health, okay?"

His statement was laced with such strong emotion that she nodded. It was sounding like this was his hot button. Maybe someone had gotten hurt on his watch, and he was feeling guilty about that.

He pointed at the far side of the parking lot. "I'd like to give Otter's vehicle a quick look before we leave."

Emory followed him to a faded blue Ford Mustang hatchback. It was covered with misty film from the ocean and a light layer of sand and didn't look like it had been driven today.

Blake rubbed off the film on a side window and peered inside. "Definitely not the vehicle used to abduct Cait. But Otter could've rented a car for the abduction. I'll have Trent request rental records and video from local car rental places."

She looked over his shoulder to see fast-food items from McDonald's and other litter on the floor. "Wrappers might be from last night, though."

"Or older." Blake pushed away from the car. "He's not the neatest guy."

"Unfortunately, you can't arrest him for being a slob or his nasty looks."

"Exactly. If that was possible, our prisons would really be overcrowded." Blake chuckled, though it seemed forced.

He spun and headed for his vehicle. She kept up with his fast pace, and once in the car, he drove quickly through town. His in-dash system announced an incoming call from Trent.

Blake answered. "You're on speaker, and Emory's in the vehicle with me."

She shot him a look. Why would he have to warn Trent about her presence? Could it be because of the conversation on their way out of the conference room that Trent obviously didn't want her to hear? Were they keeping something from her? Or could it be as simple as Blake being concerned that Trent might be calling about another investigation?

She wasn't a suspicious person by nature, but something seemed wrong. She'd have to keep an eye out for any glances or sketchy looks between the pair.

"You won't believe this," Trent said, sounding out of breath as if he was running. "A man showed up a few minutes ago and claims he's Caitlyn's adoptive father."

"Seriously?" Blake glanced at Emory, his surprised expression matching her feelings.

"I know, right? Said his name is Mark Abbot. Also said she left angry at him, and he came to check up on her. Found the seal we put on her door and came straight here."

"Put Mr. Abbot in an interview room, and whatever you do—" Blake floored the gas, "don't let him leave before we get there."

Blake wasn't shocked when Caitlyn's father jumped from his chair and rushed Emory, but Emory startled.

"Cait, oh, thank God. I thought something terrible happened to you." He reached out to hug her, and Emory stepped back out of his reach. The man's face collapsed in pain. "You're still mad at me."

"No, you don't understand," Emory quickly said. "I'm not Cait. I'm Emory Steele. Cait is my twin."

His forehead furrowed. "What kind of nonsense is this?"

Blake pointed at a chair. "Why don't you sit down, Mr. Abbot, and we'll explain everything."

Suspicion darkened the man's gray-blue eyes, but he took a seat and kept his gaze trained on Emory. She looked uncomfortable under his intense study but took the chair across from him.

Blake sat next to Emory and looked at the man who Trent had officially confirmed was Mark Abbot. In his early sixties, he had a full head of black hair and a neatly trimmed goatee that was more gray than black. He wore khaki pants and a Minnesota Golden Gophers sweatshirt. Worry was deeply etched on his face.

At the moment Blake hated his job. Giving a father bad news about his child was a hard thing to do. He took a long breath and vowed to do his best to be straightforward, and yet, help ease this man's suffering.

Blake first introduced himself.

"And I'm Mark," the older man said. "Mark Abbot, and as you know, Cait's adoptive father."

Blake nodded. "I have to inform you, Mr. Abbot, that we believe Caitlyn has been abducted."

He gasped, and his hand rose to his chest.

Blake gave the older man a concise overview of the incident, leaving out the torture details, and then explained how Emory got involved.

He swung his gaze to Emory. "You're really Cait's twin?"

"I am," she said quietly. "DNA tests confirm it. I didn't know I was adopted until I confronted my mother this morning."

"Your parents," he said, sounding so sad. "They're just

like Faye and me. We could never find the right time to tell Cait about the adoption."

"Did you finally tell her, or did she find out some other way like I did?" Emory's rapt gaze was locked on Abbot.

He shook his head in wide, sorrowful arcs. "Faye passed away a few years ago, and I finally decided it was time to clean out her things. Cait was helping me. In the process, she ran across a copy of the adoption certificate. She hasn't really spoken to me since, but has put all her focus on finding her birth parents."

Abbot tightened his hands, and his fingers turned white. "Then about a month ago, she said she'd traced her grand-mother here, and she was quitting her job and leaving me behind to move here and get to know her." He shook his head. "She hadn't even connected with her grandmother. Not a single conversation, and she ups and moves. I tried to talk some sense into her, but we fought big time. I was sick to my stomach over it all, so I came out here to try to make up. Then I found the seal on her door." He collapsed, sliding down in his chair as if he couldn't hold up under the terrible weight.

Emory rested her hand on his, her eyes filled with the man's misery, probably her own misery, too. She had to be empathizing with him big time.

"Do you think her abduction has to do with her birth family?" Abbot asked.

"Perhaps," Blake said. "But it could be something completely different."

Emory removed her hand. "Did you get a bracelet, ring, frame, and comb-and-brush set that you were supposed to give to Cait?"

Abbot nodded. "In fact, it was in the box where Cait found the adoption information." He shook his head. "I have no idea why these things were important though."

Emory nodded. "Did the bracelet have numbers on it and do you remember the numbers?"

"It did, but we put it in the file and then promptly forgot about it. Cait asked if I knew what the numbers meant, but I don't. I wish I did."

"Tell me about her research job at the University of Minnesota," Blake said.

"She was researching how tagged fish respond to sound and light deterrents mounted on the gates on the Mississippi River."

"And what did this project hope to find?" Emory asked.

"The sound and light deterrents are supposed to stop invasive fish but let other fish pass. She was supposed to find out how it was working. Or something like that." He pursed his lips and eyes narrowed. "I didn't really understand all the fine points."

Emory tipped her head, obviously in thought. "So she could've uncovered something that someone didn't want her to discover."

Blake had thought of the same thing, but in a broader scale. "Or she could have learned something totally unrelated to her project."

Abbot rubbed his hand over his narrow jaw. "I don't know if she did, but can you talk to her boss about that?"

"Yes," Blake said. "I fully intend to. Can you think of another reason someone might want to abduct her?"

Abbot's mouth fell open for a second but he quickly recovered. "What about this grandmother she came here to get to know? Have you found her? She might not have been happy to see her."

Blake shook his head. "This is the first we're hearing about a grandmother. Did Cait share her grandmother's name?"

"No." Abbot looked even sadder if that was possible. "Nothing. She said it was none of my business."

After seeing Emory's anguish this morning, Blake could easily imagine a person reacting like that. "You can be assured we'll look into it."

Abbot frowned. "Then that's it, I guess. Unless she took up with some guy that I don't know about, and he's violent. One of a father's big fears, you know?"

Blake nodded. He wasn't a father, but he'd worked enough investigations where women suffered at the hands of violent men. He didn't want to ask the next question, but he had to in order to find Caitlyn. "Can you think of any information she might have that someone would want to hurt her to obtain?"

Abbot quirked a brow. "You mean like question her about something?"

Blake nodded. "And perhaps even use force to get her to talk."

Abbot's face blanched, and he shot up in his seat. "Are you saying she was tortured for this information?"

"I don't have proof of that," Blake said, trying not to totally panic this father. "I just believe she might have information that someone else wants but she's refusing to provide it."

"I don't know. The job. Her birth family. I don't know." Abbot fell back and clutched his hands together. "I just don't know."

"Tell us about the adoption," Blake said, feeling bad about having to keep badgering this man.

"Nothing to tell really. Pretty straightforward through an adoption agency and our attorney. We'd registered and waited for about a year. Then one day got a call telling us we had a baby daughter. Nine days old." A broad smile found his face. "Was the happiest day for me and Faye. I guess we never wanted to jeopardize that, and that's why we didn't tell Cait. We should have. I know that now. But then..." He choked, and his eyes misted over.

Blake wished he could assure this father that his daughter would not only be okay but that she would come back to him after all this was over, but Blake couldn't do either. It hurt like crazy to feel this way, and he desperately wanted to change things for them. And change things for Emory and her mother, too. But how could he—a guy who'd put up a solid wall with his own parents—help other parents and children? No, he best stick to finding Cait. That was in his wheelhouse. He at least had a chance at succeeding there.

"What's the name of the adoption agency and your lawyer?"

"If you give me paper and a pen, I'll jot it down for you."

Blake took out his notepad and pen and slid them across the table.

Abbot quickly scribbled on the paper and pushed notebook back to Blake. "I don't have the agency's phone number, but they should be in the phonebook."

"Thank you," Blake said, knowing full well that Nick would be tracking down the agency and attorney, and he definitely wouldn't be using a phonebook.

"I'm glad to call my attorney to instruct him to share our files, but good luck with the agency. They wouldn't give Cait any information when she asked so I doubt they'll share with you."

Blake agreed. He had no proof her abduction had to do with the twin's adoption, so he didn't have probable cause to subpoena the records. But that didn't mean he would just let it go. He stood and handed his card to the worried father. "Please do call your attorney and thank you for coming in, Mr. Abbot. Call me if you think of anything else."

"That's it? All?" His shocked gaze met Blake's. "You're not going to do anything else?"

"You can be assured we're doing everything we can," Blake said with full confidence in his team and their investigative skills.

But the outcome? The result? He had no control there, and he prayed he could get beyond that too bring Cait Abbot home where she belonged.

13

Blake sat, head down over his laptop, filling out a warrant request, and Emory commiserated with the frustrated way he pecked at the keys. He'd phoned Cait's former supervisor at the University of Minnesota, but the man insisted on a warrant before answering any of Blake's questions.

Trent had departed for McDonald's to pick up video footage and promised to bring back the file and lunch. That was an hour ago, and Emory felt useless in this investigation. Even if Sam and Sierra recovered potential DNA, Emory wouldn't be allowed to process it, doing the one thing she did very well. So what good was she to Cait?

A knock sounded on the door, and Lorraine poked her head in. "Is now a good time to bring you up to speed on Cait's social media accounts?"

Blake waved his assistant into the room.

She carried a notepad, and instead of sitting, she took a dry erase marker and went to the whiteboard. She noted Facebook, Twitter, Instagram, SnapChat, Pinterest and YouTube then turned to face them. "Cait is active on each of these sites. Facebook has cooperated from our warrant, and I've been reviewing her posts. She'd posted at least once a day, but that stopped abruptly when she moved to Cold Harbor. Not a single post since then, but before that, she documented her search for her birth parents. Emory, you may want to look at that for your personal interest."

"I will, thank you, Lorraine." Emory smiled at the able assistant.

She smiled back, her ocean-blue eyes lighting with warmth. "Caitlyn—Cait as she calls herself on social media—also joined several Facebook groups for people who learned they were adopted as adults. She asked a lot of questions over the last year on how to find her parents, but she didn't share details of her search in those groups. Just how she felt about hitting roadblocks. Finding little successes. Getting her DNA processed at Veritas. Etcetera."

"So nothing to help then?" Blake grumbled.

"Oh, I didn't say that." A smug smile lit her face. "I found two friends who live in Cold Harbor. A guy, Eric Young, and woman, Jacie Nicholson. From what I can tell, they're a couple."

Emory shot Blake a hopeful look. "These could be the people who helped her move. She might have confided in them about her search for our family and why she came to Cold Harbor."

"I thought the same thing, so I made sure you had their pictures, names, and favorite hangouts." Lorraine handed a packet of paper to each of them. "I know you can look up their DMV records to get their addresses, but I thought this might be good background information. FYI, they both work near the marina. Jacie at the Anchors Aweigh Restaurant and Eric at the Crab Shack."

"I recognize those restaurants and not just from dining there," Blake said. "There are charges for both places on Cait's credit card bill. In fact, they're about the only other charges except for books on Amazon and groceries."

So Emory's sister was a reader. "What kind of books?"

"Fiction. Romance." Blake scrunched his nose up.

"Hey, nothing wrong with a good romance," Emory said.

Trent entered the room, carrying McDonald's bags and the room filled with a savory smell. Emory had to admit she had a soft spot for their french fries, and her stomach grumbled.

"Go ahead and hand out the food as Lorraine finishes bringing us up to speed on Cait's social media," Blake told Trent then shifted his attention to Lorraine. "Does Cait ever mention Emory in her posts?"

She shook her head. "No details about what she learned, if anything, about her birth parents on any social media site. Pinterest is filled with her decorating ideas and clothing. YouTube, she created a few playlists. Mostly Christian music."

Emory raised a quick prayer of thanks that her sister was a Christian, too.

Lorraine tapped Twitter on the board. "She uses Twitter to follow politics and social activism, and connect with her fellow U of M coworkers when she worked there."

Blake opened his sandwich wrapper. "Anything controversial that might be a reason someone would abduct her?"

"Maybe." Lorraine shifted the folders she held. "She belongs to a group trying to preserve and improve the Mississippi River. Most notably, right now they're trying to buy a one-hundred-fifty-acre closed golf course and restore it to a critical habitat. But developers are fighting them as it's prime real estate for residential development."

"A hundred fifty acres on the river?" Blake squeezed a packet of ketchup onto his wrapper and looked at Trent. "Sounds like a solid motive for abducting Cait. I don't see this as our primary lead, but get Newton looking into it."

Trent nodded, and Emory assumed Newton was another detective.

Blake dipped a fry in the ketchup. "Anything else on social media?"

Lorraine shook her head. "I'll keep monitoring to see if anyone posts to her accounts."

"Good work." Blake smiled at his assistant. "Let me know if you see anything."

"Thanks, Lorraine," Emory said and turned her attention to her meal.

"I didn't know you'd be in here, so I left your salad on your desk," Trent said.

"Thanks for picking it up." Lorraine smiled and hurried from the room.

A fry in hand, Blake faced Trent. "McDonald's video pan out?"

Trent set his burger down and wiped his mouth. "Otter was there like he said, but that doesn't rule him out for the time of abduction. I've left messages with his buddies on the way over, but odds are good they'll ignore them, and I'll have to go roust them out. And I'll want to interview the bartender anyway as the friends will likely lie for him."

Blake swallowed. "What about Cait's recent emails? You have them printed for me yet?"

Trent nodded. "Let me grab them from my desk."

He got up and left the room.

Emory chewed her fry, enjoying the saltiness, and swallowed. "I'm going to look at Cait's social media. Maybe something will catch my attention that Lorraine ruled out." She wiped her hands then got out her phone and logged into Facebook.

Blake's hand rested over his sandwich as he watched her. "You have a Facebook account?"

She looked at him. "You sound surprised by that."

"You just don't seem like the social media type."

He really had established a preconceived notion of who she was, surprising since he was so open-minded in the investigation. "And what type is that?"

"You know. Outgoing and real sociable."

"I'm going to pretend that wasn't an insult."

"No, wait—I didn't mean it as one."

She laughed. "I know you didn't. And if you must know, I only go on Facebook when Angela tells me she's posted something that I need to look at. Thankfully, that hasn't been for a few weeks. Otherwise, I'm a pretty solitary kind of person, so you were right."

"Me, too." He picked at the fries in the paper container. "Especially with the social media. I'd rather die than participate in that. But other than spending time with the Blackwells, I pretty much work."

What a wasted life. Wait. How could she think that? She lived a similar life. Work. Work. And more work. Hang out with Angela in her downtime—which was rare—and go out with Angela only when she dragged her along. When Sam lived in Portland, they'd gone out a few times. She hadn't been so focused on her work in D.C. She went home at the end of the day and did things.

But her partnership required more. Or was she letting fear from the attack keep her from missing out on life? From missing all that God wanted for her in life?

Am I, God? Missing something...like a relationship with someone like Blake?

Her Facebook page opened, and she let her thoughts go. She had plenty of time to think about her own life after they found Cait. She searched the page and was surprised to see a private message and a friend request. She clicked on the message first.

"A message," she blurted out. "It's from Cait."

Blake leaned closer, and Emory held out the phone so they both could read the message that was dated a week prior. Cait shared her picture and explained that she thought they were twins. "She wanted to meet. To have our DNA compared."

"I'll bet the friend request is from her, too," Blake said.

She clicked over to the request that was indeed from Cait and quickly accepted her friendship then registered as Cait's sister. They truly were sisters. Sure, Emory had seen the science. Saw the pictures. Found the leads. But this very simple task connected them in a concrete way. Tears wet her eyes and started rolling down her cheeks. She grabbed a tissue from her backpack.

Blake watched her carefully, his concern evident in the tightness of his expression. "What is it? What's wrong?"

"She's my sister," Emory said between sniffles. "Truly my sister."

Blake scratched his cheek and stared at her.

Right. She was confusing him. She dabbed her eyes, careful not to smudge her mascara. "I can't explain why doing this made it really sink in more, but it did."

Blake let out a quick breath as if he'd been holding it in worry for her. "Maybe because it's not related to her abduction, but it's part of everyday life. Something you can easily identify with."

"Probably." She thought about the connection more and shook her head. "I don't get it. Just don't get it."

His expression tightened again. "Get what?"

"Why would God let me find out about Cait only after she's been abducted, and I can't get to know her? I can't even meet her—might never be able to meet her."

Blake pressed his finger over the creases in his sandwich wrapper, his gaze fixed on his hand before raising it to her face, his eyes narrowed. "I can tell you what my mom keeps telling me. She says God puts us in exactly the situation that challenges us to grow. You know, so we get to know Him and grow our faith. That He can use problems to change our perspective. Not only about life, but about Him, too."

He sounded so skeptical that it hurt Emory's heart. "Sounds like you don't believe her, though."

He shoved his food away and leaned back. "I do...deep down. But when I see someone suffering, I want to take it away. Not let them go through it."

"That's a natural response for anyone who cares about other people, but suffering is when we grow, right?" She hated to admit that, but she knew it was the truth in her life. "I mean, watching Angela go through life after losing Will, I can see how much stronger she is."

He frowned. "But still, couldn't she get stronger another way?"

Emory had often wondered the same thing. "Sorry, I don't have any answers to that. I don't know that anyone does except God."

"Yeah, and I guess that should be comforting, but honestly, I don't really find comfort in it."

Emory took a moment to think about what she was going through right now with Cait missing. Would going through this situation make Emory a stronger person in the end? And how would it end? She couldn't bear to lose Cait without ever having known her, but Emory knew it was a real possibility.

Her appetite vanished and she packed up her food. "I hope God doesn't think I'm strong enough to lose Cait."

Blake pressed a hand over hers and met her gaze. "You know I'm doing everything I can to find her, right?"

She nodded, but still fear consumed her, and she had to do something to make progress. She freed her hand and turned back to Facebook. She posted a heartfelt plea on her timeline asking her friends to report any sightings of Cait to the local sheriff's office or call her as she was in Cold Harbor working closely with his office.

She looked at Blake. "I know this is a long shot, but I had to do something."

He nodded, and went back to his laptop. Wanting to get to know Cait, Emory started scrolling down her sister's posts. She read about her job. Her church. Her adoptive father. But like Lorraine said, Cait hadn't posted anything about her new home, job, or moving to Oregon. She did post details as she searched for her birth family, but never mentioned when she'd succeeded in finding a lead, so Emory couldn't learn anything new from that either. But she could recreate all of the steps Cait had posted.

Emory set down her phone. "I think we should have Nick follow the steps Cait took to locate our family. He's bound to have the same results, and he might find someone who knows more about our adoption."

Blake tipped his head and didn't respond right away. "Could work. *If* she didn't leave out a step and posted every-thing she did."

"Still, it's worth a try, right?"

"Absolutely." He smiled.

Emory could easily let herself get lost in that smile, but she jerked her gaze away to text Nick, telling him she'd email her Facebook login information so he could access Cait's feed. She followed up the text with two separate emails so that her password wasn't in the same message as her login.

He replied. *Glad to do it, but how will I ever resist posting something on your feed?*

She laughed at the winking face emoji he'd attached, and Blake glanced at her.

"Nick's humor." She shared his comment.

Blake smiled, but his attention quickly changed to Trent who entered the room.

"Cait's emails." Trent handed a folder to Blake.

Blake told him about Lorraine finding Cait's friends on Facebook and tapped the folder. "I'll review these then head out to interview the friends."

Trent nodded. "Let me know what you learn."

Blake stared up at his detective, admiration for the man in his gaze. "And you keep me updated on any new leads while I'm out."

"Will do." Trent departed.

Emory met Blake's gaze. "I'm going with you to talk to the friends."

"I assumed you would."

"What?" She mocked surprise. "You won't try to stop me?"

"I hired you, didn't I?"

Actual surprise at his willingness to take her along hit her. She shook her head. "Just when I think I know you, you do something totally out of character."

He held her gaze. "Is that a good thing?"

"A very good thing," she said before thinking, then quickly added, "A bad thing, too, because I like you too much for my own good."

14

Blake split the stack of emails with Emory and tried not to stew over her comment about liking him too much for her own good. What did she mean by that? Did she think knowing him was a bad thing? He thought he'd proved that he was more than the one-dimensional person that Sam had warned Emory about. But maybe he'd failed at that with his bossiness and demands.

"Look at this." Emory glanced up from the email she was reading. "Someone was threatening Cait back in Minnesota. Telling her to lay off the golf course project or else. To stop making people think because she had a PhD in Aquaculture and Aquatic Sciences that her opinion was worth more."

He quickly read the email and wished he thought the lead was as promising as Emory's excited gaze told him she did. "This is dated a month ago. If she didn't continue working on the project after she moved, I can't see it being a reason to abduct her. Still, I'll text Detective Newton to look into the email when he researches the group."

"Thanks," she said, but didn't sound all that thankful.

He'd likely disappointed her, but he had to put his resources where he believed they had the greatest return.

He grabbed his phone and fired off the text to Newton and went back to his stack of emails.

Trent had printed them in order from oldest to newest and Blake had taken the top off the stack so his were more current, but he still had to read through many of them before finding one with promise.

"Okay, this is recent and interesting." He looked at Emory. "Remember Cait's hobby of photobombing news stories?"

Emory nodded.

"She continued doing it here." He slid the email with a picture of Cait captured in the background of a news story on crabbing on the Oregon Coast. "Email is from a viewer who's attracted to her. More than that, actually. The language is stalkerish. We'll have to track down this account to see if we can find out where the message originated. Email providers aren't always the most helpful, though."

"Nick can track it faster than you can imagine. I'm texting the email address to him." She grabbed her phone and tapped the screen, her concentration fierce. She started to look up but her phone vibrated in her hands. "He says he'll have an ID by this afternoon at the latest."

Blake shook his head. "You really are the wonder team."

"We've hit our stride for sure, but there's so much more we could be doing. In fact, we're thinking of expanding and adding a few new partners to the group."

Now *that* he found interesting. "In what areas?"

"We'll first interview for a strong investigator. Someone to coordinate our efforts and point us all in the same direction when we're working multiple aspects of an investigation for law enforcement. This investigation would be a good example. If we had someone to coordinate and assign all of these different needs that come up, we could be more efficient and prioritize the most promising leads first."

"I could see that." He considered their group and what they might need in an investigator. "You'll want a former LEO for sure."

She nodded. "We've been thinking former FBI."

His mind raced through the possibilities. "I may be prejudiced here, but a detective might be a better bet. The FBI probably doesn't come knocking on your door all that often, right?"

"Right."

"But locals do, so why not hire someone who's more familiar with the kinds of crime the locals need help with?"

"Good point. I'll mention that at our next staff meeting."

Blake felt oddly pleased that she respected his opinion enough to bring it up at their meeting. He also wondered if he should throw his hat into the ring if they ever did decide to add the job. He could easily imagine working with this team. Imagine having a more normal work life and not having the responsibility and pressure of managing a large staff.

And then what? Have a ton of free time to do what? As his discussion with Emory pointed out, he didn't have much of a life outside of his work. So what if he changed jobs? Even in the private sector he could work nonstop. Emory proved that.

"I'm done reviewing my emails," she said, bringing him back to the task at hand. "Nothing else of interest, unless you consider the fact that she purchases a lot of her things online interesting."

"I suppose we could be looking at a delivery driver who took a shine to her." He took a second to think. "But she wasn't home during the day, so that seems unlikely."

"She might've had a weekend delivery."

"You're right, and I saw a few packages on her table.

Even if a driver didn't take an interest in her, the delivery drivers might have seen something."

He typed a text to Trent telling him to check into the packages. "Okay, I'll look up Eric's and Jacie's addresses." He opened his laptop and entered the names into the county database. "We have three Eric Youngs. Can you look in that packet from Lorraine for his picture for comparison?"

She grabbed the papers, and he printed the three records and moved on to Jacie. As he expected with the unique name, there was only one Jacie Nicholson in the county. He printed her address and picked up all the pages from the printer in the corner. He returned to the table and spread out the pictures in front of Emory. She set several of the social media photos beside them.

Blake leaned over her shoulder, and despite his wayward mind wanting to focus on her nearness, he studied the pictures of Eric. He tapped the second one. "That's our guy."

"Agreed."

"And Jacie's driver's license pic matches her Facebook pictures, too." He snatched up the papers. "We'll start by going to their homes. If we don't find them there, we can head to the restaurants where they work."

He held the door for Emory, and on the way out of the building, he stopped to grab his long guns and fill Lorraine in on his plan. They were on the road headed to Jacie's house in minutes. Emory laid her head back on the seat and rubbed her forehead.

He was concerned about her getting a bad headache since she didn't sleep enough last night, and she barely ate any breakfast or lunch. "Headache?"

"Not yet. Just tension that I'm trying to stop from becoming one."

"I totally get that. Seems like someone's life is always hanging in the balance in this job and everything is urgent."

She shifted in her seat and focused on him. "When we talked about faith, you mentioned understanding about being mad at God. Has something on the job made you angry with Him?"

She remembered his comment? He'd fired off the response without thinking. For some reason she seemed to bring up things he didn't want to talk about. This was one of them, and he didn't know how to respond, so he clamped his mouth closed before he said something he'd regret.

"I know," she said. "It's a personal question, and it's none of my business. I just thought you might want to talk to a stranger about it. You know, get an unbiased opinion from someone you won't have to see in the future."

She had a point, but he wasn't about to encourage a personal connection with her. She might only be here for a few days, but he could easily see if they opened up with each other that it could lead to a deeper relationship.

"I'm good," he said trying his best to sound nonchalant. "But thanks for offering."

He caught a flash of hurt in her eyes and felt bad, but moved them on anyway. "What about you? Want to talk about why you're mad at God?"

"No and yes."

"It has to do with your unease in getting into vehicles," he stated, though he was guessing.

She gave him an incredulous stare.

"I see you check and double-check the back seat before you climb in a car," he said. "It was worse this morning when it was dark, but you still do it and tense up every time."

"Yeah," she said, but didn't elaborate.

"Did someone break into your car?"

"Yeah."

He didn't like the one-word answers, but he would take

them to mean she didn't want to tell him anything more than he wanted to share with her. He needed to respect her privacy just as he hoped she would respect his. He focused on the road and didn't speak until they reached Jacie's small beach bungalow where an older Jeep was parked in the drive.

"Looks like she's home." He pulled to the curb. "Remember, her first reaction will be to think you're Cait."

"Thanks for reminding me. I keep forgetting that there's another person who looks exactly like me." She smiled at him.

He was unreasonably happy that she wasn't holding her earlier disappointment against him. He shifted into park. "I know you and Cait are identical, but I'll bet now that I know you better, I'll be able to pick out the difference when we find Cait."

"I can't wait to find that out." Her smile widened into a soft dreamy number that sent his heart beating harder.

He reached for the keys and got out before he gave in to his emotions and touched the side of her very beautiful face. It hit him then. He was fighting his attraction to this woman, but it also was great to feel something positive again. Felt better than he could put into words. How had that happened?

Is this you God? Pushing me? Making me come out of my funk to figure my life out? Because if it is, I sure don't think I'm in the place for this right now.

Would he ever be? He hadn't given such a thing any thought of late, simply accepted his lot in life. But now? Now what? Maybe it was time to reconsider. To listen to God again. To hear what He wanted for his life.

Maybe. And this woman at his side was the reason for stirring up these thoughts. These emotions.

As he escorted her up the short sidewalk, the cool ocean

breeze washed over them, and Emory lifted her face to it, a sweet smile tipping her lips. He wanted to forget all about their desperate need to find Cait and just enjoy her smile for a minute. But Cait needed him.

He shook off his thoughts and marched faster toward the white cottage with crisp blue accents. A hammock hung on the porch filled with colorful pillows, and he could imagine swinging here looking at the ocean day after day, at peace with the world. Maybe a woman like Emory at his side.

Enough.

He knocked on the door and stood back. He heard quick footsteps on the other side and the door opened. A tiny redhead stood looking up at him with wide eyes then swung her gaze to Emory.

"Cait, is everything okay?" Apprehension lingered in her question.

Emory held out her hand. "I'm not Cait. I'm her twin, Emory."

"Oh my gosh, she found you!" Jacie swept Emory into a hug.

"Not exactly." Looking uncomfortable, Emory pushed free. "Can we come inside for few minutes?"

"Is everything okay? Did something happen to Cait?"

Blake pointed inside and put on his expression that he used at traffic stops to discourage arguments.

"Yes, come in." She stepped back. "Have a seat."

Blake took a look around the small cottage decorated the same whites and blues as the exterior. It definitely had the feminine touch with no sign of a male living in the household. Emory sat on the white slipcovered sofa, and Blake sat on the far end. Jacie perched on the edge of a matching club chair.

"I'm afraid we have some bad news about Cait," Blake

said right off the bat. "We have reason to believe she's been abducted."

"No. Oh, no." Jacie's face paled, emphasizing freckles dotting her cheeks.

Blake shared the basics of the abduction, but left out the torture. No way she needed to hear that, and he didn't want it getting out to the general public. "Do you know of anyone who might want to abduct her?"

Tears formed in Jacie's eyes. "I've only known her for a few weeks, but she's the sweetest person. No one would want to harm her."

"When Emory identified herself, you mentioned that Cait had found her," Blake said. "Did Cait share her adoption with you?"

Jacie nodded eagerly. "And her search for her birth family. She'd found her grandmother but had yet to locate her parents or Emory."

Emory explained how she learned of Cait. "Do you know where I can find our grandmother?"

Jacie clutched trembling hands in her lap. "Cait said she lives in a remote area. In an old cabin surrounded by huge trees. But that's all she said."

"Nearby?" Blake asked.

"Oh, yeah...yes." Jacie bobbed her head. "Near Cold Harbor for sure. That's why Cait moved here."

"What about our grandmother's name?" Emory asked. "Did she tell you that?"

Jacie gnawed on her lip. "Cait may have mentioned it, but I don't remember."

If Cait had indeed confided in Jacie, Blake was disappointed in her faulty memory and hoped that Eric would know the name. "Do you know how long ago she located her grandmother?"

"Before she moved here," Jacie said. "But I'm not sure when."

"Anything else you can tell us about Cait or the adoption?" Blake could only hope that Cait had given Jacie a few details.

"Um...well..." She tapped her chin. "I think her grandmother said the parents went missing." She wrung her hands. "I don't remember the details. But Eric will. He has a memory like a steel trap."

"Eric?" Blake asked, playing dumb.

"Eric Young. We're dating. A couple." She blushed. "He's friends with Cait, too. In fact, he met her first. At the marina. He's totally into boats and lives on one. It's his day off. Mine, too. We schedule them the same so we can do things together. I can ask him to come over."

Blake shook his head. "I'd rather go see him."

"But I—"

"If I talk to you together, you may mix up your stories." He smiled to soften the blunt words. "Not on purpose. It just happens. One person starts talking. The other embellishes. Suddenly, the story changes."

"Oh, right. Okay. I could see that."

Blake shifted, readying himself to depart. "We'll head over to Eric's place as soon as we finish here. I'd appreciate it if you didn't call him or talk to him. It's better if we just arrive and he's able to tell us what he knows."

"Oh...yeah...sure. I can see that, too."

Emory shifted on the sofa. "Did Cait talk about her work in Minnesota?"

"Not with me," Jacie said. "But I know she did with Eric since he's into fishing and stuff."

Blake thought that sounded legitimate. "What about her hobby?"

"Photobombing? Yeah. We all went with her a few

times." Jacie rolled her eyes. "I never got the thrill of it. Especially when some weirdo tried to come on to her."

"Did he physically contact her?" Blake asked.

"No. Just email, but that was creepy enough." Jacie shuddered, and Emory looked equally repulsed.

Blake got their distaste, but now he was wondering if that break-in of Emory's car also involved her being attacked. He felt sick to his stomach at the thought. If it was true, and he ever came face-to-face with the guy, Blake would mess him up, that was for sure.

He focused on Jacie. "Do you know who sent her the email?"

"No, all Cait said was that she deleted it and blocked him."

"Anything else you think that can help us?" Emory asked.

Jacie shook her head.

Blake got up and waited for Emory and Jacie to stand before heading for the door.

"It's good to meet you, Emory," Jacie said. "Please know that I'll be praying and ask the others at my church to pray, too."

"Thank you." Emory hugged Jacie. "We need your prayers more than ever."

15

Blake pointed the vehicle toward the marina, and Blake hoped that Eric would know the grandmother's name and even more. He assumed Emory was thinking the same thing. He expected her to chatter on about her grandmother, but she'd been quiet. Likely reflecting on what it meant to her life. He wanted to ask, but if she wanted to share, she would be talking, and he would respect her privacy.

He pulled up to the dock, and they made their way down to the dock marked with a large C. A tall, thin guy stood on the bow of a boat that Blake thought was far too small to live on. At least for Blake. He needed more space than that.

As they approached, Blake checked the slip number to confirm this was Eric's boat.

The guy looked up from his mop and waved at them. "Cait, hey. I thought you were off for the day. At least Walter said you didn't come in."

"Eric Young?" Blake asked, though the man matched his pictures.

A worried look knotted his high forehead below a receding hairline. "What's going on, Cait? You know me."

Emory stepped closer to the boat. "I'm not Cait. I'm her twin, Emory."

He gaped at her. "For real?"

Blake didn't waste time but explained about Cait's abduction.

"Oh, man." Eric shoved his fingers into his short hair. "That's awful. Do you know who did it?"

Blake shook his head. "That's why we're here."

"You think it's me?" His voice squeaked high, and he dropped down onto a bench.

"No. No," Emory quickly said. "But we're hoping you might know who would want to hurt Cait."

His eyes tightened. "You talk to Floyd Otter?"

Blake stepped closer but made sure to keep his tone neutral. "Why do you mention him?"

"He's been like stalking her since she started her job." Eric shook his head. "Okay, maybe not stalking exactly, but bugging her, and then when she fired him, watching her. I caught him hanging out nearby a few times."

"Do you think he's dangerous?" Blake asked.

Eric placed his hand on a nervously shaking knee. "Not really, I suppose. Just more annoying."

Blake had to agree and decided to move on. "What can you tell us about Cait's grandmother?"

Eric frowned. "Not much."

"Cait never mentioned her name?" Emory asked sounding disappointed.

He shook his head. "At least not that I remember. She found her before she moved here, and I know she went to see her, but she didn't really say much about it."

Blake took a deep breath. "How about where the grandmother lives? Cait tell you that?"

Eric's head bobbed in rapid nods. "Some cabin in the

woods. Kind of a hermit is how Cait described her. In the Cold Harbor area is all I know."

Blake worked hard to keep from letting his disappointment show. "We interviewed your girlfriend, Jacie, and she said that Cait's parents had gone missing."

"Yeah, yeah." Eric's forehead furrowed. "She mentioned that. But again not the details, just that she was looking into it."

Blake had to wonder if her search for answers was the reason for the abduction. "Was law enforcement brought in when the parents went missing?"

Eric pursed his lips. "She didn't say. She really didn't mention much. Like it was too painful to talk about."

"And did she ever talk about her past work in Minnesota?" Emory sounded as disappointed in this interview as Blake was feeling.

"A bit. She was really into the environment and was working on a project to reclaim a closed golf course on the Mississippi. She still stayed in touch with the group and wrote articles for them."

"Did you know about her unusual hobby?" Blake asked.

"Photobombing you mean." He chuckled. "Jacie and I did it a few times with her. Was fun." He suddenly sat up straight. "Until some guy got creepy about it. Found out about Cait's activist work in Minnesota and got her email somehow. Sent her a creepy message. So she stopped."

"Was that email the end of this guy's contact?" Blake asked.

"Hmm, yeah. As least as far as I know, but I suppose he could've come looking for her."

That email was definitely worth checking into. "Anything else you can tell us that you think might help us find her?"

He shook his head. "No. No. Not that I can think of. But I'll give it some thought and call if I do."

"Thank you." Blake handed over his business card.

"I hope you find Cait and glad to meet you Emory." Eric scratched his neck. "The resemblance is crazy."

Emory nodded, her face unreadable, as she turned to depart. Blake desperately wanted a strong lead in this case to find Cait, but he also wanted one to erase the worry furrowing Emory's forehead. The more he got to know her, the more he wanted to protect her and put a smile on her face. But that would only happen when he located Cait alive and well, and he couldn't do that on his own. He needed help. His team. The Veritas team, too.

And God, Blake had to admit. He needed God more than he had in a long time.

Father, please. I know I've been silent for a long time and don't deserve anything, but for Emory's sake, let us find Cait soon —and still alive!

Emory so desperately wanted to find a lead to help them locate her grandmother and Cait, so when Trent opened the conference room door, a smile on his face, a surge of hopefulness pulsed through her. Sam and Sierra passed him to enter the room, and Trent closed the door behind all of them.

Excited at the possibilities of a lead, Emory got to her feet. "Please tell me you found something Helen missed."

Blake cleared his throat. "I'm hoping for the same thing, but not for Helen's sake."

Emory didn't want any new discovery to mean trouble for Helen for not locating it in the first place, but if it did, Emory would go to bat for her.

Sierra set her kit on the table. "Actually, we did find a few additional items, but Helen was instrumental in helping us."

Emory didn't know if that was true or if Sierra was being diplomatic. She was always sensitive to other people and would do something like that. But either way it didn't matter. They had new evidence, and Blake wouldn't blame Helen for failing on the initial crime scene processing.

"What did you recover?" Emory sat and the others followed suit.

Sam tugged out a paper envelope. "A broken fingernail. I looked at pictures of Cait and she most always had hers polished. This one is jagged and unpolished so could be from our suspect."

"We can run DNA comparison to the blood. And to DNA from the hair recovered from our only suspect." Emory shared about Floyd Otter.

"He also fits the suspect's description from our eyewitness." Trent shared Otter's description.

"We found a few blond hairs at the scene." Sam said. "The strands are longer than a typical male so we thought they might have come from a female friend or even someone who lived in the apartment before Cait, but from your description of Otter, the hair could be his."

"We should consider the fact that the suspect could've dyed his hair to throw us off track," Sierra said. "I'll want to look at all the samples to rule that out."

"Will you use SERS for that?" Sam asked.

Sierra nodded.

"Explain for the lay people please," Blake said.

"Surface-enhanced Raman spectroscopy. It's a surface-sensitive technique that enhances Raman scattering by molecules absorbed on a surface."

"Oh, right, yeah. That's clearer." Blake rolled his eyes.

Sierra chuckled. "Just know if the hair's been dyed, I should be able to tell you the type of treatment and even the manufacturer of the product."

"That could be valuable info." Blake looked quite impressed now, and Emory was so proud of her partner's knowledge and skills in using a cutting-edge technique.

"We also lifted a nice sample of saliva from a corner in the shower," she continued, smiling.

"Seriously." Emory shook her head. "Her abductor wore coveralls likely to contain evidence transfer. Why would he do something stupid like spit in the shower?"

"Because there's no such thing as a perfect crime," Blake said. "In the heat of the moment, criminals react and do things they can't plan for."

Sierra nodded. "And thankfully they do, or they might never get caught."

Emory agreed. "Since everything you collected today will be processed for DNA, it'll be done in my lab. I know I can't participate in running the samples, but I'd like to check in with Lara to be sure we're on track with everything. If we could get Gage to let us use the helicopter, I can drop off the new evidence, review things with Lara, and be back here in a few hours."

"He will. I'll make sure of it." Sam got to her feet and stretched out her back, likely sore from bending over evidence all morning. "Just let me make the arrangements."

"Thanks, Sam." Emory smiled at her friend. "I don't know what I'd do without great friends like you and Sierra."

"And you'll never have to find out." Sierra squeezed Emory's hand and helped cement the bond they'd developed this year.

Sam waved a hand and made her way to the corner of the room, phone already at her ear.

"I'll schedule a quick partner's update meeting while I'm

there, too," Emory added. "I need to follow up with Nick on several things, plus I'd like to pick everyone's brains for additional investigative ideas."

"Glad you're doing that before Mama Maya hunts you down." Sierra laughed and started gathering the evidence bags.

"Mama Maya?" Blake asked.

Emory grinned. "You met our managing partner, Maya Glass. She's kind of a mother hen. She's responsible for looking after the business and lets that cross over into our personal lives sometimes."

"Oh, I get that," Trent said, eyeing Blake.

"I don't do that."

"Um...yeah." Trent gave an uneasy smile. "You kinda do."

Blake actually looked stunned but rolled his eyes and shifted his gaze to Emory. "I'm coming with you to Portland."

"But why?"

"*A*, I want a law enforcement officer present while you're in the lab. When this case goes to court I don't want the opposing lawyer to have any reason to call our forensics into question. And *B*, I want to be there for your update meeting."

"Makes sense," she said, though she actually hoped he'd say "and *C*, because I want to be with you." Even if that was true, which she had no reason to believe it was, he wouldn't mention it in a meeting like this if he mentioned it at all.

He shifted his attention to Trent and recounted the interviews with Jacie and Eric. "If Emory's parents really did go missing, someone might have reported it. I need you to go back through missing persons files around Cait's and Emory's birthdate."

"Will do." He pulled a folder from a stack he'd carried in

with him and passed it to Blake. "The phone records for the last two months. I've chased down all of the calls. There doesn't seem to be anything related to Cait's disappearance, but I know you'll want to give it another look."

"I will. And let's go back a few more months. Hopefully, Cait called her grandmother, and we'll locate her that way."

"You got it."

Sam turned. "We're set. Coop's available to fly you to Portland and wait to bring you back tonight. We can head to the compound now."

"Can I talk to you a sec before you go, boss?" Trent asked.

Emory got to her feet. "We'll wait for you outside."

In the hallway, Sierra faced Emory. "What do you think he has to say about this investigation that we can't hear?"

"Might not be about Cait's case at all," Sam said.

True, but Emory couldn't help but think they were keeping something from her. She got that feeling earlier. She hoped she wasn't right, but only time would tell.

16

Blake drove the old pickup toward the Veritas Center, Emory by his side and Sierra next to her. He hardly even noticed the drive. His gut had been tied in a tight knot since Trent told him about the background check on Emory and tightened even more when Trent called after they'd landed in Portland.

Blake didn't know how to handle the news. Trent had completed his background check on Emory, and she checked out fine. But—and this was a huge, monstrous *but* for Blake—Trent found a police report filed in Portland. Emory had been assaulted by her former boyfriend. He'd broken into her car, hid in the back seat, and choked her with a rope. She honked her horn and a passerby stopped to intervene. If not...

Blake couldn't even begin to think about that. He wasn't responsible for protecting her like he'd been for Danielle, but it triggered his guilt feelings and added a strong dose of fear to them. If he hadn't planned to come to Portland on this trip, he would have once he'd heard from Trent. He wanted to be with Emory. To ease that fear she had when getting in a vehicle. If he was totally honest, he wanted more than that with her, but what, he didn't know.

"Um, Blake," Sierra said. "You gonna sit there staring all night or come in with us?"

He blinked to see he'd parked out front of the Veritas Center and felt like he was coming out of a fog. He had no idea how he'd even driven there. Not good. Not good at all. And on top of that, he hadn't come to any conclusions about whether he should tell Emory he knew about the attack or not.

"It's good to be home." Sierra climbed out.

"I never get tired of coming back to this amazing lab." Emory scooted out after her.

Blake grabbed the keys and got out, too, jogging to catch up to the pair who were nearing the front door.

The security guard stood waiting for them, holding the door, a smile on his face. "Evening, ladies and Sheriff."

"Pete," the women both said, fondness for the older man in their voices and smiles.

Emory even squeezed the guy's hand, and Blake was jealous. Not that he thought she had any interest in this older man, but Blake wanted her to be this comfortable and free with him.

"You'll have to sign in, Sheriff," Pete said.

"Seriously?" Blake eyed him. "Even if I'm with them?"

Pete firmed his shoulders. "Even then."

Pete went to the desk and grabbed the iPad. Blake filled in the form while Emory and Sierra started up the steps, chatting. If he didn't already feel like an outsider, he would now.

He gave the device back to Pete, after clipping on the visitor badge, he charged up the steps after the pair. His boots thudded on the steps, disturbing the serene atmosphere.

Emory pressed her finger on the print reader, and the door clicked open. This time when they passed the Toxicology and Controlled Substance Unit, several people including Maya were working despite the time of day. Emory and Sierra waved at Maya then Emory stepped to her own lab and opened the door.

Lara looked up at Emory. "Oh good. DNA from the Abbot crime scene just finished processing so you can review the reports. We have a male and female profile. Male from the handkerchief, female from the other blood samples."

"Any matches?" Blake asked.

"Female's profile matches Caitlyn Abbot." Lara frowned. "Unfortunately, the male profile didn't return a match in CODIS."

Blake had been counting on the DNA panning out and didn't like this news at all. "So if the evidence we brought tonight is a match to that male profile, then we're no further ahead."

"Evidence?" Lara asked.

"We recovered a fingernail, saliva, and hair samples." Sierra set down her kit and took out the evidence bags. She handed two to Lara. "Here's the saliva and fingernail, but I'm dividing the hair samples so I can check for dye."

"Thank you for working late again." Emory smiled at her analyst. "You are absolutely the best."

"Remember that at review time." Lara laughed.

"I'll get these samples split and retagged for the evidence log." Sierra grabbed her kit and stepped to the nearest empty worktable.

Emory moved closer to Lara. "So how are you doing with the workload?"

"I've got it under control. The MPS DNA is on target, and I've managed to keep up with our regular work schedule." She shoved a hand into her hair, revealing her blond roots. "If the samples you brought in are as straightforward as they seem, I should be able to get them both running tonight and still get a few hours of sleep."

"I'm glad for that at least." Emory squeezed Lara's arm. "I'd tell you to come in late tomorrow, but since I'm heading back to Cold Harbor tonight, I really need you here to supervise."

Lara waved a hand. "If this drags out, that's another story, but short-term I'm fine."

"You'll let me know if it becomes a problem for you?"

"Sure." She headed to another work area.

Emory looked at Blake and held out the papers in her hands. "I'm going to review profiles."

"You think you'll find something there?" Blake asked.

She shook her head. "But our procedures include me reviewing and signing off on all profiles. Even these."

Emory went to her desk. Blake followed her, his mind still conjuring up a rope curled around her neck. He wanted to help her find a way to put the attack in her past like Danielle had done. His sister had gone to counseling for a long time, and she was eventually able to move on. He wondered if Emory had sought counseling, too.

She perched on the edge of her chair and ran her fingers down columns on the page.

"I suppose it'll take twenty-four hours to get results again." He leaned against the wall.

"Could," she said, still looking intently at the paper in front of her.

"I don't get it. How can it take that long when the rapid DNA machine finishes in a few hours?"

She looked up but kept her finger in place on the page. "Remember we only do cheek swabs in that machine and the DNA doesn't need to be extracted, purified, or quantified

169

by an analyst because those swabs contain the necessary DNA. But when we get a sample from a crime scene, the analyst has to go through all of those steps. About half of all samples that you think will contain DNA don't. We don't yet know why, but it's a fact. So depending on the sample we receive, those steps alone can take up to twenty or more hours."

"And the ones we brought in tonight?"

"Like Lara said, it should be pretty straightforward, and she should be able to complete it in less time, but I can't be certain of that." Emory tapped the overflowing inbox on her desk. "You might want to take a seat. I have quite a few profiles to review."

He had work to do as well. "Mind if I use one of the tables to look at Cait's phone records?"

"Help yourself." She smiled and leaned forward to examine her work.

She said she worked all the time, and it appeared as if she could easily get wrapped up in it—like he did. He could see she would never leave this job, so even if he could manage to start a relationship with her, it would have to be long-distance. Or he would have to make a change in his employment. He'd been disillusioned for some time, but could he really leave law enforcement behind? Because if he couldn't, then staying in his current position where he set the tone and mood for his work was the way to go.

Shaking his head over even thinking about a relation-ship that would likely never get off the ground when he should be working, he went to one of the lab tables and took out the call logs. Trent had very neatly noted the party's identity and their association to Cait by each number. Also, he noted if he actually called the person and the result. Trent was extremely organized, and his reports were always thorough. He truly was a fine detective, and Blake was proud to have him on his team.

Blake continued down the list for the recent weeks. Cait made very few phone calls, and the ones she did make were for utility companies and her landlord. She texted with Eric and Jacie quite often. Just basic texts about planning to meet up or stresses or joys in her day. She loved Walter like a father, and she did mention Otter, but she sounded like she believed he was harmless. If she spoke to her grandmother, it wasn't via cell phone as there were no phone numbers that Trent hadn't been able to explain in the last two months. That seemed off to Blake, but Eric told them that the grandmother was like a hermit so maybe she didn't have a phone.

Sierra started packing up her things and got up. "I'll get started on the hair samples, Emory, and see you at the meeting."

Emory waved her hand and mumbled "thanks" but didn't look up. Blake nodded as Sierra passed and turned his focus back to the calls. When he finished and concluded nothing needed additional investigating, he sent a text to Trent thanking him for the thorough job and asking if he'd checked out rental agencies to see if Otter rented a car, and if he followed up with Gladys on whether she saw him outside Cait's townhouse on Saturday.

His answer came right away. *No rental cars under the name Floyd Otter, and I've got Newton reviewing video from rental companies. Gladys confirms seeing Otter. Says she doesn't think he's the man who abducted Cait. She says she can't be sure, though. Any updates there?*

Blake tapped his response. *DNA profiles from the blood match Cait and unknown male. No CODIS match. Heading into update meeting with partners soon. Will call after.*

Roger that, came the reply. *FYI the packages at Cait's house were delivered last Monday. Got the warrant for her boss in MN. Emailed it to you.*

Thanks, Blake responded. He found the email, forwarded the warrant to Victor Miller, the supervisor, and then dialed. When Victor answered, Blake tried to sound pleasant when he really wanted to race through his questions and have the guy answer as quickly.

But Blake needed to remain calm to keep from worrying the man. "First, can you confirm Caitlyn Abbot's employment with your office and explain the project she was working on."

Miller shared Cait's dates of employment and told him the same thing that Mark Abbot had mentioned about the project, only with more detail that Blake honestly didn't understand.

"But certainly none of this has to do with her abduction," he added confidently. "As this wasn't a controversial project at all."

He wasn't going to like Blake's next comment. "But the golf course project *was* quite controversial."

"I'm sorry, I'm not familiar with that project."

Blake reviewed what he knew about the golf course redevelopment. "You really didn't see the news articles regarding Cait's involvement with the golf course?"

"I may have seen something. But again, it's not related to her work here." He was so dismissive, Blake couldn't determine if he was telling the truth or not.

And it was clear Blake wouldn't get anywhere with that topic, so why beat his head against a wall? "Why did she leave her job there?"

"She said she had family in Oregon and wanted to move there to be with them. She took a job at a marina. Can you believe that with her qualifications?" He sniffed. "Such a waste."

"Can you think of anyone who would want to abduct her?" Blake asked.

"No, I honestly can't. She was a likeable person who got along with everyone. She could be pushy at times, but only when she wanted to get a point across."

She sounded like Emory. "Anything else you can tell me about her?"

"Not that could help you find the person who abducted her."

"If you think of anything please call me." Blake disconnected, and he looked up to see Emory switch off her desk lamp and shrug her backpack over her shoulder as she stood. She crossed over to Lara. "I've signed off on the reports. I've got a partners' meeting in thirty minutes and want to freshen up before that. I'll make this up to you, I promise."

Lara smiled. "You know you don't have to do anything. I'm glad to help."

"I know, but I want to." She turned and met Blake's gaze. "I'm heading up to my condo until the meeting. Do you want to stay here or come with me?"

He very much wanted to go with her, but it would probably be better if he wasn't alone with her in her condo, or he might say or do something he'd later regret. "I have some other files to review. So if you or Lara don't mind, I'll hang out here."

"I'm good with it," Lara said.

"Okay." Emory looked disappointed. "I'll come back and escort you to the meeting."

He nodded, and after giving him a long look, she started for the door. He watched her leave, and it was all he could do to stay seated and not follow her. What he clearly needed to do in the next half hour was get his head on straight. He couldn't let his interest in her interfere with finding Cait, or she could pay for his unprofessionalism with her life.

~

Emory had to admit she was disappointed that Blake decided to stay in the lab. Still, she knew it was a good thing. At least her brain thought so, but her heart wanted him with her. How had she gone in a few short days from being put off by his demanding commands to having feelings for him?

She got off the elevator and trudged down the hallway. Her lack of sleep last night and the go-go-go of the day was starting to take its toll. Perhaps she would do more than freshen up. She could take a quick shower so she was wide awake when she faced her partners.

She crossed the skybridge, the night above cloudy and the stars hidden. She loved this walk at any time of day in any weather condition as it reminded her of God's universe and how vast it was. If He could create and rule such a large universe, surely He could help her with her problems.

Mood lifted from that thought, she hurried down the hall to her condo. She reached out to unlock her door, but it was ajar.

"What in the world?" Had Angela left it open? Or had one of her partners been in here and left it unlocked? She couldn't imagine they would need to stop in, but Angela could have thought the door caught when it didn't.

Emory pushed the door all the way open, flipped on the light, and her knees went weak. Someone had ravaged through her things, her family room a mess of tossed furniture, books, files, and other personal items all mixed together in a jumble on the floor.

How had anyone breached their security? Gotten into

this building? She could hardly believe it, but she wouldn't let them get away with it.

She reached for her backpack, grabbed her gun, and entered. "If someone's in here, I have a gun. Come out with your hands up or I will shoot you."

She wished her voice sounded more confident, but it shook from the fear she was barely keeping suppressed. She listened for a moment. Heard nothing but the heat whooshing through air vents. She entered and swung into the hallway.

"I mean it, I have a gun." She waited for a response.

Silence.

She stepped into her spare room. Everything was upturned, the closet emptied of clothing, and the mattress slashed. Torn open. Mutilated.

Fear ramped up and took over. Consumed her.

She tried to turn, to move on, but couldn't. Her feet were frozen, her legs even weaker. She sank to the floor. Panic took hold. She touched her neck. Remembered the noose. She couldn't go any further.

She scrambled to the corner out of sight. Dug out her phone. Dialed Blake.

"Miss me already, huh?" he joked.

"My apartment," the words came out on a strangled breath and sob.

"Emory what is it? What's wrong?"

At the sound of his concern, she started crying. "S-s-someone broke into my apartment. T-t-trashed it. Oh, Blake, I'm so afraid. Help me. P-p-please help me."

"Where are you?"

"S-s-pare bedroom. I couldn't go on. I tried. B-b-but..."

"Get out your gun. Stay put. I'm on my way, honey. Hold on."

"Stay on the line with me. P-p-lease."

"Of course. Lara, I need you to get me access to the elevator. Now!"

"Sure," she said and Emory heard her running footsteps.

"I'm in the hallway, honey." His comforting voice came over her phone. "Heading for the elevator. The call might cut out when I get on."

She heard him breathing fast as he must have been running.

"Okay," he said. "Lara has the car on the way. I'll be there soon."

"C'mon, c'mon, c'mon," she heard him mutter and then a ding.

"Boarding the elevator now."

She sat shaking, waiting. Hoping he'd continue, but he said nothing. "Blake?"

No response. The call had dropped. She wanted to call him back, but surely she could tough it out for a few minutes.

She wrapped her fingers around the grip of her gun and held it at the ready. If anyone but Blake came to her door, she would shoot. At least she hoped she would, but honestly, she didn't know if she had the nerve to fire at something other than a target.

17

The minute the elevator doors split, Blake thought to call Emory back, but if her phone wasn't on silent he could be alerting an intruder to her location. He couldn't take that risk.

He barreled down the hallway and out onto the skybridge, rushing wildly like he was ducking defensive guards intent on tackling him in his college quarterback days.

He arrived at her wide-open door and drew his weapon.

"Emory," he called out. "I'm here. Stay where you are until I get to you."

Blake hated alerting an intruder to his presence, but he couldn't let Emory mistake him for the intruder and shoot him. He crept down the hallway and looked into the first room.

Emory cowered in the corner, her gun raised in trembling hands. Her eyes were wide in fear. His heart shattered, and he wanted to run to her. To sweep her into his arms, but he had to clear the place first to safeguard their safety.

"I'm here, honey," he said trying to sound lighthearted. "You can put your gun down now."

"My b-b-bedroom. I couldn't..."

"I know. I'll go clear it and be right back. Okay, honey?"

"Okay."

He started down the hall. Searched a bathroom then moved on to the master bedroom. He found it torn apart, too, but quickly learned that the intruder had gone. He checked the third bedroom, clearly Angela's room, trashed but empty. He holstered his weapon and went back down the hallway.

"It's okay, honey," he called out as he walked to alert Emory that he was coming back. "The intruder is gone."

He turned the corner into the spare room. She'd lowered her gun to the floor, wrapped both arms around her knees, and rested her forehead on them. She was sobbing. Gut-wrenching sobs that tore at his heart.

He lowered himself to sit beside her. He pried her hands free and took her into his arms. She clung to him, her face pressed against his chest. Her body convulsed in deep sobs.

"Shh," he whispered holding her close. "I'm here now, and I won't let anything happen to you. I'll stay by your side until all of this is over."

She looked up at him, her beautiful eyes blotchy, and her face tear-streaked. "P-p-promise?"

"I promise." He tightened his arms protectively around her.

She started crying harder again.

His heart constricted over the increase in her angst. "Did I say something wrong?"

She shook her head and swallowed hard then took several deep breaths, her crying stilling. "I h-h-ate being so weak. This isn't m-me."

He exhaled. "Everyone would be afraid at a time like this."

"Even you?"

"Sure."

"I don't believe you."

He took her hand and placed it on his chest. "Feel my heart racing. I just do this more often so I know how to handle it better than you."

Her gaze raised to his face again. "You're a good man, Blake Jenkins, and I appreciate you."

He rubbed a thumb over her cheek to swipe away her tears, but couldn't think of a thing to say because more than anything he wanted to kiss her, and he would never take advantage of her vulnerability.

She took several long breaths and let them out, her body trembling less now. "I was attacked last year. In my car. By my old boyfriend. I've been afraid ever since then." She shook her head. "He's in prison, and I know he can't hurt me, but I still have this irrational fear, and it's really starting to hinder my movements. Not to mention making me an anxious wreck."

"I'm so sorry," he said and felt guilty for not telling her about Trent's background check. But he wouldn't tell her now and risk upsetting her even more. "I hate that you had to go through that and it's still impacting your life."

"This break-in won't help make it better."

"Have you gone to counseling?" he asked gently.

She shook her head and sat back. She tugged on her shirt to straighten it like she was straightening up her life at the same time.

He took her hand and held it tight. "It's none of my business, but my sister, Danielle, was attacked. She went to counseling and it helped her recover from the trauma."

She nodded and didn't seem offended by the suggestion. "I've been thinking about going for some time. But part of me fears if I have to relive that moment with someone again, I'll lose it and not come back."

"Would you like me to pray with you?" he asked, knowing it was the only thing he could do to help her.

Her eyes widened. "I thought you were mad at God."

"Turns out I've been talking to Him since you came into my life."

"Me? I'm the reason you're praying?"

He met her gaze and for the first time in a long time, he didn't shy away from what he was feeling. "You're going through a really tough time. I've come to care about you and hate seeing you suffer like this."

"Then yes, please. Pray." She sounded so needy, so weary, that he gathered up her other hand, too and offered the most fervent prayer he could muster. He had to believe that God would work all of this out for Emory because any other solution was unbearable for Blake to consider.

The partners remained stirred up over the break-in, and Blake didn't blame them. They lived in a building with state-of-the-art cameras and locks, plus they had security guards. The place was as secure as it could be for a building that had to remain open to visits from clients, and yet, an intruder had found his way in, trashed one of their condos, and burst their safety bubble. But biggest of all, it had hurt one of their own. Not physically, but the strain from witnessing her condo thoroughly torn apart lingered in Emory's tight expression and pale skin as she sat at the conference room table with her partners.

Blake so desperately wanted to hold her and comfort her again. He felt the same overwhelming guilt as when Danielle had been assaulted, but it went even deeper now. He couldn't have predicted or stopped the break-in, but he could've gone up to the condo with Emory. Instead, he'd thought of himself first. His feelings. That's when people got hurt. He knew that, and yet...yet, he'd fallen into the trap again.

She needed him to do better. To be stronger. To button down those emotions and be the lawman she needed. Starting now, that's what he would do. And that meant swallowing down his desire to hold her.

He shoved his hands into his pockets, leaned against the wall, and waited for the first partner to speak.

Maya sat forward, her posture rigid. "This has to be related to Cait's abduction. There's no other logical explanation."

Kelsey's eyes narrowed. "If so, that would mean Cait's abduction has to do with their adoption."

"That's still kind of a stretch, don't you think?" Grady scratched his jaw.

"Not really," Blake jumped in. "It's the only thing that connects the two of them, so either Emory's break-in is a coincidence—and I don't believe in coincidences in an investigation—or it's related to their birth."

"Still, it's not enough probable cause to subpoena their adoption records from the Abbot's adoption agency or the state," Nick said.

"Unfortunately, that's true," Blake replied. "But their attorney is forwarding their files to Trent and maybe we'll find a lead in there."

"Maybe," Nick said, but his suspicious tone said he didn't really believe that.

"You may not be able to pursue the records right now, but you know I'll be all over Emory's place with a fine-tooth comb," Sierra said in a steady, low-pitched voice. "And we could find a solid lead there."

Blake firmed his stance. "We should be calling the local

authorities, and they'll want their own people to handle the scene."

"Not happening. We'll process Emory's condo and *then* call." Maya crossed her arms and eyed him. "You have a problem with that, you tell me now."

"Relax." Blake held up his hands. "It's not my jurisdiction so I'm only offering my opinion. I still recommend making the call, but I won't force you."

"Why? Why do you want us to call?" Emory asked, her voice quiet and reserved like she could barely sum up the effort to speak. Her adrenaline had worn off and she would need to crash soon.

"Because I want to see the person who scared you half to death put behind bars," he said, trying not to reveal his emotions and scare or alert the others to his deep concern for Emory. "If any of you enter the scene again, what you recover may not be admissible in court. Means your intruder could skate on charges brought against him."

Emory turned to Maya. "Then we'll report it and hope they'll let us do the forensics. We've done plenty of favors for the locals, and they owe us. Time to call one in."

Maya gave a clipped nod, but he could tell she didn't like the decision. "I'll call them as soon as we break up here."

"I've got the security video up," Nick said, and the video from the Veritas Center's back door started playing on the wall-mounted flat-screen TV.

Blake watched as Nick fast-forwarded through the recording. They all agreed that with a security guard posted twenty-four seven at the main entrance that the intruder could only have gotten in via the rear door where a guard didn't routinely stand watch.

Nick returned the video to normal speed, and at twelve-thirty in the morning, the camera caught a tall, muscular man walking up to the building.

"He's wearing a Tyvek suit and rubber boots." Blake didn't need to say that aloud as everyone could see the man's clothing and had to know it matched Gladys's description of Cait's abductor.

Blake moved closer to the television. Looking around, the man approached the door, lock-picking tools in hand, and the camera caught a clear image of his face.

"Freeze that," Blake demanded.

Nick stopped the video.

"Definitely not Otter," Emory said.

"Run it through facial recognition, Nick," Maya commanded.

Blake glanced at her in surprise. "You can do that here?"

A knowing grin crossed Maya's face. "Nick can do anything."

"Maybe not anything, but..." Nick returned her grin with a wide one of his own, and his fingers clicked over the keyboard.

Blake turned his attention back to the intruder. "Blond hair. Broad face. Tall and muscular."

"Also like Gladys described." Emory wrapped her arms around her waist as if protecting herself from the intruder. "He's wearing gloves."

Sierra nodded. "So he likely didn't leave any prints, which is where we normally start on a scene as prints can lead to an ID. Since he's wearing gloves, we'll switch things up and look for trace evidence first."

"Maybe you can compromise," Blake said. "Let the local forensics team do the prints since you don't think they'll pan out anyway."

"Are you kidding?" Sierra gaped at him like he had two heads. "No. We run it all. No offense to local criminalists, but you should know by now that we have more experience and greater skills.'"

"I should, shouldn't I? After all I've been told that enough." Blake laughed, and thankfully instead of being upset at his comment, the team joined in with him. Even Emory smiled. These people might be overly self-assured, but from what he'd witnessed and heard from other LEOs, they'd earned the right to be confident in their skills.

Nick looked up. "Okay, got the facial recognition running."

"Thanks, Nick." Emory rested her hands on the table, and Blake hated to see they still trembled.

How long would it take for her to get over this? Could she even live in her condo again? He sure hoped she could.

"Odd that he takes protections again," Sierra said. "The gloves, Tyvek, and boots—but then doesn't hide his face from the camera. He spit in the shower, too, and I'm beginning to think he's not the brightest bulb."

"Bright enough to evade the super team so far." Blake folded his arms across his chest. "My team, too."

"Hasn't anyone noticed the most worrisome thing in this video?" Grady scowled at the screen. "The guy has a gun strapped to his side."

Blake *had* noticed that but hadn't yet commented. "You're the gun expert. Can you tell us anything about it, and if it might be traceable?"

"Back up and zoom in on it, Nick," Grady instructed.

The video rewound, and Nick paused on a still shot of the weapon and zoomed in.

Grady got up and strode to the TV. Blake noticed the strength with which he carried himself, but wasn't surprised. A weapon's expert, especially one on an elite team, would fire all makes and models of guns in his tests, and likely was a gun enthusiast himself. Firing the big guns would be easier with a muscular frame like Grady's.

He squinted at the screen. "Interesting. It's an old Walther PP."

"Not PPK? "Blake asked, referring to the most current and common Walther model.

"Exactly." Grady turned to look at them. "This baby was made starting in 1929 for the German police and was dubbed Polizei Pistole, which is where the PP came from. This isn't the kind of gun a lowlife thug carries. Depending on condition, it can fetch a couple grand. And the holster alone is worth as much."

"So we might have a gun collector here," Blake stated. "Or a guy who works for a gun collector."

Grady frowned. "Honestly, I can't see a collector lending a weapon like this out or even using it himself. But then, maybe the abductor was hoping it would be less traceable than a modern-day weapon. Or we could have a gun that was passed down in a family, too. They might not know the value, just that they have a handgun to use."

"I think we should get the intruder's picture out to the press," Emory said. "And mention the gun. See if we get a tip."

Blake nodded. "Since Cait was taken in Cold Harbor, we'll start there. Nick, I'll need you to get that video to Trent right now."

"On it." Nick bent his head to his computer. "And if you somehow manage to get a better picture of this guy, I have algorithms that will search the net for information on him."

Blake got out his phone. "I'll call Trent right now so we make the ten o'clock news."

Blake quickly gave Trent the information and approved the overtime that would be needed to have deputies man the phone line. They would get calls. Tons of them. Whenever law enforcement put out a plea to the public, crazies came out in full force. Blake's team would have to sift through the calls to find any actionable leads. He stowed his phone in time to see Emory suddenly sit forward.

"What if Angela had been home instead of staying with my mother?" She lifted her gaze to Blake and shuddered.

His heart wrenched with her pain, but he wouldn't go to her like he wanted to do. It might make him feel better but would only make things worse for her.

Sierra put an arm around Emory's shoulder. "God was watching out for both of you."

"All of us," Kelsey added, worry evident on her face. "With as late as we sometimes work, any one of us could have run into him in the hallway."

Maya nodded, and it was obvious that all of them were still freaked out by the break-in.

Blake didn't want to linger on that. "While we wait on the facial recognition, Nick, why don't you update us on the items you're working on?"

"Sure thing." He sat back and draped an arm over the chair next to him. "The adoption agencies are a bust. All of Draywall's old records were destroyed in a fire. That's actually what put them out of business. The owner was nearing retirement, and he didn't want to rebuild. And I hate to admit this, but I haven't been able to track down any records from Steele's attorney."

"You, unable to do something?" Maya gaped at Nick.

"I know, shocking, right?" Nick chuckled.

"And the agency the Abbots used?" Blake asked to keep them moving.

"They're still in business, but it'll take a subpoena to get the files." He paused and locked gazes with Blake. "And you still don't have probable cause for."

"You're right, but I still have hope that we'll find what we need for them and the state records."

Nick gave a clipped nod and slid a stapled packet of

papers over to Emory and Blake. "I finished Cait's background check. Nothing remarkable there. She's never been arrested. Not even a traffic violation on her record. She's quite the activist and has participated in many protests, but peaceful ones. Until a few weeks ago, she worked for the University of Minnesota and has lived in Cold Harbor only two weeks. The first week in a hotel and then she rented the townhouse where she was abducted. Her credit is top-notch, and she has a healthy savings account. The abduction could be about that, I suppose."

"There haven't been any attempts to use her bank cards," Blake said.

"Okay, so not that." Nick gave a nonchalant shrug. "She did abruptly pay out her lease in Minneapolis and leave town. The landlord said she told him that she had family in Cold Harbor, and they needed her. He also said there was a guy who'd been stalking her. He'd called the police on the guy who was arrested. He wasn't sure if he was convicted, but he hasn't been back. I requested information on the stalker and will let you know what I find out."

"Good work, man." Blake smiled, but he had to dig deep to find one. "And what about her computer files?"

Nick took a long breath. "I'm nearly done reviewing the hard drive image. The first thing I do when starting with an image is to recover recently deleted files. They often give us the best lead."

"And did that work here?" Blake asked.

"Yes, and no." Nick rubbed the back of his neck. "I recovered a series of emails between Cait and her supervisor discussing an abandoned golf course on the Mississippi."

"We heard about this project in her Twitter feed," Blake said. "And saw an email from an unknown person warning her to back off. We didn't know the supervisor was involved. In fact, he claimed he didn't even know about the project."

"Then maybe we have something here." Nick made strong eye contact. "The supervisor was telling her to leave the group as the powers that be at the university didn't want the negative publicity associated with them. Seems since she was already working on a project that involved the Mississippi, that the press tried to link the two projects together and quoted her as an expert."

Nick slid another packet down the table to Blake and Emory. "The emails progress from a kind request to end her association with the project building up to heated demands and threats, telling her she'd be fired if she didn't stop working on it."

Blake added the packet to his things to read later. "The email we saw wasn't from the supervisor."

"Yeah, I saw the email you're talking about. It was spoofed to look like it came from the email account Emory texted to me, but it didn't. I'm tracking the message, but so far I'm bouncing from proxy server to proxy server."

"Which means what exactly?" Blake asked.

"It's like when you get a package and see in the tracking information that it went through a bunch of different hubs. This is the same, only it arrived in her inbox via a ton of different servers. So it takes time to track it back to the original sender."

"Means the sender was trying to hide his tracks," Maya said.

Nick nodded. "And he's very skilled at doing so."

Emory shifted to face Nick. "Do you think the development company who's trying to buy the property could be behind Cait's abduction?"

"Taking and holding her would stop her from working on the project, but I'm not sure it explains the torture." Nick pressed his lips together. "I'll keep after it, and let you know what I find."

"Anything else of interest on her computer?" Blake asked.

"Yeah. I saved the best for last." A grin erased Nick's angst. "Someone installed a keystroke logger on her machine. In case you don't know, that's software designed to capture and log everything a user types on their computer keyboard."

Most interesting. "Any way to tell who installed it?"

Nick shrugged. "A vulnerability in her outdated browser was used to remotely install the logger. My team is tracking that, too, but it's also an issue of proxy servers."

"Why would someone want to record her keystrokes?" Emory asked.

"That's the question of the hour," Nick said. "But if I had to guess based on what I've found on the image, it's to track information about the golf course. There's just nothing else in her files that would have either a blackmail or proprietary information payout, which is what someone behind a keystroke logger would want to find."

"You'll keep after that for us, too, right?" Blake asked.

"Of course."

"I'm impressed, man," Blake said. "Good job."

Nick puffed out his chest and smiled at Blake.

"Not to interrupt your bromance here." Maya laughed. "But what about her Internet history, Nick? Anything interesting there?"

"There's a good deal of information related to the golf course and social media, but she spent the rest of her time researching her birth history. She was looking for her parents. And like the landlord said, that's what brought her to Cold Harbor."

"Her grandmother, right?" Blake asked preempting him from having to explain.

Nick nodded.

"We have no evidence that Cait called her grandmother. Did you find any communication with her?"

Nick shook his head. "Which is odd, right? If I planned to quit my job and move cross-country, I would have emailed or talked to her."

"She could've used her work phone or another computer," Grady suggested. "Like her work machine in Minnesota or a computer at the marina."

"Still, unless she has an email account we don't know about," Nick said. "I would have found the emails. And it would be highly unlikely that she just used the other machines to talk to the grandmother."

"But say she did," Blake said. "Can we find that out?"

"Yes, it's possible to recover the information." Nick paused and pressed his lips into a fine line. "But only *if* the university has a program designed to monitor Internet usage."

"The marina owner was really helpful, and I'm sure he'll cooperate and let us image his computer," Blake said. "I'll ask Trent to arrange that, and then also request a warrant for her machine, the university's network, and the Internet history for her phone."

Nick nodded. "It's entirely possible that the IT staff has wiped her machine and you're not going to find anything. All depends on what they used to erase the drives."

"Once Trent has the warrant," Blake said. "I'll have him put their tech staff in touch with you."

"Two other things I'm working on for you. The onesie brand was sold in too many stores at the time to narrow it down to anything useable. Sorry. It's a dead end. And on tracing Cait's search for family via Facebook, I put my best tech on it. He'll write up a history of the search for you as soon as he finishes. But I should warn you. It already looks like she didn't post some steps as there is no logical way she got from one step to another in several cases. So it might be an incomplete history."

"Any idea how long that will take?" Blake asked.

Nick shook his head. "Especially with the gaps."

"Thanks for being so thorough as usual." Emory ran her gaze over the group. "Now that everyone is up to speed, any other ideas on how to proceed?"

"I'll put some feelers out on the Walther PP," Grady offered. "I can check to see if one's been sold recently or if my contacts know any collectors in the Cold Harbor area. But you should know, it's not that rare of a gun so it might not pan out. And since we still haven't pinned down a motive for the abduction, our gun owner may not reside in the area at all."

"Don't forget we have Emory's condo to process." Sierra sounded hopeful.

Blake didn't know if she really felt that way or if she was putting on a good front for Emory.

Nick's computer dinged. All eyes went to him as he was looking at his screen.

"The facial recognition?" Emory asked.

He nodded and pounded a fist on the table. "Nothing. Nada. No match, and we're back to square one."

18

Sitting next to Blake, Emory listened to the rhythmic thump of the helicopter's rotors and was glad to have left her condo behind and in Sierra's care. Emory tried to leave her fear behind with it, but the overwhelming panic traveled right along with her.

She'd spent the first hour of the flight reading the reports from Nick, and then reviewing the video Sam sent of Cait's place. Emory was glad to see where her sister lived, but seeing the blood spatter in the bathroom? That was too much, and Emory stopped watching. Now she had nothing to occupy her mind. Not even Blake. He was busy reviewing information from Trent, and she wished he would put it away and put his arm around her.

She couldn't let go of seeing the blood spatter. Of seeing her place trashed. But she had to or she'd lose it. Maybe she should concentrate on remembering Blake's strong arms cocooning her in her guest room. She'd felt so safe when he was holding her that her terror had soon dissipated. Surprised her. Totally. She hadn't wanted a man near her, much less touch her since the attack, and now she was relying on one for comfort.

"There's something I have to tell you," Blake said, and his narrowed gaze scared her.

"What? Is it Cait?"

He shook his head and took a long breath. "I knew about your attack before you told me."

"You did?" She eyed him. "But how?"

"Trent did a background check on you."

Her mouth fell open, and she didn't know what to say, so she just stared at Blake for a long moment. "I knew you were hiding something from me."

"I wasn't really hiding it so much as not knowing how to tell you. It's routine in an investigation. You know that, right?"

She lifted her chin. "Then why not just tell me about it?"

"I didn't want to give you something more to worry about. I'm sorry." He tried to take her hand, but she pulled it away.

How foolish could she be? Falling back into the same behavior. She'd thought Robby was a good guy at first, but after two months his true colors came out. Was Blake the same way? He seemed honorable, but some issue put a wall between him and God, and now he kept something from her. Neither could be a good sign. She ought to know. She was running from her own things.

"You seem a million miles away," Blake's voice came over her headset startling her. "Sorry. Didn't mean to scare you. I just...you have to understand. I care about you, but the investigation still has to come first. And I know you want that, right? For Cait?"

She nodded.

He placed his hand over hers, and she let it stay this time. She looked into his eyes, and her awareness of the feelings she'd developed for him hit her hard. Not feelings for his good looks. Nor his strength. Not even his protection.

But the compassion and caring she saw in his eyes. He'd been there for her during her struggles. This news was but a blip on a very clean radar, and she wouldn't hold keeping her background check a secret against him.

"I care about you, too," she said and couldn't believe she'd admitted it aloud.

Heat suddenly flooded his coffee brown eyes. She felt herself being drawn closer to him by a magnetic pull. She knew rationally that no such thing existed, but she leaned even closer. He cautiously cupped the side of her face, his touch igniting a fire in her heart. His skin was rough but warm, and his touch incredibly gentle for the tough-as-nails lawman.

He leaned closer. His head lowering. He swatted his microphone away. He was going to kiss her, and she wanted him to. Badly. She reached up to move her mic.

"Touchdown three minutes," Coop's voice came over the headset.

Coop, right.

She lurched back, and so did Blake. He shook his head as if chastising himself. She should be doing the same thing, but she couldn't think of even one reason right now why it would be bad to kiss him. She shifted to stare out the window for the last few minutes of the flight, taking long breaths until the heat in her face subsided and she felt calm again.

The moment Coop touched down, Blake opened the door. He stood waiting to help her down, but she couldn't touch him again. She jumped down on her own and gulped in the salty ocean air.

Blake, his gaze pensive, got his keys out. The jingle tinkled in the clear skies in Cold Harbor and in the quiet, star-filled night. A romantic night. A perfect night for a stroll with Blake.

"C'mon," he said, his tone gruff. "I'll drop you off at Sam's place on my way out."

He opened his SUV door for her, and she got in, tiredness settling deep into her bones. Despite her yearning for this man and wishing to stroll through the night with him, she yawned.

"It's the adrenaline wearing off." His tone had softened. "You need a good night's sleep."

When he got behind the wheel and pointed the vehicle down the drive, she faced him. "You need to get some sleep, too."

"Yeah, I'll catch a few hours."

"Promise me you'll try for more than a few hours."

"I'll try."

"And you'll call me if anything develops. No matter the time."

He pulled up in front of Sam's cabin and shifted into park. "I hate to disturb you when you need to sleep."

"If something happens, I want you to." She clutched his arm. "Promise me you will."

He rested a hand over hers and looked deep into her eyes. "I want to do what's best for you. I hope you know that."

"I do. I honestly do." She smiled at him.

He sucked in a breath and jerked his hand away. "If you know what's best for you, you'll get out of this vehicle before I kiss you."

"One harmless kiss wouldn't be such a bad thing," she said, surprising herself.

He looked at her long and hard then. "That's the problem, honey. It wouldn't be a harmless kiss, and we both know it."

∼

The ringing of Emory's phone pulled her from a deep sleep, and she fumbled for the device on the nightstand. She blinked and looked around at the strange room.

Oh, right. Sam's guest room.

Emory grabbed her phone and noted it was four a.m. as she answered. "Hello."

"It's Blake. Sorry to wake you, but I promised."

She came instantly awake and sat up. "What is it?"

"We found the car used to abduct Cait."

She let out a long sigh of relief.

"It's being towed into the shop right now," he continued. "I've called Sam, and she's coming to process it. I thought you might want to ride along with her."

"Yes, yes. Thanks for calling me. See you soon." She hopped out of bed and went into the family room. Sam, hair wet from a shower, stood in the adjoining kitchen making coffee. The nutty scent filtered through the air, and Emory couldn't wait for a cup.

Sam swiveled, rubbing her eyes. "Coming with me?"

Emory nodded. "Do I have time for a quick shower?"

"Absolutely. The evidence isn't going anywhere." Sam turned back to the coffee.

Emory raced from the room and got the shower started. She made the water as hot as she could stand, and though she was in a hurry, she took a few minutes to soak in the warmth. And a minute to thank God for the lead. Maybe she needed to take a page out of Blake's book and start talking to God more. Maybe in the talking she'd let go of her anger at Him for allowing her to be attacked, and her new frustration over Cait being abducted. Emory could only hope.

You know why You let this happen. I don't. I want to know. Want to make sense of it. Help me to do that. To let it go. And let this be the lead that takes us to Cait.

Refreshed, she turned off the water and toweled dry.

She chose practical jeans and a Veritas T-shirt in deep purple to wear, and then dried her hair and put on a hint of mascara.

She looked at herself in the mirror. She wanted to add more makeup, but what for? Or, more likely, who for? Blake?

No. She wasn't going there. She put on her glasses and grabbed her backpack. In the kitchen, she discovered Sam had made scrambled eggs and toast. The roasted scent of coffee drew her to the island where Sam had plated the food, and it waited with a tall glass of orange juice. Emory really didn't want to eat—just get going.

"Don't look at me that way," Sam said, fork of fluffy eggs poised at her mouth. "It's going to be a long day, and we need to fuel up."

Knowing Sam was right, Emory sat next to her friend. "Thank you for this. I didn't have much dinner so this is great."

Sam crunched her toast, a thoughtful expression on her face.

Emory stabbed her fork into the eggs. "So what do you think you'll find in the car?"

Sam swallowed. "Not sure. Blake said it was stolen, and Trent has already woken up the owners to get elimination prints."

"They must not have appreciated that." Emory took a sip of the coffee. "Has Trent even slept since he caught this case?"

"I don't think so." Sam eyed Emory.

"What?"

Sam blew on her coffee mug. "Just looking to see if there's some interest in Trent. He's a real catch, but I see he does nothing for you."

Emory gaped at her friend. "You can tell that just by looking at me?"

"Yeah. You forget I know you." Sam took a long sip of coffee. "Are you still not ready to consider dating again?"

"I didn't say that."

She spit her coffee out. "I get it now. It's Blake. It's not just that's he's interested in you—you have a thing for him, too. Seriously, Blake?"

"I didn't say that, either."

"You don't have to." Sam set down her cup and clutched Emory's hand. "You're as red as a beet."

Her face *was* burning, and that she couldn't hide. For some reason she felt like she needed to defend him. "He's not like you described him. I mean, yeah, he's tough. Has his rules and all, and he's not likely to bend them, but he's *so* much more than that. If he hadn't been there when I found my condo trashed, I..." Tears pricked her eyes, and she didn't want to get her glasses all fogged so she stopped talking.

Sam held up her hands. "Hey, I believe you. I've always been on the opposite side of things with Blake, so we've butted heads. But he's been friends with Gage for eons, and that says a lot for Blake's character."

Emory set down her fork and took a moment to gather her thoughts. "Doesn't matter. Nothing's going to happen. I'm still hung up on the attack, and he's wrestling with something he won't even talk to me about."

"But he's interested, too. I'm right about that."

Emory nodded and felt herself blush again.

"Well, girlfriend, all I can say is I found a way to be with Griff, so you can find a way to your happily ever after, too." Sam patted Emory's hand and got up. "I'm going to pour a travel mug. You want one?"

"Absolutely. Thank you." Emory was also thankful that Sam dropped the subject of Blake. She'd bring it back up, Emory was sure of that, but now Emory just wanted to gobble up this food and get going. She inhaled as much as she could, rinsed her dishes, and they set off into the foggy night for the police station. They found Blake in his office, his expression enthusiastic as he hung up his phone.

"Finding the car may bust this investigation wide open." He got up and met them at the door. "Guy must've bought Cait a change of clothes and left these in the car." He held out a plastic evidence bag with a pair of women's blue jeans. "Walmart tag still attached."

"And let me guess," Sam said. "He was caught on the store's security footage."

"We think so. I'm heading over there right now." He grabbed his jacket from a chair and looked at Sam. "Helen's already in the shop with Trent."

Sam shifted her forensic kit to her other hand. "I'll head right out there."

"Can I come with you?" Emory asked Blake.

He nodded without even a hint of a question.

Sam shot a look between them, and a wide smile crossed her face.

Blake studied her, blinking a few times as he did. "What's up with that grin?"

"Oh, nothing," she said as she walked away. "Hope you two enjoy the trip."

Blake turned to Emory. "What's going on?"

She shrugged, though she knew full well that Sam enjoyed seeing the attraction between them. "So Walmart."

"Yeah, let's go." He led the way out to the secured parking lot and his vehicle. "We only have one Walmart and it's on the far side of town. Without traffic, it won't take long."

He stopped to gather his long guns and mount them in the car, then quickly got them on the road. She almost asked why he thought he would need the guns tonight, but then he'd taken them with him on every trip, so she assumed it was standard procedure.

A misty rain dampened the car and the intermittent wipers scraped across the windshield in an annoying squeak. After her discussion with Sam, Emory felt shy around him and simply listened to the wipers and the police calls coming in on his radio instead of trying to make small talk.

He glanced at her. "Sleep well?"

"Yes, thank you," she answered, sounding so awkward she cringed. "Did you get any sleep at all?"

"An hour. But I'm running on the thrill of the lead right now." He grinned at her, a boyish grin that set her pulse kicking up.

"Do you really think Cait's abductor was dumb enough to make this mistake?" she asked, saying the first thing about the investigation that came to mind.

"Yeah, I do."

"And you're sure the car owner didn't buy the jeans?"

"Positive. Trent asked them when he woke them up to tell them about the car."

"Then I'm excited, too. If we can get a clear image of this guy, Nick can run it through facial recognition."

"Or the guy might have paid with a credit card, and we can trace that." He fell silent, maybe thinking that they would find Cait and wrap this up tonight.

She would love that. Love to find Cait and get to know her sister. Emory could easily imagine the moment they met. A big hug. A sigh of relief. And joy. Not only for finding Cait, but Cait knew their grandmother, too, so Emory would be able to meet her.

And what about Blake? Emory would have to leave him behind to go back to Portland. She didn't like that thought very much. In fact, her stomach ached thinking about it.

Had she already let herself get too close to him? She sure hoped not.

They pulled up to Walmart and met the loss prevention manager named Sal, a gorilla of a man with inky black hair, waiting for them right inside the door.

"Come with me to review the feed." He spun on rubber soled shoes that squeaked on the polished tile floor.

They marched to the back of the building through nearly deserted aisles. Emory often wondered about twenty-four-hour stores. She'd stopped in late at night at times and rarely saw many customers, and it didn't make sense to her for them to remain open. But her dad once said staying open was of value as they were stocking the store at the same time and supervisors had to be there anyway. She doubted Sal was working the wee hours of the morning, though, and the night manager had probably called him in.

Sal opened the door to a small and very messy office with a wall of computer monitors. He sat behind the middle one. "I'm pretty sure this will be your guy. Found him by pulling up transactions for the women's jeans in the last few days then narrowing it down to purchases made by a man. Only one guy who bought women's jeans. As you can imagine, that's not common."

Blake and Emory moved behind him, and he started playing the video time stamped at eight-thirty p.m. on the night Cait was abducted. A man stood calmly at the register, handing over cash to pay for a stack of clothing that included the jeans. Emory immediately recognized him as the guy who broke into her apartment. She clutched Blake's hand and looked at him. He nodded his understanding.

"As you can see," Sal said. "He bought several articles of women's clothing and paid with cash so you won't be able to track him that way."

"What about following him out of the building on your exterior cameras?" Blake asked.

"Already have that cued up for you." He rolled to the next monitor and started another video playing. "Car's an early model silver Accord. No plates, which I found interesting."

But totally fits Gladys' description and the car in the evidence bay that Sam and Helen were processing right now.

Emory watched as their suspect marched purposefully toward the silver sedan and slid behind the wheel. He was so calm when she would be terrified that someone might stop her. He'd even held the door for an elderly woman as he exited, and appeared as if he was on an everyday shopping trip, not buying clothing for an abducted woman.

Emory scanned the car, looking for Cait, but the man was alone. Or she could still be in the trunk. Nausea threatened Emory's stomach. How horrible for her sister. Having been tossed in a trunk like baggage.

For the first time, Emory let fear over not finding Cait in time take over, and she couldn't breathe in the small space. She bolted for the door and ran through the store to drag in the ocean air blowing through the parking lot.

God, please. Please. Please. I need to find my sister. I need her alive. Please help us find her. Please.

19

Blake could barely abide seeing Emory so upset. He didn't know what in the video caused her to panic, but she was struggling to breathe and was crying at the same time.

"Hey," he said as he came up beside her. "Just breathe or you'll hyperventilate."

In front of her, he modeled slowly breathing in and out for her. She followed his lead. In and out. Over and over. Until she started breathing normally and lifted her gaze to his. "What if we don't find her? She's counting on us."

"I know, honey. I know." He drew her into his arms, and her crying ramped up. "We just have to keep thinking positive thoughts, or we'll be no good to her."

He gently stroked Emory's back and held her until her tears stopped. He leaned back and looked at her tear-streaked face. He wanted to swear. To hurl something. This woman, this amazing woman, didn't deserve to go through such anguish.

God, where are You? Why let this happen?

Right, why ask? Blake knew better than that. God didn't promise answers to these kinds of questions. He expected people to trust Him to have their good at heart. Blake could understand that in his brain. It was his heart that was having such a hard time. But why? Blake had a great dad. One who truly did have Blake's best interest at heart, so he'd seen God on earth through his dad. If Blake could trust his earthly father who wasn't perfect, couldn't he trust a perfect heavenly Father?

"God's got this, honey," he said, honestly believing that now, no matter where the investigation led. "We can trust Him."

"I don't know if I can." Her chin wobbled.

"It's okay. I can, and I'll help you." He lifted her glasses to the top of her head and brushed away her tears. "And we *will* find Cait."

"How can you be so sure after another dead end?"

"It's not a dead end. At least not totally. Remember what Nick said. If we got a better picture of the suspect he would run his search algorithm. We now have a better picture."

"Right, yeah." Her eyes brightened. "There's hope then."

"And maybe Sam and Helen have found something in the car, too." He smiled to try to ease her worry.

She took off her glasses then used them to push her hair back from her face and propped the frames back on her head. "Then you need me to stop being such a big baby, and we need to get going."

"Not a big baby. Just a concerned sister." He took her hand and led her to his vehicle.

On the drive, Emory called Nick. Thankfully, he was still up working, and the moment they got back to the conference room, she sent the video to him while Blake helped Trent cue up the inside video on the larger screen.

"This guy is way too calm in the face of potential discovery," Trent said.

Blake nodded. "He's either not smart enough to know he's being recorded, or he's calculatingly ruthless and doesn't care."

Trent frowned. "Let's hope for not being very bright."

Blake nodded as Cait wouldn't fare well under the other scenario.

Trent squinted at the screen. "Looks like he's carrying under his jacket."

Blake saw the telltale bulge under the suspect's sweatshirt but that wouldn't help them other than to know he was dangerous. Blake moved on to the man's tattooed hands. Blake looked at Emory. "The video's too fuzzy to really make out the tattoos on his hands. Do you think Nick can clean up the image?"

"I'll text him and ask."

Blake replayed the video. Once, twice. A third time. Looking for any lead. Nothing else jumped out at him or Trent.

Trusting God with finding Cait got more difficult with each playing, but Blake had told Emory he had enough faith for the both of them, and he never broke a promise. So he prayed again. More earnestly this time.

The conference room door opened, and Detective William Newton poked his head in. His wide, chubby face was etched with fatigue, but his eyes still looked alert. "I'm about to go off shift, but wanted to make sure you got the information for a call pertaining to the suspect's picture on the news."

"Let's have it," Blake said.

"The guy who called says a man matching the photo moved in next door to him a few weeks ago." Newton lumbered into the room and passed a piece of paper to Blake. "House is a rental property. Neighbor said our suspect moved in and started remodeling the place. Lots of construction noises. He said there was something off about the guy, but he didn't have anything to base it on, just his gut. That and the fact that he immediately covered all the windows in black paper. Then yesterday morning, the neighbor was walking down their shared drive, and he heard a woman whimpering inside the house. Still nothing he could report the guy for, but now he said the place has gone quiet. The man's car is out front, but there's no movement inside or out since the neighbor heard the woman crying."

Newton took a deep breath, his large belly rising with the motion. "I got the plate number from the man's car and looked it up. A blue Ford Focus. Was reported stolen a week ago."

"Makes sense that he wouldn't use his own vehicle even after ditching the Honda," Trent said.

"Good work, Newton. Go home and get some rest, and we'll follow up on it." Blake dismissed Newton with a nod and got to his feet. He looked at Emory. "Trent and I'll go check out the property. I need you to stay here."

Emory firmly met his gaze with a challenging one of her own. "But I have to come with you. Cait could be the woman he heard crying, and I want to be there."

"Sorry," he said and honestly meant it. "I was fine with you accompanying me to most of the interviews, but this isn't the place for a civilian. Not only could it be risky for you, but while trying to apprehend a dangerous suspect we would have to think about protecting you. That could lead to mistakes. Costly mistakes." He kept his focus trained on her and tried to convey his sincere apology for leaving her behind.

"Okay. I'll stay here." She looked disappointed but understanding at the same time.

He resisted giving her the hug of thanks that he wanted to offer. "You can help out by checking in with Nick to see if he's making any progress, and I'll call you the minute I know anything."

"Promise?" Her gaze locked onto his.

He had to work hard not to get lost in her big brown eyes. "Yes, I promise."

He signaled for Trent to exit, and Blake followed him out of the room. "I'm not taking any chances with what we might find. Grab your go bag. I'll get the long guns and meet you at my vehicle."

Trent headed toward the exit. He kept a bag in the trunk filled with everything a deputy might need on patrol. Blake had his own bag in his vehicle, and he stopped to grab his trio of long guns.

Outside, he mounted them in the back of his SUV and slipped into his body armor. Already wearing his Kevlar vest, Trent joined him and tossed his bag in the back and laid his rifle beside it. Blake slammed the hatch just as Lorraine pulled into the lot. She quickly got out, concern in her expression as she approached them.

Blake told her where they were headed and played down the danger, but she'd been in her job long enough to know that a visit like this could go south in no time at all.

She squeezed Blake's arm. "I'll pray for your success."

Blake nodded his thanks. They could use all the prayers they could get. "I left Emory in the conference room. She's uneasy about this visit and worried about Cait. Would you mind checking in with her?"

"Will do." Lorraine peered at him for a long time, but he didn't know what he was hoping to find. "The two of you take care, you hear?"

Blake nodded and got behind the wheel. He wished the sun was up already as approaching this house in daylight would give them a better picture of what they were facing, but it lingered at the horizon, a faint reddish glow hinting at the bright orb's intention to rise.

Blake handed the call report to Trent and got his vehicle moving. "Give the neighbor a heads up so he doesn't try to insert himself in our approach."

"Roger that." Trent dialed his phone and tapped his finger on his knee. "No answer." He left a concise message. "Sure hope once he gets the message, he'll stay home."

Blake shook his head. "I never did understand why people who phone in tips often think they have a right to join in a search or visit the place or person they reported."

"Me neither, but happens often enough. Especially when it's a neighbor."

"Isn't that the truth," Blake grumbled. "We run into both extremes. Those who can't be bothered to help and those who go overboard. Let's hope this guy's in the middle, and he acts accordingly."

Blake listened to the radio calls for the rest of the drive, proud that the men and women with such professionalism in their tone worked for him. Still, a heavy measure of job fatigue impacted his life. No one but another sheriff or LEO in the upper ranks had a clue what it meant to be in charge of such a large group of law enforcement officers. The responsibility for life-and-death situations on a daily, sometimes hourly, or even a minute-by-minute basis left a heavy weight on his shoulders.

"That's it," Trent pointed ahead. "The blue house."

Blake pulled to the curb shy of the property and did a quick risk assessment. The house was two-story, older with large porch, a small front yard, and shared a driveway with the adjacent house just like the neighbor reported. And also as he'd described, the stolen car sat at the curb out front.

Blake shifted into park, but left his vehicle running. He didn't know what they might find, and with a RunLock system installed in his SUV, he could lock the door and leave the engine safely running.

He got out and met Trent at the back of the vehicle. "I won't risk losing this guy. The report of a distraught woman gives us exigent circumstances. No knock and announce. We breach the house and take him by surprise."

Trent cocked his head. "You're reaching there, aren't you? She hasn't been heard recently."

"I am, but Cait could be inside, and I don't want to wait for a warrant, so I'll take the risk." Blake grabbed a battering ram, and his assault rifle. Trey picked up his rifle, too, and they made their way toward the house.

"No light," Blake pointed out. "Hopefully we'll catch him fast asleep."

They climbed the steps to the porch. Blake wasted no time and swung the ram, splintering the door. It flew open, slamming into the wall and bouncing back. The horrific smell of death instantly hit Blake square in the face. He dropped the ram and covered his mouth.

Trent gagged, and his hand flew to his mouth, too. "Smells like we're not going to need our weapons."

Blake nodded, his stomach tight. "The only question right now is, who died?"

Emory alternated her gaze between the wall clock and her phone sitting on the table, willing it to ring and hear Blake announce that he'd found Cait—*safe*. But the clock's minute hand ticked slowly toward thirty minutes since Blake and Trent's departure and nothing else happened. Well, that and

Emory's stomach tightened more and more with each passing minute.

Sam pushed open the conference room door and entered. She looked around. "Where is everyone?"

"Gone to follow up on a lead." Emory recounted the phone call and wasn't surprised to hear her own voice filled with a mixture of fear for Trent and Blake, and eagerness for finding Cait. "This may be it. We might find Cait."

"I hope so." A deep frown creased Sam's face as she sat.

Emory didn't like that look one bit. "What's wrong?"

She didn't speak for a minute as if she was searching for the right way to say what she had to say.

"Just say it," Emory said impatiently.

"We found blood in the trunk."

A wave of nausea hit Emory, but she played down her response. "Nothing we didn't expect."

Sam nodded. "I know, but sometimes confirming things hits home on a level we can't explain."

God had certainly given Emory plenty of instances to understand that. Like hearing from Blake that she might be adopted, but then, when her mother confirmed it, the emotions hit Emory in a whole new way.

In her worry for Cait, Emory had put that issue with her mother on the back burner. What was she going to do about her mom?

Sam leaned forward. "You want to share what's put that mega frown on your face?"

Emory resisted sighing. "I'm thinking about what I should do about my mother. My adoptive mother, that is."

Sam met Emory's gaze. "I know you're devastated at her not telling you, and you may not want to hear this, but take it from someone who spent years away from her parents because I was too stubborn to make up with them. She loves you. Wants what's best for you. Go see her as soon as possible. Work this out. And just love her."

Sam made a good point, but Emory was still hurting inside. "I'll think about it."

Sam's eyes narrowed. "Do more than think. *Act*. You never know what might happen, and you won't have the chance."

"You're right. I at least need to go see her." Emory smiled to ease Sam's worry. "I'll go right after we find Cait."

Sam nodded. "On that note, I'd like to get the blood samples to Veritas ASAP. I was going to run that past Blake before calling Gage, but since he's not here, I'll just call Gage and deliver them."

"Sounds good."

Sam wrinkled her nose. "Now that was less than enthusiastic."

"Sorry, I just keep thinking about what the neighbor said about not hearing any sounds from next door since yesterday morning. What if he did have Cait there, but then he killed her?"

"No. No." Sam shook her head. "We can't think that way, sweetie. We have to stay positive."

"I know, but sitting here, waiting and waiting, my mind wanders. If I'm not thinking about my mom, or Blake and Trent's safety, Cait's consuming my brain."

Sam firmed her shoulders. "Then maybe we should talk about leads and about other things we can do if Blake doesn't find Cait at this house. That will not only keep your mind occupied, it could help find her."

"You're right. I need to keep busy instead of watching the clock." Emory pushed up her glasses. "I do have an idea that we haven't tried. You know how Nick likes to write his Internet searches? What if we take all the addresses involved in this investigation and have him run a search for a connection?"

"Sounds like a great idea."

Glad to be doing something, Emory hurried to the whiteboard. She grabbed a red marker and jotted down addresses for Walmart, the locations where both stolen cars were found and where they were stolen from, and lastly, she noted Cait's and her own address.

Sam stared at the board. "I really think you have something here."

Emory turned to look at her friend. "You're not just saying that to make me feel better, are you?"

Sam shook her head. "It's a known fact that criminals often don't leave their own neighborhoods if at all possible. So if our suspect stole cars near where he lives, this might help us find him."

Emory went to a county map mounted on the wall. She picked up map pins and stuck them in all of the locations then stood back.

Sam came up behind her. "They're all in the same general area."

"So maybe you're right. Maybe I'm on to something, and Nick can figure out the connection." She called him.

When he answered, she quickly explained. "Do you think this might work?"

"It's possible," he replied, not sounding nearly as excited as Sam had been about the idea. "It's a long shot. If you had a person's name to add to the mix, that might help. But go ahead and text the addresses to me and let me know if Blake comes up with the man's name at the house, okay?"

"Sure, thing." Emory tried to keep her enthusiasm, but even she could hear it disappear from her tone. "Were you able to run the improved picture through facial recognition?"

"It hasn't returned a match, but it's still running. So are the Internet searches."

She mentally ran through the investigation to come up with other outstanding leads. "What about Cait's Minnesota computer? Has Trent gotten info to you on that?"

"He has. Unfortunately, they don't have a program to monitor Internet usage, but the tech is overnighting an image of her hard drive for my review."

"And Cait's search for our family?" she asked, hoping this might give them even more to go on.

"My tech is still working on it." He paused for a long moment. "You know you don't have to keep checking with me, right? I'll call the minute we have a lead of any kind. Even the smallest one."

"Sorry. I don't mean to put pressure on you. It's just..."

"Hey, I get it. She's your sister. I'd be doing the same thing."

"Thanks for understanding, Nick." She hung up, took a picture of the whiteboard holding the addresses and sent it to Nick. Before she could stow her phone, it rang. Hoping Blake was calling, Emory eagerly looked at the screen. Seeing Lara's name, Emory's excitement fell, but she answered anyway.

"Glad I caught you this early in the day," Lara said. "The MPS DNA for Caitlyn and unknown subject came back. They're twins, as the earlier report suggests, but Caitlyn has five mutations that the unknown subject doesn't have."

"So we have proof positive that Caitlyn was the one abducted and the unknown twin wasn't at the scene," Emory stated though there was no need as Lara would fully understand the implications. Emory wasn't surprised by the news, but there was no way she could have known that their DNA would indeed be different. "Email the reports to me."

"Will do," Lara said, her enthusiasm still in her voice. "Hope this information helps find the missing woman."

Emory doubted the report would do anything to help find Cait, but at least she could now prove to Blake that she hadn't been at Cait's townhouse. Since Blake had gotten to know her, she doubted he would need such proof, but she could be wrong and only time would tell how he would react to the news.

20

Blake entered the house and tried not to hurl. They made their way through the front room that appeared to be a living room, but held a ratty old mattress and some male clothing in a heap on the floor. The closer they came to the back of the house the stronger the smell grew, and his stomach roiled even more.

In the dining room, he spotted the body, a tall and muscular male with blond hair lying face up. His eyes were wide open and vacant. Dried blood trailed from his nose and mouth into pools on the floor. Beside him lay a half-smoked marijuana joint and an ashtray filled with butts, some cigarettes, and other tiny joint remnants. Tattoos covered his hands.

Blake took a good look at the swollen face. No question this was the guy from the Walmart video and the one captured on video outside the Veritas Center. And he fit Gladys's description. Blake stared down on the guy who had likely abducted Cait. The condition of his body said he'd been dead for more than twenty-four hours.

Blake thought about the lack of sounds from the woman since the first night. He got a sick feeling in the pit of his stomach, and it had nothing to do with the smell. He signaled to Trent that he was going to continue to clear the house and moved on. In the kitchen, he found dirty dishes heaped in the sink, but it was the sight in the adjoining family room that brought his feet to a stop.

A large cage made of fencing material had been installed in the space. Likely the construction noises the neighbor reported. A cot sat in the middle of the six-by-six wire room. Blood-soaked clothes lay on the floor. Women's clothes. A bright yellow blouse on the top of the pile. Cait's blouse as reported by Gladys.

She'd been held here. Held in this makeshift prison. Could she still be in another room?

Rifle raised, he picked up his speed. Trent kept up as they cleared the rest of the house. They found three bedrooms upstairs but they were empty with no sign of having been used. The bathroom the same.

"Outside," Blake said, and together they moved into the small backyard and quickly determined that no one was in the yard or the small garage.

Blake was at once relieved and worried. Relieved that Cait hadn't been killed like the man inside, but worried for her safety. He wanted to rush into the house and search the guy's pockets for ID, but procedure dictated that no one touch the body without the ME's approval. No way Blake would break protocol and risk their future court case tied to this investigation, but he would light a fire under the ME and get him out here ASAP.

He holstered his weapon and worked hard to keep his tone upbeat when he turned to Trent. "Get on the horn to the ME and get him out here fast. Then cordon off this scene. Since this is a rental property, I'm going to find out who owns the place."

And call Emory to fulfill my promise. He didn't much want to tell her about the deceased suspect, but he'd promised.

He jogged down the street to his SUV. On the way, he radioed dispatch and requested two patrol cars to block off the street and to have one of the deputies act as officer of record to document persons coming and going from the crime scene.

He climbed into his vehicle and entered the street address in his laptop. The search returned the name Ulrick Obenauer. Blake looked the guy up in the DMV database. He had a shaved head and narrow jaw, was five foot six and weighed two hundred fifty pounds. Not at all like their suspect. He could be connected to the investigation or an innocent landlord.

Blake got out his phone and dialed Nick at Veritas. "I need your help."

"You mean in addition to the algorithm Emory just asked me to run?" He sounded confused.

Say what? "What exactly did she ask you to do?"

"To see if I can find a connection between all of the addresses in the investigation. Like the place where the cars were stolen and recovered, the house you're at now, etc."

Great idea. "I still want you to do that, but first, I need you get me every bit of information you can find on an Ulrick Obenauer. We found our suspect in the house owned by Obenauer. Unfortunately, the suspect is dead and can't tell us anything."

"Bad luck there," Nick said. "I'll get right on the search and report back."

"Thanks, man." Blake hung up and dialed Emory.

"Did you find her?" Her voice held a deep urgency.

Blake felt her pain and wished he could give her good news. Or at least be by her side to tell her. "Sorry. No.

There's evidence that she was held here, but she's gone now."

"I was so hoping she'd be there." Her voice had dropped to a whisper of disappointment.

He didn't want to tell her about the suspect either, but she had a right to know. "We did find the man who abducted her. He's dead. Not sure from what. No obvious sign of murder, but he was bleeding from his mouth and nose. The ME will have to give us cause of death."

"His name?" she asked, her voice louder now.

"We don't know yet. We're waiting on the ME to arrive so we can search the body and take prints." He blew out a long, frustrated breath. "I need to get off the phone now and get Sam and Helen out here."

"Sam's right here. I'll give her my phone."

"Great." He tried to sound upbeat again. "I may not be back to the office for some time, but I'll keep you updated."

"I wish I could come over there." Her voice trembled.

His heart squeezed, and he wanted to drive to the office to comfort her. But the best thing he could do for her was process this crime scene and find Cait. "There's nothing you can do here."

"Okay." Her easy capitulation when he expected her to argue broke his heart. "I'm giving the phone to Sam now."

A shuffling noise filled the phone, and then Sam came on the line. "You need me there?"

"You *and* Helen. We have a suspicious death scene." He gave her additional details and made sure she had the address.

"I'll go grab Helen and some supplies," Sam replied, sounding confident and strong. "And we'll be on the way."

Blake hung up and climbed from the vehicle in time to see a car pull up and park in front of the neighbor's house. A guy dressed in blue scrubs got out and approached Trent who was stringing yellow tape across the driveway and in front of the other house.

Blake hustled over and intercepted the neighbor before he reached Trent. Blake held out his hand to the tall, lanky man with thick blond hair and a narrow face. "Sheriff Blake Jenkins."

"Dirk Guttman." The man shook hands, his grip stronger than Blake expected.

"Did you call in the report at seeing our suspect next door?"

"Yes." He ran a nervous hand over his hair. "Can I assume by the yellow tape that you found something bad?"

Blake nodded but wouldn't offer any additional information. This man would know when the ME arrived and carried out the body that someone had died and likely assume he'd been murdered.

"It's not the woman, is it? I mean if she was hurt and I didn't do anything, I'd never forgive myself."

Blake wouldn't give any details about what they did find, but he could relieve this man's worry. "We didn't find a woman in the house."

"Good. Good." He let out a long breath.

"Tell me what you saw."

"Just what I reported. A guy moved in. Started remodeling the house."

"Did you see him do that?"

"He blacked out the windows right away. I saw him carrying supplies and heard the tools." Guttman shook his head. "I thought it was a good thing. Like maybe he bought this place, and it wouldn't be a rental anymore. We've had a bunch of less-than-savory people living there in the past, and I was hoping, you know?"

Blake nodded. "Did you see any other men with him or cars around?"

He shook his head. "But then I'm a nurse and work the night shift—seven to seven—so he could've had company while I was at work."

"When exactly did you hear the woman crying?"

"Yesterday morning. I was coming home from my shift. Put out the trash and walked the drive back to my garage. Sound came from that window." He pointed at the window near the cage. "I went to bed, got up around four, and went out to pull in the trash cans before leaving again around six-thirty. No sound at all from next door."

"Anyone else live with you who might have seen something?"

Guttman shook his head. "I live alone. But check with Nadine on the other side. We all keep an eye out for each other, and she might've seen or heard something."

Blake offered his business card. "Call me if you think of anything else."

Guttman took the card. "Did someone die in there?"

"I'm not at liberty to discuss the investigation." Blake walked away and was already forming his statement to the press in his mind. He would have to make one before the day was out, that was for sure.

He ducked under the crime scene tape and watched the ME Martin Yablonsky pull his van to the curb. The rotund man with thinning gray hair got out along with his assistant who was a nearly white-haired male with very long legs.

Blake met them at the walkway and shook Yablonsky's hand.

"Your detective said we have a suspicious death," he said.

"Follow me." Yablonsky needed to form his own opinion, so Blake refrained from commenting on the scene and led the way to the door. He stopped on the porch for the three of them to put on booties and gloves that Trent had left out there. Trent had Yablonsky and his assistant sign in on the log before entering the house.

Blake flinched at the smell. He would love to open a window but that could contaminate the scene. At the body, he stood back and let Yablonsky make his examination, but Blake took a better look at the place as he waited. An older home, it had seen better days. Paint was stained in many places, and the walls dirty. The landlord obviously didn't care about how his house looked and didn't maintain it.

Yablonsky squatted, and Blake was always surprised at how agile he was for his size. He turned the victim's head. "Interesting. Something caused him to hemorrhage."

"Looks like he was smoking pot," Blake pointed out. "Could it do that?"

"Highly unlikely." He picked up the joint lying next to the body, sniffed it, and handed it to Blake. "Take a whiff of this. Doesn't smell like any pot I've ever smelled."

Blake got it close enough to his nose to eliminate the body odor and took a whiff. Yablonsky was right. The deceased wasn't smoking pot. "Any idea what it might be?"

Yablonsky shook his head. "We'll bag it and run it for analysis."

Blake nodded his agreement. He wanted to take this sample to Veritas to process, but they could be dealing with murder here, and he didn't want anything to potentially cause an issue when the killer was brought to trial. "Mind searching his pockets for ID?"

Yablonsky got up and nodded at his assistant who started with the front pockets. "More joints."

Blake held out his hand. "I'll take them into evidence."

The assistant dropped the joints into Blake's hand, then he rolled the body, releasing a smell that nearly took Blake to his knees, but the assistant didn't even cringe. Blake covered his nose and stood fast, but his stomach was churning. He hadn't lost a meal since his first homicide investigation, and he wouldn't embarrass himself by doing so now.

"Back pockets are empty," the assistant said. "No ID."

Par for the course.

"Your crime scene photographer here yet?" Yablonsky asked.

"I'll step outside and see." It took great willpower not to run out the front door, but Blake took his time and passed the cage for a better look. No sign of blood spatter or any other indication that Cait had been tortured in this location. And no sign that she'd been murdered here, thank God.

He continued to the door, and when he hit the porch not only was he relieved at the fresher air but at seeing Helen pull the county van to the curb. The patrol vehicles had also arrived, and Trent had stationed one of the deputies at the sidewalk. Trent turned and climbed up to the porch.

"No ID on the body," Blake said. "ME will do prints, and Sam can lift DNA, but I need you to rip this place apart for any hint to his identification. Not that there's much to look through, but the pile of clothes might hold his ID."

Trent gave a solemn nod. Sam and Helen joined them on the porch.

Blake held out his hand. "ME found these joints on the victim. It's not pot, and we need to get this analyzed. The ME thinks our victim suffered from a hemorrhage, and odds are good that it's from whatever we find in these."

"Could be tainted synthetic pot." Sam got out an evidence bag.

"I've read about the synthetic stuff but don't know a whole lot about it," Blake said.

Sam opened the bag and held it out for Blake. "The synthetic marijuana is often sold in gas stations and convenience stores. With pot being legal in Oregon it isn't common here, but there have been cases reported across the country where it's been laced with synthetic warfarin."

"The blood thinner?" Blake dumped the joints into the bag.

"And rat poison. That would certainly cause a hemorrhage." Sam sealed the bag. "You should know, we found blood in the trunk of the car, and I need to get that to Veritas. I'll make sure Maya gets this, too."

Blake nodded his thanks. "FYI, we don't have an ID for the deceased or a motive for why he took Cait. I'll need the victim's DNA and prints. And be on the lookout for any information to help with ID. Now get moving so you can get pics before the ME removes the body."

They both nodded and stepped into the house.

"I'm heading out to interview the landlord," Blake told Trent. "Scene's all yours."

Blake got in his SUV and could barely stand the smell that came along with him. He grabbed an emergency blanket to cover the seat and opened the window. He wanted to go straight to the landlord's place, but a stop at home to shower and change was the first priority. Then he hoped very soon to learn the name of their suspect from the landlord, and finally have a strong lead in bringing Cait home alive.

21

Emory paced the conference room. Back and forth. Step after step. She'd nearly worn a hole in the tile. Okay, fine, no hole, but she'd been on her feet for thirty minutes now waiting for Blake's return. He'd gone to interview the landlord and texted to say he was on his way back. She so desperately hoped he would return with the suspect's name.

He opened the door, and the rigid set of his jaw and posture told her he'd struck out.

"No information?" she asked, but knew the answer before he replied.

He shook his head. "Our suspect paid the landlord six months' rent in cash for one month's use. Only stipulation was he wouldn't fill out an application."

"And the landlord went for it?"

Blake nodded. "Turns out he's not the most scrupulous of landlords."

All hope fled, and Emory felt like she carried the weight of the world on her shoulders. "So now what?"

"We hope they find something else at the crime scene or in the car that provides the deceased's ID." He frowned.

"And we go back through our leads to see what we've missed."

His phone rang. "It's Nick."

She watched as he answered and listened, his expression running the gamut of interested to disappointed.

"Fits what I learned when I talked to him," Blake said. "Anything on the image you're searching for or the addresses Emory provided?"

Blake tilted his head as she listened. "Okay. Well, thanks for trying."

He hung up. "I had Nick run a background check on the landlord, and he confirmed he wasn't the most upright guy. Also the image from the video didn't return a match in facial recognition."

She sighed. "These dead ends have me on edge. I mean, we keep hitting brick walls and I don't know how much longer they'll keep Cait alive."

"Maybe it's time for me to try to get her adoption records from the state and the Abbot's agency."

"But how? We don't have any more proof that this has to do with our adoption than we did before."

"I know, I just..."

"Need to do something, right?"

He nodded. "And we don't have a lot to go on right now, so I'm feeling even more helpless."

Her phone chimed.

"Ooh. Ooh." She could barely contain her excitement as she reached for it. "That's the ringtone I assigned to the DNA searches I kicked off at the lab the other night."

She read the message and shot her hand up. "Yes!"

"What is it?" Blake asked.

"I got a few hits on my searches."

"Exactly what did you find?"

"All the alert tells me is that there are matches to my

225

DNA. It might mean we found a match to Cait, but it could also mean a match to someone related to us. Maybe even my grandmother. I need a computer I can use to log into my program so we can find out."

"Use my office!" He rushed to open the door.

She hurried down the hall and smiled at Lorraine as she passed.

"Looks like someone's on fire." Lorraine laughed.

Blake didn't respond but pushed past Emory to his computer and logged into their network. He backed away. "Go for it."

She sat in his chair, and he looked over her shoulder. She was aware of him standing so close but got straight to work as she was eager to see who her DNA matched. She opened the program she'd written with Nick's help and clicked on the first match.

"Cait," Blake said. "Go on to the next one."

He was right. She'd matched to Cait at an obscure ancestry site. Emory clicked on the second link. Same thing, only a different site.

"Keep going," he urged.

She hadn't seen him this frantic before. It scared her, because she knew it was fueled by desperation for a lead. She clicked on the link and blinked twice when she saw a different name.

"Who's Naomi Layton?" Blake asked.

"I don't know." Emory quickly reviewed the report.

"What does the mtDNA test measure?"

"Mt stands for mitochondrial. It's often called a female or maternal lineage test."

"It's that specific?"

She nodded. "Both men and women have mitochondrial DNA, but mtDNA is passed on from the female within the lineage and is very unique to that female line."

"So this is a woman you're related to," Blake said. "Your mother?"

Emory shook her head and tapped the screen. "Look at the birthdate. This has to be my grandmother's DNA."

"Then scoot over and let me look in the county property records for a Naomi Layton."

She rolled the chair out of the way, and his fingers flashed over the keyboard as he entered the information into the database.

"Bingo," he said, meeting her gaze, a fire burning in his. "We finally have your grandmother's address."

≈

In Blake's SUV, Emory smoothed her hands over her pants and wished she'd had time to change and clean up instead of arriving to meet her grandmother with the mess of the day all over her. She ran her fingers through her hair and separated tangles.

Blake glanced at her. "You look fine."

Emory cast him an irritated look. "*Fine* isn't good enough for meeting my grandmother for the first time."

"Then let me upgrade my statement. You look beautiful." He smiled.

"You're only saying that because of my comment."

"No, I'm only saying it because it's true."

She narrowed her gaze. "Then why didn't you say it first?"

He didn't answer right away, his thumb tapping on the wheel. "Because I'm trying my best not to notice how gorgeous you are."

"What?" She stared at him. "Why?"

"I'm attracted to you. You know that. And I don't want to be. Can't be."

"Why not?"

He blew out a long breath. "Because I can't be attracted to any woman. I'm not free to have a relationship."

"What?" She gaped at him. "You're with someone?"

"No. No." He held up his hand. "It's not that."

She watched him for a long time, waiting for him to elaborate. But in true Blake form, he clammed up. She recalled everything he'd said to her about his personal life and landed on the only possibility. "It's because of the reason you're mad at God."

He nodded, but didn't speak.

"You want to tell me about it?" she encouraged.

"Not really." He flipped on the blinkers and turned onto a narrow road. "We're almost at your grandmother's place."

"So later then?"

"Maybe."

"Now I can see the man Sam told me about." She sighed. "Stubborn. Closed off."

"Yep."

And that was all he said, his focus firmly fixed on the road. She watched ahead for her grandmother's house. Better to pay attention to something she could have an impact on instead of looking at the solid wall of stubborn.

The sun had all but disappeared under the thick canopy of trees, and the tires rumbled over the gravel road that climbed into the mountain's foothills. But it soon opened to a large clearing with a small log cabin and several outbuildings. An older model Blazer was parked in front of a single-car garage.

This was her grandmother's house. Her grandmother! Emory forgot all about Blake's refusal to talk and tried to take in the scene all at once, but couldn't sit still. Eager for answers about her parents, she hopped out of the car before it even stopped rocking. She raced up the steps and pounded on the door.

Blake caught up to her. "Take a breath and calm down, Emory. Remember we have a purpose for being here other than for you to meet your grandmother."

"Right. Right," she said the words, but they didn't even pierce her excitement over meeting her grandmother.·

The door opened, and for the first time in Emory's life, she looked into the face of another living person that held her similar features. She nearly passed out with the earth-shattering joy lifting her heart.

"Cait, darling. What a wonderful surprise." Her grandmother swept her into a hug.

Emory didn't correct her right way, but enjoyed the embrace of her own flesh and blood. Oh, what joy. What peace. Coming home for the first time.

Her grandmother leaned back, and Emory memorized every inch of her face. Wrinkles sure, but underneath Emory spotted her own high cheekbones. Her eyes the same chocolate brown though dulled a bit by age. Her grandmother wore glasses, too, wire-rimmed. She had a warm and welcoming smile, and she was thin, not plump.

She shifted her focus to Blake. "Sheriff. Is there something wrong?"

"I'm not, Cait," Emory blurted out. "I'm Emory, and Cait's been abducted."

Her grandmother's face lost all color, and she stumbled then grabbed the doorframe.

"I'm sorry." Emory clutched her grandmother's arm. "This is a shock. I should have asked to sit down before telling you."

"Let's do that now." Her grandmother swept Emory into the house with her and led her to a worn plaid sofa. They sat together, or more like fell onto the sofa.

Emory scooted closer to her grandmother. She knew she was staring but couldn't help it. "You're really our grandmother?"

"I don't have official proof. Cait was going to have our DNA tested at some place called the Veritas Center."

"Oh, my gosh! That's where I work. I wonder if it's in the queue. Why didn't I think to check? Give me a second to call and ask." Emory got up and had to move to the corner of the room to get a signal. She dialed Lara. "Check the log for DNA samples submitted by Caitlyn Abbot."

"You think she sent in other DNA?" Lara asked.

"Yes, for her grandmother."

"Hold on, I'll check."

As Emory waited, she heard her grandmother offer Blake coffee or water. Emory turned to look at her grandmother again. Emory didn't need the official DNA. She could see the resemblance. It was just breathtaking.

Blake accepted her offer of water.

She rose and came to Emory to cup the side of her face. "And you, darling granddaughter? Water or coffee?"

Emory pressed her free hand over her grandmother's aged one.

"Water," she managed to choke out a throat clogged with so many emotions.

Her grandmother removed her hand, and Emory felt alone.

"Got one in the queue," Lara came back on the line. "Submitted four days ago."

"Get it processing now." Emory demanded.

"Okay," Lara sounded hesitant.

"Sorry," Emory said. "Please. Can you get it processing now?"

"Of course. I'll get the results to you as soon as possible."

"Use the RapidHIT." She eyed Blake. "Sheriff Jenkins will sign off on that."

He nodded.

"Call you soon." Emory disconnected the call and stowed her phone. "We should have the results in a few hours."

"Now, Granddaughter," her grandmother said when she turned with two tall glasses of ice water. "Tell me what it is you do that you can order such a thing just like that."

"I'm a partner at the Veritas Center, and I work with DNA."

"A DNA expert," Blake said, sounding proud of her, surprising Emory. "Tops in her field."

"Well, isn't that something." Her grandmother handed her the water and led her back to the sofa. "Both of my girls such smart scientists."

Feeling unreasonably pleased over such a simple compliment, Emory took a sip of her water to hide her emotions from Blake's watchful gaze.

Her grandmother gave the other glass to Blake and returned to the sofa. "Now suppose you tell me what happened to Cait."

Emory set down her glass and lifted her grandmother's papery soft hand, but Blake took over, sharing only the barest of points, for which Emory was thankful. She didn't want her grandmother to be even more upset. "We believe it might have to do with the adoption, but we can't be sure."

"And so you tracked me down."

Emory nodded. "When was the last time you saw Cait?"

"The day she took the sample. She said it was just a formality, but she wanted proof for when she finally found you." She shook her head. "Isn't it so ironic that she sent the sample to you to process and had no idea you were right there all along?"

Emory nodded. "And that she chose us at all. There are so many mail-order labs she could choose from."

"I think that's a God moment for sure."

"Me, too." Emory smiled and was glad to hear her grandmother believed in God. "Can you tell me about my parents?"

Her grandmother frowned, and her chin trembled. "I can't tell you a thing about them beyond the week of your birth. They left here with the two of you, and I never saw any of you again...until Cait showed up at my door."

"Tell me more about that," Blake encouraged in a soft tone that Emory appreciated.

"I lost my Bert to cancer when Olivia—your mother, my daughter—was five. She never really recovered from losing her dad and could never settle down. She developed a wanderlust. She met your father—Charlie, his name is Charlie—in high school, and he shared her love of travel. They got married right out of high school, bought an old VW bus, and took off, doing odd jobs to pay for gas and food."

She paused and shook her head. "I didn't like it, you know. My only child gone most of the time. But they'd come back home every so often. Stay for a week and then head out again. When they came home with Olivia eight months pregnant and big as a house, I thought maybe they'd stay. But when you were little over a week old something happened. Olivia wasn't her usual easygoing self, and Charlie seemed worried. At the time I thought they were just adjusting to parenthood, but then they left, and I never heard from them again."

Tears filled her eyes, and Emory's eyes responded in kind. She hated seeing her grandmother so tortured. "Did you call the police?"

"The sheriff's office." She looked at Blake and took a long

cleansing breath. "They took a report, but since Olivia and Charlie had a habit of leaving to parts unknown, they couldn't do much other than put out an alert for their van and visit the few places I knew they liked to hang out when in town. For the first few years, I kept going back to the sheriff. Asking him to raise the alert again. And he did."

"Tell me about the places they liked to hang out," Blake said.

"There was an Indian restaurant downtown called Little India, but it's gone now. And they loved the beach. Not the clear sunny days, but when it was rainy and gloomy. Plus they loved to hike in the woods. Hiked all around here, but they had a favorite trail."

"Do you know the name of it?" Emory asked.

"Nothing like that." She waved a hand. "It never had a name. It's barely even a trail."

"How do we find it?" Blake asked.

"I can show you on a map. I still have the one I used to show the sheriff when they went missing." She pushed to her feet and walked stiffly to a large rolltop desk in the corner. She came back with a thick file and sat back down.

She patted the folder. "This holds all the postcards and letters they sent me from their travels in the early days. I made copies for the sheriff, so it should all still be in their file if you want to review it."

She opened it and for a moment seemed lost in the past and so incredibly forlorn that Emory patted her grandmother's shoulder. "It's okay, Grandma. Can I call you Grandma?"

"Oh child, yes. Of course." She squeezed Emory's hand and went back to the folder where she drew out a worn map. "Thing's nearly falling apart. I've looked at it so many times hoping something would jump out and grab me, but nothing ever did. I just keep wondering if I'd been able to remember more if..."

Her voice broke, and she sniffed as she spread the map out on the table. She pointed to a spot marked on the map with a bright red X.

"I know that area," Blake said. "But I didn't know there were any trails there."

"It's an old logging trail and most people don't know about it. That's why they liked it. They could be alone. I went up there with the sheriff. Nothing there, really. Just a clearing at the top of the trail. But Olivia said she could totally relax and feel closer to God there than most anywhere. With her traveling and seeing so many new and different things, I always worried that she might give up on her faith. The fact that she kept spending time up there when she came home gave me great comfort."

Blake took out his camera and snapped pictures of the map. "But as you said, the sheriff checked it out."

She nodded.

"Have you been back there since that visit?" Blake asked.

She shook her head. "It's too painful, and now my old arthritic knees couldn't possibly make the climb."

Her comment made Emory acutely aware of how few years she may still have with her grandmother. "After we find Cait, can I come back to visit you?"

"Well, of course you can, child. I hope you will. Often."

"You can count on that." Emory said with certainty. She meant it, but she also knew she could be coming back to tell her that Cait had been hurt or worse. Or they'd found their parents, and they were no longer living. So many possibilities, Emory could hardly breathe.

"One more thing, Mrs. Layton, and we'll get out of your hair," Blake said. "Do know anything about bracelets that your daughter instructed the adoptive parents to give to the girls?"

No. No I don't."

"Do the numbers forty-five, twenty-eight, and twenty-two mean anything to you?"

She shook her head. "I haven't a clue about either of those things."

"What about an engraved silver frame, comb-and-brush set, and ruby ring?"

"Oh, yes, yes. That was a gift from Charlie's parents." She frowned. "They've since passed, or they would be thrilled to see you girls."

"But you're sure they didn't give us bracelets?" Emory clarified.

"I can't be sure, but if so, I never saw them. Charlie was so proud of those gifts because he'd had a difficult time with his parents before you two were born and was thrilled they'd reconciled. So I would think he would've shown the bracelets to me if they were from his folks."

Blake nodded. "Before we go, can you think of anything, anything at all, as to why Cait might have been taken?"

She shook her head. "I sure hope it's not related to her parents, but it seems awfully coincidental that they all disappeared."

Emory thought the same thing, and it scared her as to what they would learn going forward.

Blake got to his feet and handed over a business card. "Call me if anything comes to mind."

Emory and her grandmother stood and hugged. Emory felt so comfortable with this woman that she didn't want to leave, but Cait needed her. "I'll let you know the minute we have news of Cait."

"Thank you, my darling." She smoothed Emory's hair. "I know God has her and you in His hands just like he's had my sweet Olivia and Charlie all these years."

Emory smiled. "That's what gives you comfort, isn't it? Your faith in God?"

She nodded, but Emory still saw sadness that went soul-crushing deep. She held her grandmother's hand. "I'm so glad I got to meet you and can't wait to see you again."

Emory turned and walked away, hoping when she returned that she would have nothing but good news for her grandmother. Near the car, she looked up at Blake. "Where to now?"

"We make a trip to see Sheriff Ziegler to find out if your grandmother has told us everything we need to know about your parents' disappearance."

22

Blake had always made it a point to keep in touch with his county's former sheriffs. At first he did so to pick their brains about the county. Then he learned they were a lonely bunch, missing their law enforcement days. Blake tried to keep them involved in policing the county in some way, and routinely took them out to lunch. It had been less than two weeks since he'd seen Ziegler. But still, when he knocked on the door to the small bungalow, he was shocked at how frail the old guy looked.

"Hey, old man," Blake greeted in a fond tone. "You doing okay?"

"Had a little flu bug, but I'm on the mend." He looked past Blake at Emory. "Now who's this pretty little thing?"

"I'm Emory Steele." She held out her hand. "DNA expert at Veritas Center."

"That pricey lab in Portland?" His gaze filled with respect. "Always wanted to get a peek at that place."

She smiled. "I'm glad to give you a tour anytime you want."

"I'll be taking you up on that." He shifted his focus to Blake. "Now tell me what you need, boy."

Blake nearly laughed at him still using the name "boy" after all of Blake's years as sheriff. "Mind if we come in and talk about one of your old investigations?"

He stepped back. "Just put on a pot of coffee. Help yourself on the way through."

Blake didn't want coffee, but he also didn't want to offend Ziegler, so he stopped at the counter and grabbed two cups and filled them. He handed one to Emory and waited for Zeigler to pass. "He gets a little cranky when you refuse his coffee. Take it and hold it if you don't want it."

"Is it any good?"

"Yeah he makes a mean cup of Joe." He led her into the small living room.

Ziegler was already seated in his recliner, and he waved his cup toward the matching leather couch, the liquid sloshing over the rim. He didn't notice or if he did, he didn't care. "Now tell me what this is all about."

"We just came from talking to Naomi Layton," Blake said. "That name ring a bell?"

He scowled. "'Course it does. Her daughter and husband went missing in the eighties. Never found them."

"Naomi told us about their disappearance, but I wanted to hear it from your side."

He nodded knowingly and took a long guzzle of coffee before speaking. "And did she tell you about the couple's criminal history?"

Emory gasped.

"She didn't mention that," Blake said evenly, though he was surprised, too.

"'Course she didn't." He shook his head. "Charlie started finding his way on the wrong side of the law as a juvenile. Olivia had a clean record. But I located a few people they stayed with on their past trips, and there were rumors of petty things he continued to engage in to put food on the table during their travels. But Naomi claimed he'd straightened up when the babies were born and wouldn't hear a bad word against him."

"As one of those babies." Emory lifted her shoulders. "I'd like to think they did."

His mouth fell open. "No kidding. You're one of the twins?"

"I am, and my sister's been abducted. We're trying to find her."

"I'm real sorry about that." He cast Emory a sympathetic look then focused on Blake. "You think it might have to do with the parents' disappearance?"

"It's possible," Blake replied. "We don't know. The girls were adopted by different families and haven't had any contact with each other."

The old guy might be physically frail, but he had a sharp mind, so Blake shared the investigation details.

"Wish I could be of some help," Ziegler said. "But honestly, there wasn't much to investigate. I visited the restaurant they hung out at and checked out their favorite hiking trail, but that was about all I had to go on. Put out alerts on the vehicle and updated them every year, but they just plain vanished."

Blake didn't like the sound of that. "You have a theory?"

"I figured after their world travels that they didn't want to come back to our sleepy little town." He rubbed his hand over a whisker-covered jaw. "But you gotta think if they gave up the babies there had to be a reason, right? Maybe they fell in with the wrong crowd and were worried for the babies' safety. Naomi said how much they loved the girls, so giving them up had to be tough." He lifted a gnarled finger. "Only one reason a parent who loves their kids does that."

"They're thinking of what's best for the children," Blake said.

"Exactly."

Blake sat forward. "You said you visited their favorite trail. Was that with Naomi or alone?"

"Both. She insisted I go up there with her, but then I went back with one of my bloodhounds. He sniffed the place out. Found nothing odd."

Blake didn't want to ask the next question in front of Emory, but he had to know. "Would he have lighted on a buried body?"

He shook his head. "But I gave him the scent from the parents' clothes, and he would've told me if they'd been there since the crazy rains we had. Had him sniff for the babies, too, but now we at least know what happened to them." He sighed and shifted his gaze to Emory. "Does my heart good all these years later to know you're okay."

"But Cait's not okay now, so can you think of anything?" Emory sounded desperate. "Anything at all to help us find her?"

"I'm sorry, but no." He set down his mug and tapped his chin. "I coulda forgot a thing or two over the years, so you might want to read my report. I doubt it, though. This is one of those cases that sticks with you, you know?"

Blake nodded. All law enforcement officers doing the job for any amount of time had at least one case that kept them up at night. He got up. "Thanks, old man."

Zeigler grinned and waved a hand. "See you at lunch next week."

"Wouldn't miss it." Blake took his cup back to the kitchen, and he heard Emory follow.

She rinsed out her mug and set it on the counter. "Can we visit their favorite trail?"

He rinsed his, too. "Are you thinking we'll find something there?"

"Honestly, no, but I want to visit the place where my

parents felt such peace. Might help my attitude while we're waiting to find Cait."

"Then of course we can take a few minutes to do that." He smiled at her.

She returned the smile. Wide, shy, caring—all at once—and it left him breathless. Just looking into her eyes made him feel like he'd fallen off a cliff and didn't have the power to climb back up.

"Is something wrong?" she asked.

Wrong? No. Something was very right, but he didn't know how to find his way out of his hole to pursue it.

He shook his head.

Blake opened the door for her and escorted her to his car then set out for the trail. She didn't speak and neither did he. She was likely thinking about her grandmother, Cait, their parents. He was thinking about how he could be with her.

I found something worth moving on for. I know it should've happened just because I trusted You, but...

He didn't know what else to say except to ask for help again to find Cait and for God to be with Emory. And now he had to let things rest in God's hands and believe He would help them.

At the trailhead, they started up a steep hill that he couldn't imagine many people would want to climb. Emory was breathing hard before long, and Blake slowed down to make it easier for her. He heard the gentle rush of water from a creek ahead. It was a soothing sound in this otherwise tense climb. The trail suddenly ended at a dense thicket.

"Now what?" she asked between breaths. "No trail."

He looked the area over. "This may have grown in over the years or the clearing is off to the side. We'll just head into the woods."

She braced her hands on her knees to breathe more deeply. "You sure we won't get lost?"

"I'll mark our GPS coordinates so we can find our way back." He grabbed his phone and took his time registering their location so Emory could rest.

When she was breathing easier, he nodded at the trail overgrown with ferns and other vining plants. "I'll head in first. Stay close behind."

He stepped off the path and took careful steps through the undergrowth with tall trees above. The going was slow as the growth was heavy and thick. He pulled up branches and vines for Emory to pass under and warned her when to step over fallen logs or large rocks. Just when he was ready to give up and try another direction, the heavy trees suddenly opened into a small clearing where the misty rain filtered down through the hazy sunshine. The shaded ground was covered in a thick carpet of pine needles. The space held a haunting beauty, and he could see why her parents loved it.

Emory came up beside him and they both turned to survey the entire area. Something caught his attention. His focus locked in, and he came to a stop to point ahead. "There."

"It's a..." Her voice fell off.

"Yeah." Blake's gut tightened. "Looks like it's a grave."

23

"What do we do next?" Emory wrapped her arms around her body.

Blake watched her carefully and couldn't figure out if she was taking such a protective stance because of the discovery or the fact that the sun disappeared and the rain intensified, making the area more unnerving than peaceful. Maybe both.

"We stay put," he said. "And I call in forensics and a cadaver dog."

"But we don't know for sure it's a grave." She twisted her hands together.

Blake knew she was trying to believe anything but that her parents had potentially been murdered and buried here. But Blake also knew the area where the soil had long ago been firmed into this mound was a grave. "The shape says we're going to find a person buried there."

"And it's not recent," the words came out in a whisper.

"We'll likely need a forensic anthropologist." He shook his head over issuing such a statement in relationship to this investigation.

He expected Emory to react in a negative way, but her only response was to dig out her phone. "Then it's a good thing we have Kelsey. Do you have a team you use for cadaver searches or should I ask her for a referral?"

"The best team in the state is Zoey Bradley and her dog Einstein," he replied. "I can get them out here."

Emory held her phone but didn't make the call. "Interesting name for a dog."

"Zoey said he was the brightest puppy she'd ever seen with such strong instincts, and the name fit. They live nearby, and if she's not working elsewhere, I know she'll come straight away."

Emory nodded. "We'll want Sam and Sierra to process this scene, right?"

Blake nodded.

"Then I'll call all of them." She focused on her phone, making the call and then lifting it to her ear.

Blake dialed Zoey who answered right away. He gave her a concise overview of their discovery, including their location. "Are you and Einstein free?"

"We are," she said. "Text me the GPS coordinates, and I can be there in thirty minutes."

"You got it, and thanks, Zoey." He disconnected and sent her the coordinates. He was confident that she would easily find them with or without the coordinates. As a search and rescue team member she knew these foothills and many of the mountains in the state better than most people.

He stowed his phone but Emory was still talking to Sam. She shoved her hand into her hair and frowned. "Please bring extra swabs and evidence bags for my use."

She sounded confident again, but he saw the lingering anguish in her eyes. He would do anything he could to make this situation better for her, but no matter his care and concern, the next few hours were going to be excruciating for her.

She lowered her phone but started tapping the screen. "I'm texting Sam the coordinates. Is Zoey coming?"

"They'll be here in thirty minutes."

"Then when I call Sierra, I'll also ask Kelsey to clear her schedule. That way once we confirm that we need her, she can make her way here."

"Maybe we should hold off on telling Kelsey." Blake didn't want to waste the woman's time if they didn't need her.

Emory looked up. "She's a single parent, and she'll need to arrange care for her son. I'd rather she did that now in case we need her right away."

Blake was surprised to hear she was a mother as he'd noticed that none of the Veritas partners wore wedding rings. "I didn't know Kelsey was married."

"She isn't." Emory's frown deepened. "Her husband was gunned down in a hotel parking lot a little over a year ago, leaving her with custody of her stepson."

"I'm sorry to hear that." So much violent loss and Blake just didn't know the purpose for any of it. Like this grave. It might not be Emory's parents, but his gut said someone had died under suspicious circumstances and was buried here. Someone's relative was likely missing and wishing they would come home. Someone like sweet Emory, a woman now searching for her birth parents. Not something Blake should focus on if he wanted to keep his head in the game. "Go ahead and have Kelsey make arrangements. I'll have Gage send the chopper to pick her up the minute Einstein confirms we have a body here."

Emory stood silently for a moment, her eyes still awash with pain, but then she lifted her shoulders and made the call.

Impressed with her ability to act in such dire circumstances, Blake followed suit, and when Gage answered, Blake filled him in on their findings. "I won't disturb the grave without Kelsey here and hoped you could send Riley or Coop to pick her up once we know what we're looking at."

"Man, that's rough." Gage's compassionate tone filtered through the phone. "Riley's just finishing a training. I'll have him start the preflight check so he's ready the minute you need him."

Blake blew out a relieved breath. "Thanks, man. I owe you big time."

"Don't give it another thought. It's what we do."

"Yeah, but not for free like this."

"Glad to do it. You know that."

"I do. And thanks again." Blake hung up and relayed the information to Emory who was watching him carefully.

"Kelsey's a go, too," she said.

Blake was touched again by the Veritas team's selfless sacrifice, just like the Blackwell team, and he raised his face to the drizzling rain to offer his thanks.

"Blake?" Emory asked.

"Just thanking God for all the help. Your team and Blackwell will be the reason we bring Cait safely home."

"You have to give your team credit, too. Trent and Lorraine have been amazing, and I know there are countless others working on finding her."

"They have, at that," Blake said, but suddenly felt weary from years of trying to apprehend bad guys and manage a large group of deputies and the associated professionals.

He took a breath and swallowed down the emotions. He couldn't let anything get to him now. Not when he needed to figure out this scene and to stay strong for Emory. "Why don't we find a place to sit out of the rain and wait for Zoey to arrive. I'll also give Trent a call to update him and have him prepare to light this place up if we don't get it processed by sunset."

She nodded, but silently stared at the mound in the swirling rain. He wanted to know what she was thinking but would never question her and potentially make things worse for her. He'd give her time and allow her to tell him if she wanted to.

She slowly swung her gaze his way, her eyes awash with tears. "Do you think this could be one of my birth parents?" Her voice broke, her words whispering into the misty air.

Blake forgot all about his need to remain professional. About not wanting to get involved with anyone and gently took her in his arms. She sagged against his chest, and he held her tightly.

"I don't know who it is, honey," he said, trying to keep the anger for the crime from his tone. "But if it's one or even both of your parents, I'll be right here by your side to help you through it."

She lifted her head, tears streaming down her face. He gently brushed them away. "Don't cry. It'll be okay. I promise."

She took a shuddering breath. "How can you promise that?"

"I can't, but God can. In His wisdom. He knows why this is unfolding this way. How it will impact you and our search for Cait. We just have to stay strong and believe that He has this."

She shook her head and stepped free of his arms. He instantly missed holding her, but didn't try to reach out for her again.

"You can really do that?" She swiped an angry hand at

her tears. "I mean, I'm a basket case, and I can only focus on the bad things happening. On the pain."

"Yeah," he said, trying to remain calm and not add to her agitation. "I get that. I've lived that way for years. Many, many years, and seeing you go through this has been like looking in the mirror."

She stood unmoving except for her gaze that intently searched his. "Tell me about what happened to you. Please. Don't shut me out again."

"Let's sit." He didn't wait for her to agree but found a fallen log under the trees' canopy and led the way. He pulled an emergency blanket from his backpack and draped the silver material over the soaked wood.

Emory sat down, the blanket crinkling under her. She hunched forward, her body shivering.

He joined her, sitting as close to her as possible. "Body heat might help with the cold." He shoved his hands in his pockets to fight the urge to put an arm around her.

She looked at him. "About your looking in a mirror."

"My sister was attacked and ended up losing her sight," he said quickly before he chickened out on telling her again. "We were young. Fighting in the car. You know, brother and sister stuff. She got mad and demanded I let her out to walk home. Cold Harbor didn't have a lot of crime back then, so I figured she was safe. But then a man assaulted her. He slammed her head against a brick wall doing permanent damage. She's been blind ever since."

Emory clutched his arm. "And you've blamed yourself all this time."

"If I hadn't let her out of the car..." He shook his head. "But then I saw all the blame going around in your and Cait's life. Parents hurting greatly and taking blame for hurting their child. But I could also see that they always had their child's best interest at heart. They didn't mean to hurt you or Cait any more than I meant for Danielle to get hurt."

Emory didn't respond at first, her focus pointed somewhere in the trees. She shifted to face him. "I can see that."

"Last night when I was trying to sleep and couldn't, I decided I was done hurting over this. Danielle doesn't blame me. My parents don't blame me. Why should I blame myself? So I finally prayed and surrendered my will." Emotions welled up in his chest, and he stopped to gulp in a deep breath. "I hadn't realized how much I was ignoring God's will for my life, but believing I was responsible for Danielle's injury was totally rebellious thinking. I didn't want to admit she'd been hurt. By taking the blame, I could run away from it and didn't have to deal with the pain of her loss."

"And now?"

"Now I know I have to go ask my family to forgive me for the years I wasted living on the fringe." He drew his hands from his pocket and gripped hers. "And maybe you can do the same thing. I mean with your adoptive mom. Life's too short for us to waste it. I know that now."

"I want to forgive her. To reconcile." Emory's gaze flitted around the area as if looking for something. Strength maybe. Or help. "I promise to pray about it. I will. Honest. But that's the best I can do right now."

"I totally understand," he said, though he was sad that she couldn't move on yet as he knew after his years in exile that handling this right now would be better for her. "It's a personal journey that you have to take at your own speed."

He heard rustling behind them and shot to his feet, his hand going to his sidearm. "That'll likely be Zoey."

A dog barked and the tiny quick footfalls came closer.

Blake was right. Einstein had arrived, and they would

soon find out if Blake was also right about a body buried in the clearing.

~

Emory stood to see a tall woman with wavy blond hair step into the clearing. She wore hiking boots, khaki tactical pants, and a heavy blue parka with a search and rescue patch on the chest. Her German Shepherd was black mixed with a deep reddish tan. Big and fierce looking, he raised his black snout and sniffed the air.

"Zoey," Blake greeted the woman. "Meet Emory Steele. The Veritas Center's DNA expert."

"Cool." Zoey smiled, her blue eyes lighting with it. "I've worked with Kelsey there."

Emory shook Zoey's gloved hand. "She'll be arriving here if Einstein confirms our find."

He tugged on the leash and looked up at Zoey with a demanding expression as if he knew they were talking about him.

"He's got kind of a big head." Zoey chuckled.

"The mound's in the clearing just ahead," Blake said.

"Then let's get to it." Zoey bent and rubbed Einstein's neck.

"Search," she commanded as she simultaneously released him and stood.

Emory watched him bolt away. "I've never seen a cadaver dog in action."

"Nothing earth-shattering." Zoey kept her focus on Einstein as they stepped into the clearing. "Basically, he sniffs the ground, and if he lights on a scent, he'll sit down and wait until I release him. And let me tell you, sitting still is hard for this guy to do."

"Why's that?" Emory asked.

"He was born a singleton—the only puppy in the litter. So he didn't have socializing with other puppies to put him in his place when he needed it. So he's brash, confident, and full of himself. And he doesn't play well with others." Her love for Einstein radiated from her face. "Makes him good at his work because he gets to work alone and receives all kinds of praise when he does his job right. Swells his head even more, so he thinks he should be in charge. I have to keep reminding him who really is."

He loped across the clearing as if not interested in searching but then bent his nose to the ground and snuffled. He searched an area far from the mound and circled a few times. Sniffed harder.

"He's got something," Zoey said.

He walked away from the area and sniffed at the base of a tree on the far side of the clearing, well away from the mound. The area was flat with a thick bed of pine needles covering bare soil.

Fascinated, Emory kept watching him. "Why didn't he sit like you said he would do?"

"The scent isn't always the strongest over the actual body," Zoey replied. "Scent can percolate down hills and gather in low spots. Animal burrows can make the scent more accessible, too. And scent can travel along vegetation roots, particularly tree roots. Where these roots surface, the scent is stronger."

Emory was confused. "But then how can you tell when he's hit on an actual body?"

"He'll tell us. Just wait." Zoey sounded so confident that Emory had no doubt she was right.

Einstein sniffed and circled again. Once. Twice. A third time. He suddenly stopped, his big snout pressed to the ground. He circled again, then sat and peered at Zoey.

"But that's not where the mound is at all," Emory cried out.

Zoey squatted, her focus pinned on the area where Einstein sat. "There's a slight rise in the ground over there, suggesting it has been disturbed at some point."

"Could he be detecting the scent from the mound?" Blake asked.

"Possible, I suppose, but due to the distance and landscape, it's more likely we have two graves." Zoey stood and pulled a stake from her bag.

"But it could just be an animal buried there, right?" Emory asked hopefully. She was just grasping at straws—anything not to admit her parents might be buried here.

But Zoey didn't know that, and she raised her shoulders in offense. "Well trained cadaver dogs can distinguish between animal and human remains."

Emory opened her mouth to apologize for doubting Einstein, but Zoey held up her hand. "And before you say humans are animals, that's true, but you know what I mean. I'll go mark the spot, then give Einstein a reward and break. We'll start again in a minute." Zoey marched purposefully toward her dog, who remained sitting obediently.

She planted the stake then ruffled Einstein's face. "Good job, buddy. You did it."

He barked, the sound echoing through the clearing and sending birds flapping into the air. She tossed him a chew toy in the shape of a large bone, and he caught it between his fierce jaws then dropped down and enthusiastically chewed on it.

Emory faced Blake, dread gnawing at her stomach. "Do you think we have two bodies?"

"It's possible," he said, but sounded reluctant to admit it.

"Both my parents?" she whispered as she could hardly catch a full breath.

"I sure hope not." His pain-filled eyes told her the thought bothered him a great deal as well. "You should call Kelsey and tell her she might be looking at two graves."

Emory nodded, but wanted to collapse to the ground. To pretend she was on any other crime scene. One that didn't involve her parents. But she couldn't pretend that her parents weren't in these graves. Not anymore.

This was real. Very real. And she had to brace herself for bad news.

24

Einstein had gone back to work and also lit on the mound, sitting down as if protecting the body below. Two people or more were buried in the two graves, and the reality drained Emory of strength and forced her to take a seat on the fallen tree. Trent had arrived with Sam and Sierra, and he and Blake had strung yellow crime scene tape, cordoning off the area, and the plastic fluttered in a strong breeze, flickering and clicking in an annoying cadence.

Dressed in white coveralls and blue booties, Kelsey had arrived, too. She'd tamed her curly hair into a bun, typical when working a scene. Emory always admired her friend's graceful movements and focused on her long slender neck and willowy shape as she quickly erected a white canopy over the grave.

Emory shifted her gaze to Sierra who stood next to Kelsey, camera out, waiting to document the findings. Findings of death. Of lives extinguished under suspicious circumstances or they wouldn't be buried up here. Emory desperately wanted to pray that these graves didn't hold her parents, but then if not her, other family members who would hear of this loss, and she wouldn't wish that on anyone. Instead, she decided to do as Blake suggested and believe no matter what happened here, God had this in hand.

"I've numbered the graves to make it easier for us to communicate," Kelsey said to Sierra. "This will be number one. I'll get the canopy set up over the other grave, and then begin excavating this one."

Emory watched the pair in action. Sierra's blond hair was pulled back in a long ponytail. Emory thought she looked her age at thirty-two, but Kelsey always appeared younger than her thirty-four years to most people, and she was often questioned about her credentials. She held a PhD from the University of California and interned at the Smithsonian before coming to Veritas where her services were sought worldwide.

Emory was proud to work alongside both women—alongside all of her talented team members. She also appreciated having Blake and Sam on this investigation. They may not have the formal education that the Veritas staff possessed, but their work experience and drive made them top-notch investigators.

Emory had to get it together and pitch in to help them. She gave herself a long pep talk, offered an equally long prayer, then got up and headed for Kelsey. Emory heard her bootie-covered feet whisper over the fallen needles from the many red pines and Douglas firs in the area. She heard the wind rustle through the trees. Heard the crime scene tape flutter, but it all still seemed so surreal.

She stopped at the first canopy. "What can I do?"

Kelsey looked up from where she knelt by her tools. She'd already staked out the site and used string to divide it into quadrants for identifying the location in the grid where remains were recovered. "If you really want to help, I could use your assistance in digging. You're experienced at excavation, and the others might be too aggressive and destroy valuable evidence. But are you sure you're up for helping?"

Emory nodded, though she wasn't sure at all. "Just tell me where to start."

"We'll begin here." Kelsey got up and gestured at the large mound. "Start removing the soil and matter while I finish prepping the other site."

She spun on her heel, and Emory grabbed a short shovel with wide blade, trowel, and bucket. Using the trowel, she scraped the top layer into the shovel, dumped the leaf litter into the bucket, and then onto a clean tarp for later systematic examination. She kept digging, forcing her mind to focus on the soil and not her fears until Kelsey returned.

Emory sat back. "We have a rectangular area that's been cut into the ground."

Kelsey nodded but didn't come right out and say it was a grave. She couldn't. Einstein might have confirmed human remains, but from Kelsey's viewpoint all she could say was that the dirt had been disturbed. No matter. Emory knew in her heart that someone was buried here.

"Let's get the fill area removed so we can document the different layers." Kelsey knelt next to Emory, and they dug together, removing soil and placing it on a tarp plus running it through a sieve to look for any forensic evidence. Kelsey stopped to make notes on the layers and soil type.

Emory removed another layer, revealing a large flat bone that she believed to be the frontal bone of a skull. Her heart constricted, a vise of tightening pain, and sat back. Kelsey would go it alone now. She couldn't risk any help or the skeleton could be damaged.

She glanced at Emory. "You might not want to watch this."

"No, I do," Emory said trying to sound certain when she felt anything but.

Kelsey's compassionate gaze held Emory's. "You don't have to be so brave, sweetie. Go sit. I'll let you know when I determine anything."

Emory decided her partner was right. There was no point in torturing herself. She'd know soon enough if one of her parents was buried in this grave.

∽

Blake continued to shift his focus between Emory and Kelsey. Emory appeared as if she might pass out at any moment, so he kept plying her with drinks filled with electrolytes. Thankfully, Sam sat next to Emory on the fallen tree, holding her hand as they waited for any identifying information.

Kelsey, on the other hand, remained composed and worked quickly but carefully, gently scraping back soil to reveal bones, and then using a soft brush to expose the entire body which was fully skeletonized. No question, the body had been buried for some time. Perhaps back when Emory's parents had gone missing, but buried after Ziegler checked out the area as there's no way he would have missed this grave.

Based on the length of the skeleton, Blake thought they were looking at a male, but he had to wait for Kelsey's findings. Still, he suspected he was looking at Emory's father.

Kelsey sat back to retrieve a sketch pad, and while she did, Sierra stepped in and started snapping photos. She'd been shooting pictures all along to record the time-consuming excavation process, a record that would be used in court if Blake located the killer. A big *if* on a case this old.

Emory's phone dinged. "Text from Lara. My grandmother's DNA matched Cait. So it's official. She's my grandmother."

"That's got to feel good." Blake smiled. "Having more family."

Emory nodded, but didn't speak. She could very well be thinking that she would have to tell her grandmother that her son-in-law and maybe daughter had not only died, but had died under suspicious circumstances.

Kelsey suddenly stood and waved Emory over. She and Sam rushed across the space, Blake kept hot on their trail. Emory peered into the shallow grave, and he stood next to her, Sam on Emory's other side.

"I know you're eager for information, so I'll share what I know now," Kelsey said, her focus pinned on Emory. "But full details won't be available until I transport the bones to the lab and examine each and every one for the kind of trauma that might give us a cause of death."

"So what *can* you tell us?" Blake asked to remind Kelsey that he was the one who was really entitled to this information. Not in a proprietary way, just that he didn't want her to forget she was working for a law enforcement agency, not Emory.

"The skeleton is intact, and unless your killer is an expert at arranging bones, the body was buried shortly after death. Additionally, I can tell you this is a Caucasian male."

"My father?" The words whispered out on a strangled breath from Emory's mouth.

Sam put her arm around Emory. Blake had the urge to push it away and replace it with his own arm, but he held back.

"Don't jump to conclusions when we don't have much to go on right now," Kelsey said.

"What about cause or time of death?" Blake asked.

Kelsey shook her head. "As you know, Blake, it's the ME's job to officially rule on cause of death, but since there isn't any soft tissue left on the bones, I'll work closely with the ME."

"It's not likely anyone would be buried up here unless they were murdered," Emory said, sounding frustrated. "So how and when he died is crucial in our hunt for the killer."

Kelsey nodded. "I wish I could give you the information you need right now, sweetie, but we'll get there."

"I know you will, and I'm sorry to be so pushy."

"Be as pushy as you need to be. I can handle it." Kelsey squatted and pointed at a round hole in the skull. Blake could see the anguish in her eyes. She might be coming across as clinical and detached, but she really cared about this victim. "I can tell you he sustained a gunshot to the frontal bone."

"Likely cause of death," Blake said.

"Likely," Kelsey replied. "But that's an off-the-record observation."

"How do you know he's male?" Blake asked. "Height?"

"Not height." She pointed at the pelvic opening. "I can say with certainty the narrow girth here suggests we're looking at a male." She moved to the skull and pointed at the forehead. "The sloping forehead and brow ridge further confirm it's a male." She gestured at the area where the nose would be located. "He has a narrow nasal root and bridge, as well as a narrow face. That tells me he's Caucasian."

"Any idea of age?" Sam asked.

Kelsey sat back on her haunches and looked up. "That's more complicated. Let me explain. We classify bodies in three broad categories. Very young, teen, and adult. Based on bone growth, a body is placed in one of these categories. Primary and secondary areas of bone growth continue until the secondary areas fuse to the primary area. At this point, all growth ceases."

"How does that help?" Emory asked.

"Former studies give us approximate ages at which the bones fuse. After examining a variety of bones, I put this man around twenty-five when he died."

"My father was twenty-three when he went missing." Emory seemed to struggle to get the words out.

Blake had to ignore Emory's pain and remain an impartial sheriff investigating a case instead of a man who hated seeing her endure this agony. "Will you be able to tell us how long he's been here?"

"Hopefully, but it'll take more time." Kelsey pointed at the ribcage and looked up at them. "When bodies first decay, they're very toxic to plant life in the area. After a time, they become excellent fertilizer and plants love them. As you can see, the roots from the nearby vegetation has intertwined with the skeleton. The heavy mass of roots suggests he's been here for quite some time, but I can't pinpoint it until I analyze the surrounding soil."

"How does that help?" Sam asked.

"As bodies decompose, they leak fatty acids into the ground. The acid profiles vary over time, so analyzing them can show how long he's been dead and buried."

"But so far..." Emory wrapped her arms around her waist. "...there's nothing to suggest this isn't my birth father."

"I'm sorry, sweetie, but no. At this point, though, it could still be anyone."

"And this is going to take time."

Kelsey nodded.

"I can run DNA from a bone as soon as you can provide one," Emory offered.

"Yes, that might be our fastest method to ID him. Or facial reconstruction is possible. And the teeth are intact, so we could find out if it's your father or not by using dental records assuming your grandmother can give us a dentist with his records after all this time."

Blake firmed his stance. "But before any of that, you need to unearth the other body."

"Yes, before taking any further action, we need to know if we're dealing with two victims." Kelsey gathered her tools and crossed to the other location where Einstein had alerted. She spread out a fresh tarp and began the soil removal.

"This will take time. We should sit." Blake gestured for Emory to sit on the fallen tree.

They took a seat together, but before long Kelsey got up and started toward them. Emory shot to her feet, and Blake stood next to her, wondering what kind of news Kelsey could have this quickly.

She stepped up to them a frown on her face. "We need to call the ME."

"Why's that?" Blake asked.

"We have another body—another male—but he's been recently buried."

Emory gasped.

"Define recently," Blake demanded as he tried to process the unexpected news.

"A month, maybe less."

Emory wobbled. Blake could no longer keep his hands at his side. He took a firm hold of her elbow and helped her sit.

"I'm with you, honey," he whispered. "We'll get you through this."

She looked up at him, and the severe anguish in her eyes stopped his breath. It hit him then. Hard. He'd fallen in love with this woman, loved her completely, and from this moment forward his search was no longer just about finding Cait. It was also about finding the killer who could very well have ended their father's life and so deeply hurt this woman he was just coming to learn he couldn't live without.

25

Emory unlocked her lab door and entered, Blake right on her heels. She'd tried to come up with something positive to focus on during the helicopter ride, but all she could think about was that the unearthed man was around her biological father's age and odds were good that one of two males would be identified as her father.

Lara looked up from the lab table where she was seated. Only in her late twenties, the dark circles under her eyes made her look older.

Guilt heaped itself on Emory's shoulders and washed away her anguish for the moment. "I'm sorry about all these hours I've had you working. This is very important to me, or I'd ask another assistant to run the tests."

Lara waved her hand, and her full lips curved up in a smile. "It is what it is. Now where is the bone and DNA you need me to process?"

Emory took the evidence bags from her tote and gently handed them to Lara. For once she was thankful that Blake wouldn't let her run DNA. She didn't think she could saw into the bone to cut off a small sample and crush it into the fine powder that was needed to extract

DNA. Or even run the sample the ME had taken from the other body.

In fact, she couldn't even stay in the lab and watch the procedures. She laid out the chain of custody form for Lara to sign, confirming Lara received the samples, and then gave her the blood sample from the trunk of the getaway car, too.

Tears threatened, and Emory wasn't about to break down in front of her assistant, especially since Lara had no idea Emory was personally connected to this investigation. "I'll be with Maya or Nick if you need me."

Her assistant nodded and started unpacking the first bone sample. Emory all but fled from her own lab, the place that had always been such a sanctuary for her—especially after the attack. Now, knowing that her father's bone might be in the lab, it felt more like a torture chamber.

"Hey, hey." Blake caught up to her and took her hand. "Are you okay?"

She shook her head and looked down so he didn't catch sight of her tears. But he gently lifted her chin with his finger and looked into her eyes, his filled with a mixture of compassion and anger.

"I hate seeing what this is doing to you," he said almost growling. "And I want to support you in any way I can. What do you need me to do?"

"Just being here for me is all you can do." She stopped to gain control of the tears before she was crying like a baby. "It's a lot to handle, sure, but the fact that it's potentially my father's bone that I delivered...it's almost too much."

"You should have let Sam bring it here."

She shook her head. "It's something I had to do. I know it sounds weird. Like, on the one hand, I can barely stand to do it, and then on the other hand, I *had* to do it, but I guess emotions don't make sense."

"Yeah, I get that." He took her hands and rubbed his

thumbs over the top. "Just remember—if it gets to be too much, say the word, and we'll take a walk or something. Okay?"

"Okay." She threw caution to the wind and flung her arms around his neck to hug him tight. He circled a strong arm around her back and drew her close. She felt so safe and secure in his arms, like nothing could touch her. She knew it could, but now she understood having someone like Blake to rely on would be wonderful. But even if they could get past their issues, and that was a big *if*, he was the sheriff in a county hours away, and she would never give up her partnership at Veritas. It meant too much to her.

She eased out of his arms and smiled at him. "Thanks again. I feel better already."

He gave a formal nod, and she didn't know what had changed in his mind, but something had. She didn't have time to stand and examine it when they needed to have the synthetic marijuana joints found on Cait's abductor analyzed. She stepped into Maya's lab and found her sitting on a stool looking into her microscope.

Maya glanced up, but quickly resumed her study. "I assume you brought the joints you called about."

"We did." Emory laid the bag on the table and had Maya sign the evidence log. "How long do you think it will take?"

Maya looked up and chuckled. "You're starting to sound like LEOs who leave samples here."

"Sorry." Emory wrinkled her nose. "I don't mean to put pressure on you."

"Hey, we live for that pressure, right?" Maya smiled. "In all seriousness, it will depend on what the sample contains as to how long it will take to run in the mass spec."

Emory knew she was referring to Gas Chromatograph Mass Spectrometer, a pricey machine that was the mainstay of Maya's work. "We're headed down to see Nick next. Text me when you have the results."

"Will do." Maya picked up the bag and took it to a clean table.

Emory left her friend to do her work, and they took the elevator up one floor.

In the hallway, Blake looked around. "So this is where Nick works."

"He likes to call it his kingdom." Emory chuckled, but it was forced as she couldn't find any true humor right now. "You'll see why when we get inside."

She made her way down the hall to his domain and opened the door. The lights were dimmed for his preference, and the main lab held monitors on tables that ringed the walls. "I have no idea why he needs so many computers, but when he requests something new, he simply launches into technospeak until we can't stand it anymore, and we agree."

"I can hear you, you know?" Nick called out from the adjoining space, but his tone was lighthearted.

Emory stepped into the smaller room he loosely called an office. The space was totally disorganized with computer parts stacked in every conceivable space. His desk held a ginormous monitor, the edges covered in sticky notes that no one understood but him, and dozens of Star Wars action figures sat near his monitor. He was such a geek in so many ways but also a gifted partner when it came to running the business. He was truly a logical thinker but also practical. Two things that didn't always go together.

"Did you come to check up on me?" He gave them a lopsided smile.

She laughed. "No. If you can believe it, we're here to ask you to do even more work."

"Oh, that I can believe." He dramatically rolled his eyes.

"You all think I wave my magic wand over the computers and they instantly spit out answers, when it's actually a lot of work."

"I get it," Emory said. "People think the same thing about DNA."

"But you can at least say how long it should take. I don't have those parameters in my work. It takes as long as it takes."

"You're right, and I'm sorry if I take advantage of you."

"You don't." He suddenly grinned. "Just busting your chops. It's what I'm here for. What do you need now?"

Emory tried to smile at her friend but it fell flat. "We need one of your famous algorithms to search for crimes that my parents might have been involved in."

"Your parents?" He gaped at her.

Emory had expected the response, but still it added to her hurt. She took a long breath before starting again. "Turns out my birth parents may or may not have been involved in criminal activity. It's unclear, but the former sheriff seems to think they may have given us up for adoption because they fell in with the wrong crowd and were afraid for our safety."

"Hmm." Nick tapped his chin. "So this wouldn't likely be a petty crime. Something much bigger. Perhaps something that involved weapons."

"That's my thinking."

"Mine, too," Blake said.

Nick handed her a sticky note pad, his very favorite office supply. "Give me the dates, and I'll see what I can put together."

She took the pad and jotted down the time frame when her parents went missing.

He ripped off the sticky and put it on the edge of his monitor. "FYI, I haven't found any correlations between the addresses you gave me, but the computer is still working the problem." He picked up his Yoda action figure and turned it over and over in his hands. "And if you're wondering, that's why I need the computing power in the other room."

He chuckled and swiveled back to face his monitor. "And please, don't stand there watching over my shoulder. I'll let you know when I have something or strike out."

"Thanks, Nick," Blake said and turned to leave.

Emory followed him out to the hallway and stopped as the things they'd come to Veritas to do had been handled.

Blake tilted his head and looked at her. "What now?"

Yeah, what? Go home? Back to the lab? What? "Normally, I would say we could hang at my condo while we wait, but it's a mess."

"Then let's go straighten it up," he said quickly. "It'll keep us occupied, fix a problem, and we can talk about the investigation while we clean."

She searched his eyes. "You sure you want to do that?"

"Yes. I absolutely want to help you right your life."

She studied his expression. "Why do I think there's a far deeper meaning than just picking my things up and putting them away?"

"Because there is."

She shook her head and started off for the elevator. No way would she ask for additional information as they definitely didn't need to get into a personal discussion right now.

In the elevator, he looked at her. "Guess your silence means you don't want to talk about my comment."

She met his gaze. "Now would be a good time for the close-mouthed Blake Jenkins to show up."

His mouth fell open at her comment, and then he threw back his head and laughed, the sound ricocheting around the small car.

She was so thankful for his response that she laughed along with him, and the emotional release felt wonderful. Still smiling, she led the way to her condo. The door had been repaired just as Sierra had told her, and Emory unlocked it and flipped on the light.

A clean and organized condo sat before her. "What?"

"Someone cleaned it all up."

"My partners." Tears of gratitude replaced the sorrowful ones, and Emory had to swallow hard to stop them. "It's just like them to do something like this and not tell me."

Blake nodded. "You have an amazing support network here."

"I do, and I am so blessed by them." She stepped inside and didn't feel any of the terrifying emotions she thought would assault her when she arrived home. The fear. The anxiety didn't return. None of it.

Did it have to do with Blake standing at her side, or could she actually live in this condo again?

She faced him. "Do you want something to eat or drink?"

He met her gaze but didn't speak. "Do you honestly want to know what I want?"

Her mouth suddenly went dry. "What?"

"This." He slid his fingers into her hair and drew her head closer. "I'm going to kiss you unless you stop me."

Her heart raced, and she grinned. "Stop you? Why would I do that?" She cupped the back of his head and pulled it closer until his lips settled on hers.

His kiss wasn't tentative or questioning, but sure and strong like he'd wanted this for some time. Just as she'd wanted it. His arms circled around her, eliminating any space between them. She could feel his heartbeat thundering against her own, their kiss filling her with longing for a future bursting with hope and love. And the joy that had been missing in her life for so long.

His muscular arms tightened even more, holding her like he would never let go. And she didn't want him to. She deepened the kiss and was shocked at the low moan coming from her throat. She wanted this more than she'd known. Wanted it never to end. Never.

Blake's phone rang, and he jerked back as if he'd come to his senses. But a quick look at him told her he hadn't. His eyes were glazed over, and he looked dazed. The kiss had affected him as deeply as it had her.

He blinked hard, dug out his phone, taking in a long breath then letting it out. "It's Trent. I have to take it."

She nodded, trying to catch her breath as well.

"What do you have?" he asked Trent, his gaze still fixed on her.

She didn't know what to do with herself. She touched her lips and remembered their kiss. She'd never experienced such a deep and abiding kinship with anyone before.

He jerked his gaze away and clamped a hand on the back of his neck. "You're sure?"

Was it bad news? Had Cait been injured, found dead? Emory's warm feelings evaporated, and a cold ball of dread settled in where the joy had been.

"Search his place and report back," he said. "I'll run this past Nick and see what we can learn about him." Blake shoved his phone into his pocket.

"What is it?" Emory asked, but hated to hear the answer.

"Someone recognized the photo we put out with the media and called in to report him. The guy who broke into your condo and held Cait captive is Sid Pipkin."

"But knowing his name is good news," she cried out. "Why do you sound so upset?"

"Do I?" He shook his head. "I don't mean to. But the kiss. I didn't want it to end."

"Me neither," she admitted. "But you have to agree, it's for a good reason."

He nodded. "Let's get down to Nick's kingdom and see if adding Pipkin's name to his searches will give us the lead we so desperately need."

26

Blake didn't know Emory could move so fast, but she bolted down the stairs to Nick's lab and Blake had to run to keep up with her. She shoved open the door.

"Sid Pipkin," she said. "Add his name to all of your fancy searches. Now! Quickly!"

Blake wasn't surprised that the words rushed out of her mouth, but Nick looked up, eyes wide. "Well, hello to you, too."

"Sorry. It's just…we've identified the man who abducted Cait and broke into my condo. I know he'll be the key to finding her."

Nick's expression turned serious. "If I change the searches, they'll all have to start over. Are you sure you want that?"

"We have to do it. So yes. Go!"

He glanced at Blake.

"Agreed," Blake said, thankful that Emory's teammate would check with him, too, before acting.

Nick took off for the main lab to sit before the first computer. He logged in and typed as fast as Emory had run down the stairs. He slid his chair to the next computer.

Logged in. Typed. Slid again. Same procedure until he'd logged into five different machines.

Blake couldn't help but wonder why these computers weren't networked, and Nick could do this from his own computer, but he wasn't about to question an IT expert on his own field of expertise.

"Can't you access these all in one place?" Emory asked, obviously not as hesitant as Blake.

"Yeah, but it's far more dramatic for you to watch me slide from machine to machine." He grinned.

Emory rolled her eyes. "Yeah, you're a regular riot."

"Hey, I resent that." His grin widened. "The searches will take time to return data. Have you done a basic search using this guy's name?"

She shook her head. "We came right down here."

"Then let's do that." He spun his chair and rushed back to his office to sit at his desk. Blake followed Emory, and they stood behind Nick as he typed Sid Pipkin's name into the search engine.

"We're fortunate he has a unique name," Nick said as links loaded on the screen.

Blake ran his focus down the list of links. Social media. White pages. Other address sites.

"Check Facebook," Blake directed. "I can't tell you how foolish criminals are and how many times they share information that leads to their arrest."

Nick clicked on the Facebook link, and Pipkin's page loaded.

Blake took in the profile photo. "That's our guy. Lives in Rugged Point."

"Where's that?" Emory and Nick asked at the same time.

"About ten miles north of Cold Harbor." Blake read down the page. "He's unemployed. Didn't finish high school and is single."

"So he had plenty of time to stalk and abduct Cait." Nick shook his head and sounded disgusted.

Blake pointed at his latest post. "He doesn't believe in securing his feed. Scroll down the page so we can read his posts."

Nick slowly rolled the screen down, and Blake took in the items, mostly sharing of outrageous posts by government radicals and promoting the right to bear arms.

Nick continued to scroll. "How far do you want me to go?"

"Just keep at it," Blake said, getting frustrated that the posts were so generic.

An alert popped up on the screen.

"We already have a match in one of the searches." Excitement lightened Nick's tone. "It's the one for crimes in the area from the eighties."

"But Pipkin would've been a baby at that time," Blake said.

"Then let's see what the alert hit on." Nick clicked on the link, bringing up a news story written about five years ago and reminiscing on an unsolved bank robbery.

Blake scanned the article to catch the main points. "An Ike Pipkin and three others were suspected of the armed robbery, including a woman, but only Pipkin was arrested and convicted. The others have never been identified and the money never found."

"Sid's father?" Emory asked.

"Likely, since it came up in connection to my algorithm," Nick replied. "I'll do a quick search and let you know."

Emory looked up at Blake. "Do you think my parents participated in this robbery?"

Blake hated to think so, but... "Seems quite possible that they were two of the people who were never caught, and they disappeared with the money."

She rubbed a hand over her face. "Or their partners turned on them and killed them."

"Don't go there." Blake squeezed her hand. "Not unless DNA confirms it. Let's focus on Ike Pipkin. I'll call Trent to see if the guy's still incarcerated, and if not, if we have a current address."

Nick continued typing, and Blake ignored him to contact Trent. When Trent answered on the second ring, Blake nearly shouted out his thanks.

"Did you search Sid Pipkin's place?" Blake asked without a greeting.

"That's where I am now," Trent replied. "Nothing of interest yet."

"Any info on the guy's father?"

"Nothing. In fact, no personal items in the place at all. It looks like he just moved in. I did find a picture of Cait, though. At work."

So he really was their guy. "Get out to your computer and run the particulars on an Ike Pipkin who we believe is Sid's father."

"Hold on a sec," Trent said.

Blake heard a door slam in the background, the sound of Trent breathing harder, and then typing on a keyboard.

"He's Sid's father all right," Nick said. "And he got out of prison two months ago."

Blake didn't know how Nick found the connecting information so quickly, but it was right there on his screen.

"Ike Pipkin has been released," Trent reported. "And I have a Rugged Point address for him."

"Text me his photo and particulars," Blake ordered. "Then leave Sid's place to the techs and get over there to sit on the house. Covert surveillance. I'm heading back. Keep me informed of any movement."

"Roger that."

Blake hung up and updated Nick and Emory. "This is the break we need. I'm heading back to Cold Harbor."

Emory met his gaze. "I'm going with you."

He shook his head. "You can't come along on the stakeout."

She firmed her shoulders into a straight line. "I know, but I want to be close by when you find Cait."

As the sun rose behind heavy rain clouds, Blake parked his vehicle behind Trent's SUV in the run-down area of Rugged Point. Small cottage-style homes that had seen better days dotted the street. He ran his binoculars over the area, zooming in on the faded blue cottage Ike Pipkin had given as a rental address when he was released from prison. But Blake was skeptical. Just because Pipkin gave them this address didn't mean he really lived there.

Blake stepped into the misty rain and slipped into Trent's car and the guy didn't startle at all. He wouldn't have missed Blake's arrival, even if Blake did pull up covertly without headlights.

Trent lowered his binoculars from his spot behind the wheel. "Boss."

"Anything?" Blake asked.

Trent shook his head. "No movement, but now that the sun is coming up, we might get lucky."

Dark circles hung under Trent's eyes, and he needed a shave. "When's the last time you slept?"

He cocked his head. "I could ask you the same thing."

"I snoozed off and on during the flight. Why don't I take over, and you head home for a few hours?"

"And miss out on a take down and freeing Cait?" He fired a combative look at Blake. "No way."

Blake knew tiredness fueled his detective's sharp tongue and held up his hands. "No need for a fight. It was just a suggestion."

Trent nodded and lifted his binoculars. "I'm surprised Emory didn't insist on coming along."

"Oh, she did, but I put my foot down." Blake thought about how many times she'd argued her case on the flight, and her little pout when he'd walked out of Sam's cabin door without her. "She's hard to say no to."

"For you, maybe."

Blake shot Trent a look. "What's that supposed to mean?"

"C'mon, boss. Neither one of you is making a secret of your interest in each other."

Blake nearly groaned. "That obvious, huh?"

"Maybe not to most people, but I'm like this crazy good detective." Trent laughed.

Blake smiled. "You ever think about becoming sheriff?"

"Why would I, when you'll be filling those shoes for years to come?"

"You should give it some thought. You never know what might happen."

Trent lowered his binoculars and eyed him. "You thinking about retiring?"

Blake shrugged. "Just telling you to give it some thought."

Blake lifted his binoculars to end the conversation. He watched for nearly twenty minutes when the garage door at Pipkin's bungalow opened and a man wheeled out a garbage can. Blake zoomed in on his face. It was a slightly older version of Sid's square face, and Ike's blond hair had some streaks of silver. He carried himself as tall and tough as his deceased son. "It's our guy."

"Agreed," Trent said, his binoculars also raised. "Question is, does he have Cait inside?"

Pipkin went back into the garage but didn't close the door.

"Maybe he's going out. One of us can follow him, the other scope out the house."

"You get a warrant?" Trent asked.

Blake nodded.

A small car backed from the garage.

"Tail him," Blake said reaching for the door handle. "I'm going in."

Emory might have promised she would stay in Sam's cabin, but she was going stir-crazy. She could at least wait at Blake's office so when he found Cait, Emory would be closer. But Sam had taken her car and Emory needed transportation.

Hannah. The perfect solution.

Emory grabbed her jacket and jogged down the narrow drive with tall pines abutting it to Hannah and Gage's house. The skies were gray and rain clouds threatened, but Emory arrived on Hannah's doorstep without getting wet. She adjusted her jacket and took a long breath, then knocked.

Hannah answered the door and smiled. "Emory. What a surprise. Come in."

Emory stepped into the entryway but didn't go further. "I've come to borrow a car."

Hannah tipped her head in surprise.

"I know it's a big ask, but Sam has her car, and Blake is staking out the man they think might have Cait. Of course, I couldn't go along, so he left me here to sleep. But I couldn't, so I thought I'd head into his office and wait."

Hannah raised an eyebrow. "And you're sure that's all you're going to do? Not go after the man yourself? I mean, if I were in your shoes, I'd sure want to."

"Blake figured that, too, so he didn't let me see the address."

"Ah, yes." Hannah wrinkled her nose. "That sounds like Blake."

"So if you might let me borrow your car, that would be awesome."

"Of course. Unless you want me to drive you."

Emory wouldn't mind the company, but she heard the kids playing in the other room and didn't want them to come along. "I'm good if you trust me with your car."

"I absolutely do. Let me grab the keys." She went down the hallway and soon returned with them jingling on her finger. She handed them over and gave Emory a temporary gate code. "I'm glad to hear that Blake has a solid lead on finding Cait. You must be so relieved."

Was she? Not yet. "I will be once I can hug her."

"Let me give you one for the time being." Hannah wrapped her arms around Emory.

She felt those incessant tears starting again and quickly eased away before she broke down in front of Hannah. "Thanks for the hug. After this is all over, I hope we stay in touch. I'd love to see your precious baby."

Hannah watched her carefully. "If this thing between you and Blake continues, I'm sure we'll see you. He visits often."

Emory shook her head. "Even if we could work out the issues we have, we're both married to our jobs in different cities and not willing to give them up."

"We'll see," Hannah said with a hint of a smirk.

"You know something I don't know."

"Only that when two people are meant to be together,

God moves heaven and earth to make it happen. So different cities in Oregon isn't really a big challenge for Him." She smiled.

The more Emory learned about this woman, the more she was impressed with her strength and wisdom. "I wish my faith was half as strong as yours."

She shook her head. "You should have seen me a few years ago. A regular mess in the faith department. Give everything up to God and your life will be righted. I oughta know. As do most of the team members here. Talk to any of them, and they'll tell you not to fight what God puts in your world."

"Resistance is futile, huh?" Emory chuckled.

"Go ahead and joke, but you'll see." Hannah smiled again—a knowing smile, and Emory was starting to think Hannah totally knew what she was talking about.

So on the way to the car, Emory offered a plea to God to make things clear to her. To help restore her relationship with Him. To show her the way through her fear and find the life He wanted for her, as she was certain He didn't want her to live in fear.

Her heart felt a bit lighter, and she exited the compound and merged onto the main road. Traffic was light at this time of morning, and she settled back for the winding drive into town. She didn't have an access code so she couldn't park in the secure lot, and the spaces out front of Blake's office were filled with department vehicles. She circled the building and found a spot in the back, quickly pulling to the curb.

She took a moment to check her phone to see if Blake had called while she was driving, but she hadn't missed any calls, just two texts. One from Sam telling her that they worked all night on the clearing, and she and Sierra were heading to the compound with potential evidence they'd collected.

Emory fired off a responding text. *In town at Blake's office. Will catch you later.*

And the second text was from Maya confirming the joint held synthetic pot and rat poison. The autopsy would confirm that Sid died from the poison, but the state lab results would take weeks. Emory was so thankful for the speed at which her team could run tests. She wished that all law enforcement had rapid test results, but the Veritas Center could only help so many of them.

She stowed her phone in the outer pocket of her backpack and climbed out. As she reached for the lock, she was aware of someone quickly approaching from behind. Fears from the car attack surfaced, and she spun.

A tall, muscular man with a gun in his hand stood right behind her.

"Back in the car," he demanded. "Now."

She couldn't move except to flash her gaze to his face. The sudden recognition nearly took her breath. "Ike Pipkin. You have my sister."

"I do, indeed, and if you want to see her alive again, you'll get into the car. You drive." He waved the gun at Hannah's vehicle. "*Now!*"

Emory wanted to bolt, but she couldn't outrun a bullet, and her sister came first anyway. Emory would do anything for Cait, even climb back into the car with a man that they were sure was a killer.

Blake silenced his phone and radio to keep from alerting anyone inside the house, and crept up to the building. The blinds were closed on every window. He would have to break down a door to gain entry, and he'd rather not draw the neighbors' attention. He stepped through the gate and eased around the side of the house and into the back yard.

He had to wade through knee-high grass to the wooden door that had seen better days. He kicked it in, then drew his weapon and entered. The house smelled like rotting garbage, and the kitchen sink was filled with food-caked dishes. He started down a hall and poked his head into the first room. A bathroom with rusty fixtures.

He moved on to a bedroom. Empty. Then another bedroom equally as empty. The hall opened into a great room, and he stopped, stunned to see a cage similar to the one at Sid's place. But in the corner of this one sat Cait, her mouth gagged, her hands bound and tied to the cage, her eyes—the same dark brown as Emory's—filled with terror. Her face a dead ringer for the woman he loved. So very odd for him to see.

"Am I glad to see you," he said and nearly fell to the floor in relief to find her alive and not severely beaten. "I'm Sheriff Blake Jenkins. Let me finish clearing the house, and then I'll get you out of here."

She mumbled behind the tape and shook her hands. He couldn't make out her words, but he knew by her frantic body language that she was begging him to free her. He'd love to, but first he had to clear the place to make sure they wouldn't be attacked.

He made quick work of moving through the living room where a mattress, recliner, and old television sat, and empty beer cans were stacked in a pyramid on one wall.

Satisfied no danger existed, Blake holstered his weapon and bent his head to his radio to call for backup. Two units in the area responded, and Blake signed off.

"Before you go, you should know Detective Winfield is trying to call you," the dispatcher said.

"Roger that." He looked at Cait and his heart wrenched

again at the panic and terror on a face that was a mirror image to the woman he loved. "Let me grab a bolt cutter from my vehicle to cut the lock."

She mumbled behind her gag again.

"Don't worry. I'll be right back, and Pipkin won't intervene." At least Blake didn't think so. Maybe Trent would change Blake's opinion. On his way to the car, he dialed his detective.

Trent answered right away. "You have to—"

"Cait's in the house," Blake said and opened the back of his SUV. "She's alive and in pretty good shape."

"I—"

"If you're calling to tell me Pipkin is on his way back here, stall him. I'll have her out in no time."

"Listen!" Trent snapped. "Pipkin has Emory."

"What?" Blake grabbed the bolt cutter and slammed the hatch. "Not possible. He could never get into the Blackwell compound."

"Emory's not at the compound."

Panic hit Blake like a punch to the chest. His feet came to a stop, and he couldn't get a breath.

"She borrowed Hannah's car," Trent continued. "Drove to the office so she'd be there if we brought Cait in. Pipkin parked out back. Maybe hoping to see Emory. I don't know. He had a gun and forced her back into Hannah's car. I couldn't intervene, or he would have shot her. I followed them but got separated at the railroad tracks."

Emory. A killer has Emory.

Blake didn't know what to do, and he'd only felt this utterly helpless once in his life—when Danielle was attacked.

"Have you interviewed Cait to see why he took her?" Trent asked. "That might help us find Emory."

Right. Cait might know how to find them.

"Going back inside now." Blake ran for the house, his feet flying over the grass. "Get over here ASAP."

"On my way."

Blake rushed into the family room. Snapped the lock on the cage and charged over to Cait, carefully removing her gag.

"Why did Pipkin abduct you?" he asked, his tone far more demanding than he would like.

She opened and closed her mouth a few times then swallowed. "He wanted the bracelet and to know my twin's identity."

"Bracelet?" Blake sliced through her zip tie with a knife.

"We both got a bracelet when we were babies. They each have a set of three numbers. Hers are different than mine. Together, the pair of six digits form GPS coordinates for where my dad buried the money from a robbery." Cait paused and breathed deeply, but started crying. "I finally gave in and told him where mine was because without Emory's numbers it wouldn't help him."

"He just took Emory. How did he know who she was? Did you tell him?" Blake hated the accusation in his tone and the effect it had on the already-terrified woman.

She shook her head and swiped at her tears. "He took over my social media accounts, and she friended me yesterday. He saw her picture and immediately knew who she was. And then she posted about working with your office on trying to find me, so he thought he'd hang out there in case she showed up and he could tail her to where she was staying."

Blake slammed a fist into the cage wall.

She grabbed his other hand and held it like a death grip. "Tell me she's okay."

"I can't."

Cait swallowed hard, terror growing on her face. "He'll

be after the bracelet. Wherever she keeps it is where he'll go."

Blake thought back to the helicopter ride when Emory had taken out the bracelet and studied it. "She put it in her backpack. She probably has it with her."

Cait clutched her bloodied hands together. "If she gives it to him, then he'll know where the money is located, and he doesn't need her anymore."

27

Emory thought Trent was following them in his unmarked car, but then Pipkin forced her to race over the railroad tracks before the sign came down, and they lost Trent—if it had indeed been him back there.

"Give me your phone," Pipkin insisted.

She didn't want to give it up as Blake could track her that way, so she kept quiet and continued driving, the road turning rural and more deserted.

Pipkin jammed the cold barrel of his gun into her temple, and she caught a better look at it. Was it the Walther PP that Sid had carried when he'd broken into her condo?

"I know you won't kill me." She couldn't believe how confident she sounded, when in reality her insides were quivering. "You want something from Cait, and you want the same thing from me. Plus I'm driving, and shooting me would just be foolish."

He swore under his breath and grabbed her backpack. After texting Sam, she'd been in a hurry and had dropped her phone into the front pocket instead of putting it in her pants pocket like she would normally have done. He found the phone and opened the window to toss it out.

She heard it hit the road and shatter. Her last hope at Blake tracking her was gone like a puff of smoke.

"What do you want with me?" she asked, hoping if she knew his purpose in taking her, she could figure out how to outsmart him.

"Pull over, and I'll tell you."

She didn't want to do as he asked, but maybe if she wasn't focused on driving she might find a way to escape. She waited until a safe spot presented itself to ease off the side of the road into a graveled clearing.

She shifted into Park and faced him. "So. I've done as you asked. Now tell me what you want."

"Your bracelet."

She was taken aback by his response. "What bracelet?"

"The one your adoptive parents were given with the numbers on it."

Ah, so that was it.

He pulled a bracelet matching hers from his pocket—matching in design, but the beads held different numbers. That meant he was looking for something with six numbers, not three.

What had six numbers?

"Well," he demanded. "Where is it?"

She wouldn't let on that she knew about the bracelet and would play dumb to buy time. She tried her best to look confused. "I have no idea what you're talking about. I just found out this week that I was adopted and have a twin sister."

He rolled his eyes. "You expect me to believe that?"

"It's the truth," she could earnestly say as the last part of her statement was true. "My parents kept it a secret. It wasn't until Cait went missing and the sheriff brought me her DNA to process that I figured it out."

"I'm no idiot, lady." Pipkin ground his teeth and dug

out a handkerchief to swipe it over his perspiring fore-head. "If you just found that out, you would have confronted your parents, and they would have given you the bracelet."

He was smarter than she thought. "Not sure what you mean."

"Okay fine. Play it that way." He waved his gun. "I know you don't value your own life, but the person I have babysit-ting Caitlyn is trigger-happy. Give me the bracelet, or I make a quick phone call and she's dead."

Emory didn't believe him. Or maybe she just didn't want to believe him. She couldn't risk him having Cait killed. But what if he was lying, and he'd already killed her?

No. Emory had to believe as a twin she would know if Cait was gone. But that still didn't tell her what to do.

She fired a look around the car as if she was going to find an answer hanging in the air and she could pluck it down to escape.

Father, what do I do? If I give up the bracelet, he doesn't need me anymore. Or Cait. Tell me what to do. Please. And no matter what, watch over Cait.

Medics had treated Cait and now rolled her out the door to transport her to the hospital to be checked out. Blake wanted to celebrate the good news in finding her not only alive but in pretty good condition considering what she'd been through, but Blake couldn't focus on that with Emory missing. He *had* to find her. But first he'd needed to secure this crime scene by posting deputies outside in case Pipkin was dumb enough to return to the rental house.

"I'm sorry." Trent cast Blake an apologetic look across Pipkin's living room.

"No need for sorry," Blake said, his mind still racing over how to locate Emory.

Trent shoved a hand into his hair. "You trusted me, and I let the train separate me from Emory and Pipkin."

"Not your fault." Blake's fault. Totally. "I should've asked to have one of the Blackwell team guard her, and she would never have left the compound without me finding out."

"You had no way of knowing she was in danger at the compound." Trent stepped closer. "Or that she would leave there on her own. Or even that Pipkin knew how to locate her."

All true, but none of it eased the ache in Blake's gut. "You sure we can't track her phone?"

"Positive. It quit working right after they crossed the tracks. Pipkin must've destroyed it."

"If only we had another way to trace her." Blake started pacing, his brain mush as he frantically tried to come up with a way to find the woman he loved.

"Let's run the facts," Trent said. "That should help."

"Right. Good." He sighed a breath of thanks at Trent's logical thinking in such a stressful situation. "She was at the compound. Borrowed Hannah's car. Drove to our office. Parked. Pipkin grabbed her. Wait—that's it!"

"What?" Trent asked.

"Borrowed Hannah's car." Blake grabbed his phone and dialed Gage.

"Hannah's car," Blake blurted out after Gage answered. "You have a tracker on it, right?"

"Of course." Gage chuckled.

Blake shot a hand up in victory. "I figured after she was in danger when you met her that you wouldn't risk her safety again."

"Okay," Gage sounded wary. "So why do you want to know?"

"Emory borrowed Hannah's car to come to my office. The guy who abducted Cait overpowered Emory and took off in Hannah's car. We lost them."

"Man, sorry," Gage said. "You've gotta be totally stressing. Hang on, I've got the app on my computer, and I'll check for the car's GPS coordinates."

Blake started pacing again. Step after step. The silence ticked by, feeling like hours. Fear coiled in his stomach and turned into a squeezing fist.

"Okay, here you go." Gage rattled off coordinates. "If you stay on the phone with me, I can keep updating you."

"Perfect." Blake looked at Trent. "We have the coordinates. Let's move."

They raced out the door. Blake told the closest deputy to maintain the scene's security and Blake would return with instructions later.

He got in his SUV and connected his phone to the car information system. He punched the coordinates into his map program and glanced at Trent. "They're ten miles away. We need to move fast. Light 'em up."

Trent flipped on the lights and siren, and Blake peeled away from the curb. They raced through town, the skies dark and overcast, getting darker when they turned onto the oceanside road. Angry clouds rolled across the sky, unleashing rain in a fury on them, but Blake didn't slow down.

"Gage, update us," Blake demanded, turning on his wipers.

"They're not moving. Same location."

"Perfect. We're gaining on them." Blake pressed the gas harder, taking the dangerous ocean drive at a speed that had Trent cringing. Blake let up on the gas. He needed to reach Emory, not run the vehicle off the road onto the craggy rocks and roaring ocean below.

"What's your plan when we reach them?" Trent asked speaking loud to be heard above the rain.

"I don't know." Blake hated to admit that aloud, but he couldn't form a plan until he got the lay of the land. "We'll just have to wing it."

"Probably the only thing we can do, but boss—" Trent met Blake's gaze and held it. "Don't be in such an all-fire hurry to rescue her that you forget she's being held at gunpoint and Pipkin may not have anything to lose."

❧

Emory watched the rain pelting the car windows as Pipkin dug the bracelet from her backpack. She'd stalled until he picked up his phone and dialed. She couldn't risk Cait's life. Her own, yes, but not Cait's. And her twin sense said Cait was still alive, so she'd given in. Told him where the bracelet was located.

He dragged it out, the gun still in his other hand.

"Perfect. Now I have the coordinates I've waited thirty years to possess." A sick grin slid across his face.

"Coordinates for what?" she asked, trying to remain calm.

"Your foolish parents robbed me."

So they *were* involved. "How?"

"We held up a bank," he said not looking up. "They were too chicken to come in but did a good job as a lookout and getaway driver."

He might have declared her parents' involvement, but she still didn't want to think they were criminals. "I can't believe they would do that."

"They had to, you see." A snide smile slid across his lips. "I was in the lending business back then. They owed me a pretty penny. Said they were going to get their mommy to

290

pay it back, but she didn't have the cash. So I told them if they wanted you and Caitlyn to be safe, they'd have to work it off."

He was more of a monster than she thought. "You threatened to hurt babies?"

"Would never have done it, but they didn't know that." He chuckled. "We got a nice payday. But when it came time to split it up, they held us at gunpoint and took off."

She hated that her parents had done some bad things, but taking this guy's money? That she could get on board with. "Good for them."

"Until it wasn't." He met her gaze, that sick grin there again, oozing evil.

She lurched back, her instincts telling her to protect herself. "You killed my father and buried him in his favorite spot."

He stared at her for long, uncomfortable moments. "So you found him, huh?"

An ache that she'd never before experienced lanced her body at his confirmation of her father's death. She wanted to cry. To rail at him. But she couldn't grieve now. Not with her life on the line. She took a deep breath. Another. And another, trying to find strength to act.

"Unfortunately, he didn't remember the coordinates," Pipkin went on, oblivious to her fear. "Not even when we threatened to hurt your mother in front of him. But he *did* tell us about the adoptions and bracelets."

"So you threaten women *and* children." She shook her head in disgust. "How did you find Cait?"

"Adoption website," he answered, his tone cocky. "Knew your birthdate so it wasn't hard. Pretended to be your dad and asked her to meet up."

Oh, Cait, if only you hadn't trusted him. But Emory would likely have done the same thing. Or...maybe not after her attack. "And the other man? The one you recently buried?"

"Our other partner. Tom Viceroy. I wanted his help to get Cait to talk, but he'd gone straight. Threatened to go to the authorities and report me. I couldn't let him do that."

"And so you tasked your son with taking her?"

"Actually." He tipped his head and frowned. "If she'd cooperated and given me the bracelet and your name, we wouldn't have taken her at all."

"You would've killed her instead."

"Of course." He laughed, the weaselly sound bouncing around the vehicle, competing with the pelting rain to be heard.

She wanted to lash out at him. Hurt him. "Then your son died."

"Stupid boy." He didn't sound even the least bit upset. "Smoking that stuff when he could get the real thing. But he said he liked that high better. Shouldn't have been smoking anything while guarding Caitlyn, but you young people have no self-control." He shook his head. "I guarded her while he searched your condo. No way I was going to take a chance in getting nabbed at your place. But I should have kept watching her. Couldn't though. I'm not as young as I used to be and need some sleep. Never thought the boy would get high."

Emory left that topic alone. No way would she get him into a discussion about his son's decisions. "What happened to my mother?"

He shrugged. "She didn't know anything, so I let her go. I didn't like the thought of killing a woman back then. But she knew I'd hunt her down if she ever went home or told anyone about me."

Her mother might still be alive. A ray of hope helped temper Emory's grief.

He waved his hand. "Enough yammering on. Time to find the money."

He tapped on his phone, and she saw a map program open. He got out Cait's bracelet and started to enter the coordinates.

He was so focused on his work that his gun dipped, and he didn't seem to remember she was in the vehicle with him.

This is it. Her chance to get free. She took a deep breath. Placed one hand on the door handle, making sure she knew how to open it. Then she reached out with the other and gave his hand a forceful chop.

The gun fell to the floor.

He startled, and she jerked open her door. Bolted. Ran across the road. Down into the ditch. Tumbled, head over heels in the soggy clay soil. Righted herself and took off toward a line of tall, thick trees. The rain slashed at her face, blurred her vision. She had to be extra careful not to miss an obstacle and fall.

She heard Pipkin swearing at the top of his lungs from across the road.

She ran harder. Through soggy knee-high grass threatening to take her down. Over ruts. Her feet pounding. Her heart pounding. Harder. Faster. The cold air blasted her in the face. The rain cut into her skin, but she kept going, Faster. Faster. Over potholes. Over the grass. Small rocks.

"Stop or I'll shoot," Pipkin yelled from a location far too close for her liking. "And you know I'll do it."

He was going to kill her anyway. What did she have to lose?

She kept going. Braced herself. Waited for the gun to fire. For a bullet in the back.

"Police, drop the gun." She heard a man yell out, but

couldn't make sense of the fact that the police could even be here. How?

A gunshot split the air, and then a second one. Emory hunched forward, waiting for him to fire again and the bullet to strike. Waiting to die.

~

Emory suddenly dropped to the ground, and Blake lost all feeling in his body.

"Emory," he shouted. "No!"

He took off running. He reached the unmoving Pipkin and kicked his gun out of reach. Blake bent down to check for a pulse. None. So Blake's bullet had killed the man. A bolt of regret sliced into him, but he had no time to ponder the emotion. That was for later. He needed to get to Emory.

He plunged down into the field. Kept his gaze locked on Emory. She didn't move.

"Emory! Emory!" His frantic tone cut into the rain, into the air, into his own heart. "Are you hurt?"

She sat up. Stared at him, her expression confused.

Yes! She was alive, but dazed. His chest ached from the fast sprint across the field, but he picked up speed anyway. He reached her and dropped down next to her. He searched her body, looking for an injury. For a bullet wound. No sign of blood. Of any wound.

"You weren't shot?" he asked and wished he could control the anxiety in his tone.

She shook her head. "My legs. I was so afraid. They wouldn't hold me."

She gazed at him, her eyes wide and clouded with shock. He wanted to scoop her into his arms, but first she had to know she was safe.

"I had to shoot Pipkin. He can't hurt you." At her brief

nod of understanding, he gathered her into his arms and held her trembling body. "I'm so glad we found you, and you're alive. I couldn't bear to lose you. Just couldn't bear it."

"How did you find me?" Her breath whispered softly against his neck.

He nearly fell apart over the love he had for her and the fear that was just now ebbing, but he had to hold it together for her. "Gage put GPS on Hannah's car."

She leaned back and tried to smile, but her lips trembled. "Remind me to thank him."

"You and me both."

She suddenly pushed out of his arms, her gaze flashing up to his. "Cait. Did you find her?"

"Yes. Yes." He should have thought to lead with that. "She's being checked out at the hospital, but from what I could see she will be okay and is eager to meet you."

Emory's shoulders sagged, and he held her up. But the distance seemed too great and he let his emotions go and leaned forward to kiss her. Her lips were cold. Trembling. But he couldn't pull back. Not yet. He had to let her know how much he cared for her.

She returned his kiss measure for measure, heating his blood, and he knew he never wanted to let her go. Didn't want a life without her.

His radio squawked, the sound of Trent requesting an ambulance and backup, bringing Blake to his senses. He lifted his head to smile at her. "It's over."

She nodded. "Pipkin killed my dad. He admitted it. Buried him in the clearing. He said Dad owed him money. He threatened my parents that he'd hurt Cait and me if they didn't pay off their debt by being the lookout and getaway driver for the bank robbery. The second body is his other partner."

"I'm so sorry, honey." Blake felt her pain deep in his own heart. "And your mother?"

"He said he let her go, but she had to disappear and never come back. I don't know if we'll ever find her, but at least I know he didn't hurt her. Or least he said he didn't. I figure if he did, she would be buried by my dad."

"Let's hope that's true." He thought about Emory's situation and how hard it would be not to know where your mother was or if she was even alive. He had a mother. Father. Sister. And he'd been avoiding them for a stupid reason. Now that they'd found Cait, he would go see them as soon as he could and make amends. But what about Emory? He would put his every effort when not working to help locate her mother, but now he needed to get her out of this cold, wet field.

"Can you walk?" he asked.

"My legs feel stronger, but I'm not sure."

"Let me help you so we can go meet your sister."

Emory's eyes widened, and a smile transformed her face. "I didn't even think of that. I'm going to see Cait. Hold her. Hug her. Get to know her. And help her heal from this. We can heal together."

Blake helped Emory to her feet. He wanted to offer his services in helping her heal, too, but she didn't need him butting into her life right now. There was time to tell her how he felt later. Just not *too* much later.

28

"Come in," Emory's grandmother called out.

Emory took a long breath and pressed open the door, suddenly shy about meeting her twin. They'd gone straight to the hospital, but Cait had been discharged to their grandmother's care. An even better reunion in Emory's mind. Sure, her grandmother would have to hear about their dad, but her daughter could still be alive, and that was great news.

Her grandmother sat on her worn sofa, her arm around Cait. Emory could see the resemblance between them. One look at her sister's face was so like looking in a mirror that Emory lost all shyness and apprehension. She ran across the room, and by the time she reached the sofa, Cait was on her feet, holding out her arms.

They swept each other into a fierce hug. A peace that Emory never knew before invaded her soul, and she sighed in pure joy. Tears poured from her eyes, and she let the joy wash out all of the pain and agony until her heart overflowed with happiness.

"Hello, Mrs. Layton," Blake said.

Emory heard Blake speak, but she couldn't pull back just yet.

"Please, call me Naomi," her grandmother replied. "Now come close so I can give you a hug for saving both of my precious granddaughters."

"That's not necessary," Blake said.

"It's my house, and I'll say what's necessary."

Cait pushed back but kept an arm circled around Emory's back. "You better do as she asks. She's got a stubborn streak."

"Then she's truly Emory's grandmother." A wry smile found Blake's face as he looked fondly at Emory.

"Oh, oh," Cait exclaimed. "My sister has a boyfriend."

"It's not like that," Emory said.

Blake shot her a look filled with hurt.

"I mean, we care for each other," she rushed on to clarify and erase his unease. "But we live so far apart."

Cait shrugged. "So one of you moves."

"I know that sounds simple," Emory said, uncomfortable with the subject as she'd never even discussed her feelings with Blake. "But we both love our jobs."

"More than each other?" her grandmother asked. "Because after all you've been through, I would think you'd realize what's most important in life, and I can tell you it's not a job."

"You're right, I...we..."

"We really haven't had time to talk about this." Blake saved her. "We just met, you know, so this is all new to us."

"Well don't let any time pass. Get it sorted out. Life can be too short." Her grandmother took Cait and Emory's arms. "Now let's sit, and you tell me about this Pipkin fellow."

Emory sat on one side of her grandmother and kept stealing looks at Cait who was doing the same thing. They shared a knowing, and yet, incredulous look over finding each other.

"I think Cait and Emory need time to get to know each other, so why don't I tell you?" Blake offered.

"I see your point." Her grandmother got up and scooted Emory over next to Cait. Emory took Cait's hand as Blake started to recount Pipkin's story, but Emory tuned him out because she knew all the details.

"I met your adoptive father," she whispered to Cait. "You should call him and tell him you're okay."

"I already did."

"Oh, good. I hope you can reconcile with him."

"We already did that, too." Cait smiled. "Like Grandma said, being held captive put my priorities straight real quick."

Emory still couldn't get used to seeing her own face looking at her. She touched Cait's cheek and stared in awe.

Cait smiled so broadly, Emory was surprised her face didn't crack. "What about your adoptive parents?"

Feeling like a bucket of cold water had been dumped on her, Emory removed her hand and shared about her argument with her mother. "My father died when I was in high school, but I plan to fly back to Portland tonight and mend things with my mom."

"I can totally understand how you feel." Cait pressed her hand over Emory's. "I'd like to meet your mother."

Emory would love that. "And I want you to meet my sister, too. Angela. You could come with us tonight."

"Sure." Cait's eyes brightened with excitement. "And can I visit your work? Grandma told me you're like this big shot at the Veritas Center. Too bizarre that I chose your lab to do my DNA, right?"

Emory nodded. "I have a condo on the property. Angela

lives with me. You can stay with us, and we can all get to know each other."

Cait stared for a long moment, then shook her head. "This is totally weird, right?"

"Totally," Emory agreed.

They clutched hands and laughed together, but Emory heard Blake mention their birth mother, and her smile fell. "We have to find our mom."

"Absolutely. That's kinda why I wanted to meet your team." Cait nipped her lip. "Figured we could get them all to help us."

"Of course," Emory readily agreed. "They're the best at what they do. I have high hopes that we can find her."

"You should start your hunt by trying to get a national news story," Blake said, drawing their attention. "Once we recover the bank robbery money, they'll pick up the story. Your mother might see it, and knowing Pipkin is dead, will come forward."

"Won't she be subject to prosecution for the robbery, though?" Emory asked.

"As far as I can see, we have no proof that she participated in any crime, and even if she did, the statute of limitations has run out for the prosecutor to bring charges against her. Since they never even suspected your parents, she should be okay."

Emory flashed Blake a big smile. "Then I think the news story sounds like a great way to start."

"I want my Olivia found." Their grandmother's insistent voice cut through the room. "But you both need to take some time to heal from this traumatic situation. To find out who you are as twins before you're paraded in front of the media."

"Yes, of course," Emory said, as she knew she also needed to heal from the attack in her car, and she planned to seek counseling when she got back home and get her life sorted out.

"And we need to give Dad a proper burial," Cait said. "We have so much to do."

Emory met Cait's gaze. "But we have each other now and a super amazing grandma. That will make things we face from this day forward so much easier."

Emory said the words, but as soon as they were out, she glanced at Blake and knew neither woman could help her find the best way to deal with her feelings for this amazing man. No, that she would have to work out for herself.

And if his warm gaze on her told her anything, it said he wanted her to figure it out as quickly as possible.

EPILOGUE

Three months later

Emory finished polishing the large desk and stood back to look at the office she'd created on the third floor of the Veritas building. The desk gleamed. Matching bookshelves lined the back wall. The chairs were rich mahogany leather and ocean scenes were framed on the walls. Perfect. Just like she'd hoped when she'd ordered everything.

She went to the door and ran her fingers over the name-plate. It was like pinching herself to make sure this really was happening today.

"Relax," Cait said. "Blake will love this office and love working here."

"You think?" Emory twisted the polishing cloth in her hands.

"I think he'd be happy working any place that meant he lived in the same town as you." Cait smiled. "He's over the moon in love with you."

"I know." Emory thought she really *should* pinch herself.

"But?"

"But I worry he'll miss working in law enforcement."

"It was his choice. Said he'd been thinking of retiring for

302

some time. And as far as I can see, Blake Jenkins knows what he wants and how to get it." Cait gestured at the sign on the door. "Case in point. He's your new criminal investigator when the job didn't exist before."

"But we were thinking of adding it."

"But this soon?"

"No. Next year."

"And yet, he'll be here in a few minutes to start work." Cait cocked an eyebrow, and Emory still couldn't get used to looking at her mirror image whose gestures and mannerisms were so similar to Emory's.

"Yeah, he'll be here any time." Emory's heartbeat kicked up at the mere thought of seeing him again, and a smile found its way to her face. She'd pretty much been smiling since he agreed to take the job and couldn't stop. Didn't want to stop.

"I just wish the marina was here, too" Cait said. "But then we're only hours away from each other."

Emory looked at her twin. "I still can't believe you bought it. With your degree and all."

"If the research I plan to do doesn't work out, I'll sell the place and find a job here in Portland."

Emory opened her mouth to respond, but she heard footsteps in the hallway, and her heartbeat raced. She spun to look at the door. Blake appeared, and she thought her heart might split from the sheer joy of seeing him. He wore black tactical pants and a black collared shirt with the Veritas logo on his chest. He looked darkly dangerous, but his warm smile when he met her gaze was anything but dangerous.

"Hi, Blake," Cait said, heading for the door. "Bye, Blake."

He chuckled, but his gaze locked on Emory and stole her breath.

"Hello there, workmate." He circled his arms around her

waist and drew her closer. "Thanks for setting up the office for me. You did a great job, but I don't need all of this."

"You may not need it, but you deserve it." Would he really be happy here?

"Hey, what's with the frown?" He ran his fingers over her lips.

Her frown faded and a delicious shudder took hold of her, but it didn't erase her concern. "Are you sure you're going to like it here? I mean, you won't have the adrenaline rush of being the sheriff."

He waved a hand. "Being the sheriff was more administrative in nature. Wasn't often that I got to go out and experience frontline policing. And you know I was getting burned out on all the supervision. So yeah, a job where I'm only in charge of myself will be great."

His phone rang, and he released her to answer. "Blake Jenkins."

He listened intently to his caller, and she realized that he was looking younger. More relaxed and at peace. He really did want to do this job, and it looked like it would be good for him. Her heart swelled with happiness.

"Be right there." He hung up and stowed his phone in his pant pocket. "Maya has summoned us to the conference room."

"Monday morning status meeting." Emory put the cleaning supplies in the tote and shoved them in his closet.

When she turned, he was watching her intently. "One thing before we head down there."

He sounded so serious that her joy evaporated. "What is it?"

"This." He reached into his pocket and produced a ring box.

She gasped. "Is this...are you..."

"Proposing?" he asked as he got down on one knee. "Yeah, I am."

She clapped a hand to her mouth.

He smiled up at her. "I love you, Emory, you know that. But I also admire, respect, and think you're the most amazing woman I have ever met. Smart. Talented. Gorgeous."

"Stop. I'm just me. But *you*. You're strong and capable. Sure of yourself. And compassionate beyond measure. And handsome. So handsome." She fanned her heated face. "And I can't believe you fell in love with a lab nerd like me. But since I love you more than life, it's a very good thing."

"Um...honey. You're kind of hijacking my proposal here." He grinned and got to his feet.

She felt a blush rise up over her face. "Sorry, I just love you so much, and I never thought I would have such an amazing relationship in my life."

"Will you marry me, Emory?" He gazed longingly at her. "Be my wife."

"Yes. Yes. Yes." She threw her arms around his neck and hugged him hard.

When she pulled back, he leaned down to kiss her. His lips were warm and insistent, and he kissed her with a new level of passion. She matched him as she wanted him to know how much she loved him. He suddenly lifted his head.

"The ring. I need to get it on your finger for proof." He slipped the princess cut diamond from the satin bed and slid it on her finger.

She held out her hand and admired the sparkly diamond and white gold setting.

"Oh, Blake." She sighed and looked up at him. "The ring is absolutely beautiful. And perfect. Just like I would have picked out for myself."

"I'm glad." His smile broadened. "It'll also help me tell you apart from Cait."

"C'mon, we only tricked you that one time." She laughed as memories of their recent prank came back. "I promise I have put that part of my new twin behavior in the past."

His phone rang again, and he frowned. "Maya again, you think?"

"Yes." Emory smiled. "She can be relentless, but we all love her to death. But you...you still have time to run before your partnership in the lab becomes official."

He pulled her to him and let the phone ring. "First new rule I'm going to make as a partner is no mandatory meetings when one of the partners is kissing his soon-to-be wife."

"I can totally get behind that rule." Emory snaked an arm around his neck. "And extend it to no meetings at all when a partner is kissing the man she loves. And I plan to be doing that quite frequently, so Maya will just have to learn to be patient."

She drew his head down and kissed him with abandon. But when her phone rang, she pulled back. "Come on. I know they invited a few people over to celebrate your partnership and welcome you to the team."

She took his hand and drew him into the hallway and to the elevator.

When the doors closed, he turned to her. "Are there any rules prohibiting kissing in the elevator?"

"None that I know of."

"Then come here, woman." He reached out for her, and she slid into his arms. "I love you, Emory."

"And I love you, too."

He captured her mouth with his, and she slid a hand into his hair and placed the other one on his back pulling

306

him closer. She gave into the emotions racing through her body and lost track of time, wanting this never to end.

"Oh my gosh, you're engaged." Cait's raised voice brought Emory to her senses, and she looked up to find the elevator door had opened and Maya and Cait were watching them.

Maya stepped forward. "You weren't coming down to us so we were coming up to get you."

"Sorry." Emory wiggled her hand. "I was busy getting engaged."

Cait squealed and pulled Emory out of the elevator. She was vaguely aware of Blake following as she was led to the conference room, but the other women in the room surrounded her like ants at a picnic, *oohing* and *ahhing* over the ring that Emory could simply sit and stare at all day. That was, when she wasn't kissing Blake.

Maya took charge of the group and managed to hand out champagne flutes filled with sparkling cider. Emory was surprised to see Blake's parents and his sister, Emory's grandmother, along with her adopted mother *and* birth mother who stood side by side smiling. The news story did the trick and her mother was now back living with Emory's grandmother.

"Congratulations, sweetheart," her birth mother said.

Emory smiled at her and squeezed her hand. Her adoptive mother hung back, but Emory reached out to grab her hand while still holding her birth mother's hand. "If I know Blake, we'll be setting a date by the end of the day. So the three of us are going to have to start planning this wedding."

"Hey, now," Cait complained. "Not just the three of you."

"Right the four..." Emory caught her grandmother's gaze and then Blake's mom and his sister, Danielle's eyes, though with having been blinded, she would have to sense that Emory was looking at her. "The seven of us. And I know my partners will want to help. We'll have a regular committee to plan the day."

"Poor, Blake," Cait said, turning to look at him. "He won't know what hit him."

"Are you kidding?" Blake's mother said and smiled. "Look at him. Have you ever seen a happier man?"

Emory faced him and her heart flooded with love. "And soon he will be legally all mine."

"Okay, everyone, if I could have your attention." Maya lifted her glass. "Thank you all for coming today to welcome Blake into our family as well as to celebrate reuniting another very special family." She smiled at Emory and her extended family members. "And now we can also congratulate Blake and Emory on their engagement, too!"

"Hear, hear." Nick held his glass up.

Emory basked in the joy as all the people she loved cheered, lifted glasses, and clinked.

Blake found his way through the group to Emory and put an arm around her waist, drawing her close. She took a long, contented breath, inhaling his now-familiar minty scent and simply reveled in the moment while her friends and family sipped their cider and then broke into small groups to chat.

Emory looked up at Blake, his smile lighting up his handsome face. "I have never known such happiness."

"Me, neither." He locked on her gaze and held it, her pulse racing under his intense study. "But I know there's much more to come."

"A lifetime." She didn't care that everyone was watching, she turned to kiss him and begin that lifetime filled with love.

ENJOY THIS BOOK?

Reviews are the most powerful tool to draw attention to my books for new readers. I wish I had the budget of a New York publisher to take out ads and commercials but that's not a reality. I do have something much more powerful and effective than that.

A committed and loyal bunch of readers like you.

If you've enjoyed *Dead Ringer*, I would be very grateful if you could leave an honest review on the bookseller's site. It can be as short as you like. Just a few words is all it takes. Thank you very much.

BOOKS IN THE TRUTH SEEKERS SERIES
People are rarely who they seem

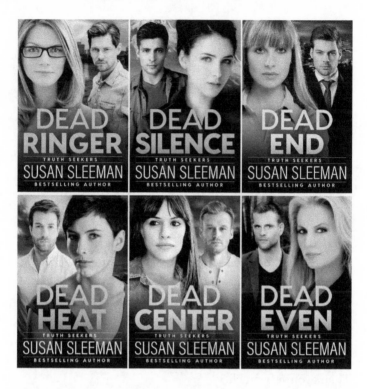

A twin who never knew her sister existed, a mother whose child is not her own, a woman whose father is anything but her father. All searching. All seeking. All needing help and hope.

Meet the unsung heroes of the Veritas Center. The Truth Seekers – a team, that includes experts in forensic anthropology, DNA, trace evidence, ballistics, cybercrimes, and toxicology. Committed to restoring hope and families by solving one mystery at a time, none of them are prepared for when the mystery comes calling close to home and threatens to destroy the only life they've known.

For More Details Visit -
www.susansleeman.com/books/truth-seekers/

BOOKS IN THE COLD HARBOR SERIES

Blackwell Tactical – this law enforcement training facility and protection services agency is made up of former military and law enforcement heroes whose injuries keep them from the line of duty. When trouble strikes, there's no better team to have on your side, and they would give everything, even their lives, to protect innocents.

For More Details Visit -

www.susansleeman.com/books/cold-harbor/

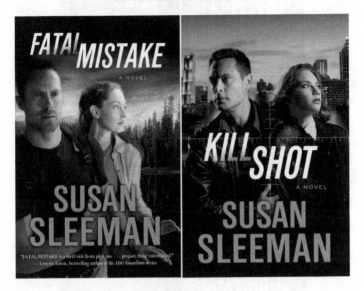

Set in Lost Creek, a fictitious town in the Texas Hill Country, a member of the McKade family has been the county sheriff and/or a deputy for the last 125 years. The series features four McKade siblings along with their grandparents, Jed and Betty McKade, and parents, Walt and Winnie McKade. In addition to law enforcement duties, they also own a working dude ranch. Walt is the soon to retire sheriff, and his children are all law enforcement professionals.

FIRST RESPONDERS

  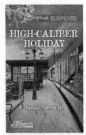

  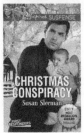

Join the First Response Squad, a six member county Critical Incident Response team, as they report to explosive emergencies and find themselves embroiled in life threatening situations of their own. And join in on the camaraderie at their home, an old firehouse remodeled to provide a home and team meeting facility for this talented team of law enforcement officers.

ABOUT SUSAN

SUSAN SLEEMAN is a bestselling and award-winning author of more than 35 inspirational/Christian and clean read romantic suspense books. In addition to writing, Susan also hosts the website, TheSuspenseZone.com.

Susan currently lives in Oregon, but has had the pleasure of living in nine states. Her husband is a retired church music director and they have two beautiful daughters, two very special sons-in-law, and an adorable grandson.

For more information visit:
www.susansleeman.com